"Anything ha[

"Holly attacked us again."

"Holly . . . attacked you?"

Amanda knelt down and placed a hand on Jer's shoulder. "When she came back from the Dreamtime, she wasn't alone. Demons or something are possessing her."

"No!" Jer gasped.

"There is more that you should know," Philippe said, also placing a hand on his shoulder. "She is in thrall . . . to your father."

The cry of anguish that came from Jer was like no sound Richard had ever heard from a human being. Out of respect, he ducked his eyes, the only gesture of privacy he could offer him.

When Jer finally spoke, though, Richard heard the steel in his voice. "I will find her and free her, if I have to kill my father and myself to do it."

WICKED

SPELLBOUND

NANCY HOLDER *and* **DEBBIE VIGUIÉ**

SIMON PULSE

New York   London   Toronto   Sydney   Singapore

First Simon Pulse edition September 2003

Copyright © 2003 by Nancy Holder

SIMON PULSE
An imprint of Simon & Schuster
Children's Publishing Division
1230 Avenue of the Americas
New York, NY 10020

Printed in the United States of America
10 9 8 7 6 5 4 3 2 1
Library of Congress Control Number 2003106083
ISBN 0-7434-2699-1

For those who hold me spellbound: Elise and Hank, Skylah and Belle, Teresa and Richard, Sandra and Belle . . . and our David, always. We all miss you, sweetie.

—Nancy Holder

To my mother, Barbara Reynolds, who has always loved me, encouraged me, and believed in me, thank you for everything.

—Debbie Viguié

ACKNOWLEDGMENTS

First of all, thank you, Debbie Viguié, for your friendship, your talent, and your dedication. And thank you to her husband, Scott, for your shoulder, your ear, and your wisdom. Lisa Clancy and Lisa Gribbin at Simon and Schuster, thank you both for all your care, editorial and otherwise. I have so much respect and affection for my agent, Howard Morhaim, and his assistant, Ryan Blitstein. For my many friends, I am so grateful—Dal, Steve, Lydia, Art, Jeff, Maryelizabeth, Melissa Mia, Von and Wes, Angela and Pat, and Liz Cratty Engstrom. Kym, you're the It girl. Thank you.

—N. H.

Thanks to my friend and coauthor, Nancy Holder, you are one in a million! Thanks, as always, to the fabulous team of Lisa Clancy and Lisa Gribbin at Simon and Schuster—what would we do without you? Thank you to Lindsay Keilers for your friendship. Thanks to Morris Skupinsky and Julie Gentile for all your love and support and my lucky contract/book-signing pen! Thank you to Super Librarian Rebecca Collacott (sorry for giving away your secret identity!). Thank you also to Michael, Sabrina, and most especially, Whisper.

—D. V.

CAST OF CHARACTERS

☾

Forces of Light
Tri-Coven: The Union of Three Powerful Covens

Cathers Coven

Holly Cathers—head of the Coven; cousin to Amanda and Nicole

Amanda Anderson—the "boring" twin; daughter of Richard

Nicole Anderson—the "vibrant" twin; daughter of Richard

Tommy Nagai—Amanda's best friend and lover

Spanish Coven

Philippe—head of the Spanish Coven

Armand—studied for the priesthood before he learned magic

Pablo—the late José Luís's younger brother

Rebel Coven

Jeraud Deveraux—warlock burned in the Black Fire; son of Michael

Kari Hardwicke—graduate student and Jeraud's former girlfriend

Aligned with the Tri-Coven through the Cathers Coven, although not official covenates:

Richard Anderson—father of Nicole and Amanda
Barbara Davis-Chin—Holly's mother's best friend
Dan Carter—Native American shaman; died in battle against the Deveraux

Mother Coven

Sasha Deveraux—mother of Jeraud and Eli
Anne-Louise Montrachet—raised in the Mother Coven; its representative
Luna—High Priestess of the Mother Coven

Forces of Darkness
Supreme Coven

House Moore

Sir William Moore—demonic warlock; leader of the Supreme Coven
James Moore—Sir William's son, who is plotting to overthrow him

House Deveraux

Michael Deveraux—warlock; father of Jeraud and Eli
Eli Deveraux—Jeraud's brother, who is following in their father's footsteps

Ancestors

Isabeau Cahors—in love with and married to her sworn enemy, Jean, she betrayed both their families; her spirit is cursed to wander the world until she kills him

Jean Deveraux—married to Isabeau; he both loves her and hates her

Catherine Cahors—Isabeau's mother; most powerful witch until Holly

Laurent Deveraux—Jean's father

Peter "Cavendish" Cathers—father of Ginny and Veronica Cathers, half-sisters

Veronica Cathers (Covey, widowed)—daughter of Peter by his second wife, Jane; ancestress of Holly Cathers and Amanda and Nicole Anderson

Ginny Cathers Morris—daughter of Peter by his first wife, Claire; ancestress of Alex Carruthers

Part One
Earth

☾

From the earth below we come
And upon its breast we live
We feed it with our death
Our bodies all we can give

Ashes to ashes and dust to dust
In Mother Earth we place our trust
And as we cycle through our years
We water it with blood and tears

ONE

ISIS

☾

We've scattered now all their bones
Ruined all their lives and homes
None can now escape Deveraux ire
As we burn them with midnight fire

Goddess hear us in the night
Save all Cahors within your sight
Help us not to count the cost
As we survey all we've lost

Seattle: Amanda and Tommy

The whole world was on fire. Trees exploded in showers of sparks, and bits of burning leaves fluttered toward the ground. They landed on Amanda Anderson's shoulders as she ran, and she did not have time to snuff them out. She could smell her hair burning, but she could not stop. She was being run to ground just like a wild animal, and she felt as small and insignificant as the squirrel that raced past her and shot up a tree, fleeing the smoke and the flames.

Behind her, unearthly screams pierced the night, howls of pain that could have come from either beast or man. She didn't turn around. People were dying, and she could not save them.

Beside her, her soul mate, Tommy Nagai, ran for his life, his breathing labored. His lungs were being seared by the same acrid smoke that was burning hers. Through the smoke she had lost sight of Philippe, her sister Nicole's true love; she hoped he was still beside Tommy, or at least behind him.

Goddess, keep us together. She sobbed, bereft and terrified, wondering if there was anywhere on the planet that such a prayer could come true. From Seattle to Paris to London and back again, Amanda and the other members of the Cahors Coven had run from Deveraux warlocks. Michael Deveraux had probably engineered the deaths of Holly's parents and attacked their family friend, Barbara Davis-Chin, so that the teenage Holly had no one to turn to except Amanda and Nicole's family in Seattle. Then he had had an affair with their mom, and Amanda was certain he was responsible for her death as well. He was closing in on Holly from all sides.

Michael's son Eli had been Nicole's "bad boy" boyfriend for a couple of years, but he had helped

James Moore, son of the Supreme Coven, kidnap Nicole and force her into marriage with James.

And now they've kidnapped her again.

And Jeraud Deveraux . . . who could say how much of all this was his fault? His own brother and father had burned him with Black Fire; he was hideous now, horribly scarred. He claimed to love Holly, but he was still a Deveraux warlock . . . and the vessel through which Jean Deveraux could attempt to finish the vendetta between the ancient, noble Deveraux and Cahors witch families, by murdering Amanda's cousin, Holly Cathers.

Michael Deveraux had won the battle, won the war. He and the forces of evil had been too powerful. Even with the Mother Coven helping them, Holly's coven had never stood a chance. Now almost everyone Amanda loved in the entire world was either dead or missing.

When Michael attacked them with his army and set their safe house on fire, Amanda had prayed all the spells and charms she could think of as her covenates scattered, racing from the burning cabin into the night. She didn't know if, with their own magic, the others had saved her and Tommy, or if it was just sheer luck that she and he had escaped into the trees relatively unscathed.

Whatever the reason, I am so grateful. So very, very grateful.

As she staggered along, defeated and terrified, she wasn't sure what she believed anymore. She used to think that the Goddess would protect them no matter what, that their powers could match that of Michael Deveraux.

That was before tonight, when James Moore and Eli had kidnapped her sister, Nicole, right out of the stronghold of the coven.

She used to believe that she could count on Holly to know what to do, even if it wasn't always what Amanda herself would have chosen. That was before Holly had been possessed by demons from the Dreamtime and had lost Jeraud Deveraux in the process. *We could have used him to fight his father,* she thought bitterly. Now she didn't even know if he was alive. *Just like everyone else.*

She used to believe there was safety in numbers, but even all the reinforcements sent by the Mother Coven had been helpless before the powers of darkness wielded against them. Now, for all she knew, she and Tommy were alone, the only two survivors of a very bad night.

We tried so hard. We tried for so long. How can it be that we failed? Doesn't right eventually prevail?

She wished she could ask Tommy some of these questions, but she couldn't spare any precious energy to speak. The flames were on their heels, racing all the faster because of the magic that was fanning them. They had to keep running. She could feel the heat fanning her back, burning her with its intensity. She glanced at Tommy. Sweat poured down his face, which was flushed. Her fear isolated her from him; though she loved him, she realized now that his love had limits, just like all love. He couldn't save her life simply by loving her. He couldn't make everything better.

But he can help me give it meaning, she thought, watching his strong back, barely visible through the smoke. *There are people worth living for. And dying for. And that's the blessing the Goddess has given us . . . and the curse. It makes us keep going . . . and makes us want to give up.*

She was exhausted. She hadn't slept in longer than she could remember, and it seemed like all she had been doing her entire life was fighting and running. *Especially running.* Maybe she should just stop and let the fire catch her, or Michael Deveraux, if he was back there. It would be so much easier. She was tired and sick of it all.

But the strange thing was that no matter how much she wanted to give up, she couldn't. A tiny spark flickered deep inside her chest—she could sense it rather than feel it—and she had no idea if that was her soul or her conscience or some other magical part of her.

I am a Lady of the Lily, she thought. *One of the Three Sisters. Holly carries most of our magic bloodline, but not all of it. I am one of the Cahors witches, even though my last name is Anderson, but Nicole and I are Cahors descendants, same as Holly.*

If something happens to Holly . . . if Nicole isn't . . . if she is dead, then I'm the only one . . .

She choked back a sob and violently shook her head. She was overwhelmed. She had already lost her mother. She refused to even consider that she might have lost other loved ones.

Nicole and I were finally getting close. She can't be dead. She has to be alive, because I can't stand any more dying.

Skeletal branches grabbed at her hair and ripped her clothes to shreds. Blood dripped down her forehead into her eyes, turning the world into a sea of heaving red. Still, she ran, and Tommy with her; and she was beginning to lose hope for Philippe.

Then, behind her, another explosion split the night air. She risked a glance back. It was massive, fissuring the earth like a nightmare earthquake. The tall copse of trees closest to her immediately burst into flames, and fireballs of branches and pinecones plummeted from the sky.

The resultant magical shock wave from the explosion threw her to the ground with such force that her ribs snapped, one by one by one, as if someone were ripping them from her backbone.

Somewhere nearby, Tommy screamed in agony.

The world was exploding; everything was blazing, even the ground. She looked up; a wedge of birds burst into flame and, screaming as one being, dropped into the firestorm that the forest had become.

Desperately she grabbed fistfuls of dirt and screamed, "Goddess help me!"

Though the fire raged around her, a centering quiet seized her thundering heart. As fear drained from her, the lack of tension was for a moment more unnerving than the terror had been. As lassitude crept over her, she felt vulnerable to further attacks.

"*Be still,*" came a voice, a woman's voice. "*Be still; I will not leave you.*"

"Goddess," she whispered. "Goddess."

"*I will not leave you.*"

Amanda wearily closed her eyes.

Maybe you won't leave me, she thought, *but will you actually help me? Can you save me?*

Then she let the darkness take her, her last thought for Tommy.

If you can't save me, can you save him? Goddess, he is my life. Can you save him? I will do anything . . .

Anything . . .

"Ssh," the Goddess urged her.

And Amanda obeyed.

London, the Supreme Coven: Sir William

Sir William Moore, descendant of Sir Richard Moore, the famed Australian governor who had brought the Nightmare Dreamtime to the arsenal of his house, sat on the skull throne and chuckled. As head of the Supreme Coven, master and servant of evil, he was exhilarated by the death and despair that coursed through his very veins as, halfway across the world in Seattle, witches died. Michael Deveraux had done well.

But not well enough. For while it was true that many of the forces of light had been extinguished, there were three yet alive whom Sir William willed dead: Holly Cathers, and the twin sisters, Amanda and Nicole Anderson.

I can change that.

And I will.

Filled with confidence and grim purpose, he rose, his ceremonial midnight robes swirling around him. He was not surprised that Michael had failed to kill the three Cahors witches. It was clear that the warlock wasn't putting his heart into it. *He still believes that an alliance between the House of Deveraux and the House of*

Cahors would give his family enough power to overthrow me. Sir William chuckled again. Michael Deveraux was about to outlive his usefulness.

He is living on borrowed time, anyway, to borrow a cliché. I'm not sure he is aware that the threads of his existence have never left my fingers . . . and that my athame can cut a man's life to ribbons with unbelievable speed.

Sir William entered a tiny stone room that was empty save for a stone washtub and a chair upon which was folded a simple white garment. He disrobed and stepped into the warm water. Magics that required ritual purification were not to be taken lightly, not even by the leader of the Supreme Coven. The water for the bath had been brought by an innocent, a young serving girl unaware of the dark purposes of her master. Likewise the pure white robe had been brought by a delivery boy who had been instructed to place it in the room so that no other hands would touch it.

As soon as each of them had left the room, their throats had been cut by Sir William's favorite, one Alastair, and their bodies hefted into the dungeon. Nothing would go to waste; the Supreme Coven's *Book of Shadows* contained spells requiring all sorts of interesting portions of the human body . . . and the skull throne could always use another head or two. . . .

The stone room and everything in it was clean and

undefiled, and unknown to the outside world. Now it was Sir William's turn to be cleansed.

Clearing his mind of all emotion, all volition, all cognition, he scooped up the water and turned to the east. He sluiced it over his head, a mockery of Christian baptism, and allowed his muscles to slacken. In the spiritual form of freefall, he humbly submitted to the Dark God, who loved him and provided for him.

While in this limbo state, he allowed the dark forces to penetrate him, and to lift from his essence another small portion of his soul. He could sense their presence, feel the removal. There was a sharp pain for a moment, like a pinprick, and then it was over.

He had very little of his soul left, but so far, he had not missed it much. In truth, from what he had seen of those who were not children of the Horned God, souls weighed heavily and drained the joy and pleasure from their hosts.

Restoring himself to his own senses, the warlock performed the same obeisance to the west, the north, and the south, to the many aspects of the God: the Green Man; Pan; the Horned One; the Outcast Son of Light.

The purification and obeisance complete, Sir William donned the white garment—*interesting that both sides use white to much the same effect,* he noted idly, *the absence of prior limitation*—and imperiously waved his hand.

A section of the wall disappeared to reveal another room. It was brilliantly clean and devoid of any contents, save for a dozen life-size clay statues of men lying in four rows of three on the stone floor.

My Golems, he thought eagerly. *So useful, so professional. I love using them as minions.*

He rewalled the room and walked to the statuary. Though they currently reclined passively on their backs, they reminded him of the massive army of Qin dynasty terra cotta figures discovered in China three decades before. Though modern archaeologists had not realized it, Sir William knew the figures served a similar purpose as the dozen now lying before him: the bidding of those who knew how to control them.

Each statue was approximately six feet tall, each one clearly distinguishable from his fellows. Their faces were fierce and battle-ready; their expressions leered and spoke of violence and evil and a love of the hunt. On each of their foreheads was inscribed the word *emet,* which in the tongue of the ancients meant "truth."

He put his hand inside his white garment. Sewn into the skirt was a pouch, and in that pouch lay twelve pieces of vellum stolen from the Cathedral of Notre-Dame in Paris during one of the Supreme Coven's many aborted raids on the Mother Coven's Moon Temple.

Inside the mouths of the Golems he placed the strips of vellum. The creatures had no teeth; they expelled no breath. Once he brought them into life, the paper would still stay in place, as Golems had no voices with which to speak. It was the only flaw in otherwise perfect creatures.

While the houses of Deveraux and Cahors had spent centuries trying to destroy each other, House Moore had spent the time studying every form of magic known to man. It had been a wise and mature path . . . and one that was personally very rewarding for Sir William, for all their knowledge had all been passed down to him. He knew the secrets of the Australian aboriginals; the holy words of the Middle East; the rituals of shamans from countless different tribes . . . and he knew the secrets of the Kabalistic schools.

Golems sprang from that tradition: the veneration of the word. From thought to word sprang all creation—the earth, the heavens, and life within shapes of clay.

Sir William slowly walked around his unholy dozen, chanting in Hebrew. He called out the seventy-two names of God recorded in the Talmud. He did so carefully, precisely, for to make a slip would mean certain death to him. Each name corresponded to a limb or organ of the creatures on the ground. Each name called a part of the clay beings into life. To mispronounce a name would result in that organ or limb being misplaced on his own body.

Into the clay creatures he poured his spirit, his will, even as he breathed words of life over them. Ancient rabbis had created Golems for holy purposes. Ancient warlocks had learned how to twist that act of creation to their own dark purposes. The Golem became an extension of its creator, and any sins it might commit were placed on the head of the "father." Sir William could not hold back a smile. *It is a good thing I don't care about sins.*

At last the final name was pronounced. With a flourish, Sir William stepped back. *"Abracadabra,"* he intoned—a sacred word used so often, it had become a shorthand parody of magical forms. Few who spoke it mockingly understood that each syllable carried within it enormous potential for destruction . . . or grace.

The twelve forms on the ground shuddered into hideous life. Slowly, one by one, they rose, terrible in form, with blank, uncomprehending stares. Truly they were empty vessels waiting to be filled, to be commanded, to be given a purpose.

Sir William waved his hand at the four of them on

his left. "You, you will seek out the witch known as Nicole Anderson, of the ancient house Cahors. Destroy her."

The four beings nodded, their eyes filling with a flicker of intelligence as they grasped their duty. Faithful servants, they would obey him.

He turned to the four on his right. "You four shall seek out the witch known as Amanda Anderson, of the ancient House of Cahors. Destroy her."

Those four nodded as well. Their faces reflected an eagerness to please, like that of dogs willing to die or kill for their masters.

He faced the four directly in front of him. "And you four shall seek out the witch known as Holly Cathers, of the ancient House of Cahors. Destroy her. Grind her bones until they are dust and then scatter that to the winds."

They nodded eagerly, flexing the muscles along their shoulders. Sir William was pleased as he looked upon his creation. They would do their job well, never stopping, never resting. They would be completely relentless, fixed on one goal only. And when they had achieved it, the three witches would be dead.

He slowly lifted his arms into the air. "Now go, my children, and do my bidding."

He tapped each one on the chest, infusing them

with magic power. Each now had the ability to teleport through space. Slowly, the creatures vanished from his sight. When the last had gone, he smiled to himself. *Let's see the Rabbis top that.*

Four of the Golems didn't have far to go. The island of Avalon was heavily warded, though. Centuries of magic protected the place from all prying eyes and intruders. It wasn't by chance that no ship had accidentally run aground on its shores. The magics used to protect the island were powerful and indiscriminate.

Therefore, when the Golems tried to teleport there, they were repulsed—violently. The four creatures stood up on a distant shore, only slightly dazed, and shook themselves off. Then, with the single-minded unity of a common purpose, they headed off in search of a boat to try to reach the island.

Seattle: Richard

I'm back in the jungle again, knee-deep in the hooplah, and it's raining hell.

That was all Richard Anderson could think as the smoke stung his eyes and the sound of explosions pierced the air. He crouched down, the years seeming to fall off him as he zigzagged his way through the underbrush, the unconscious Barbara Davis-Chin draped over his shoulder. His eyes roved back and forth, probing the darkness.

By the time Dan Carter's cabin exploded, dozens of witches Richard had never seen fought valiantly to protect Amanda, Nicole, and everyone else trapped inside. The warrior witches had failed; and many had died while he was making his break for the tree line. One of the foreign men in the cabin had died horribly, cut in half by a pincered monster. Richard was sure more of his people would have been slaughtered if the witches hadn't come to their aid.

Thank God you showed, he thought. *Thank God you fought. I'm going to make damn sure your sacrifice was not in vain.*

Without a moment's hesitation, he'd hoisted Barbara over his shoulder. One of the European men gathered Kari Hardwicke into his arms and took off without a single look back.

Richard had seen Amanda and Tommy escape toward the north. He himself was moving east to force the enemy to divide its forces. His strategy was simple: to increase the number of targets for whoever was attacking them. If everybody moved in one large group, it would be easier for the enemy to pick them off.

Where's Nicole? he wondered now. *Where's my other little girl?*

A tree exploded in a shower of sparks to his left, and he jerked his face away, shielding his eyes. A distance behind him, a woman screamed, high and shrill. Her voice was cut off suddenly, in a gurgling rasp.

Oh God, don't let that be one of mine.

Forcing himself to move on, he stepped on a branch that cracked like a rifle. Wild animals shrieked with panic as the fire burned them out.

Richard stumbled over a smoking tree root; then, as he caught himself, the ground erupted with fire. A white-hot rock smacked him on his cheek. He flinched but stolidly kept going. A second explosion shot a tree into the air like a missile; then, from the gaping hole it left behind, a scaly demon with long ebony claws yanked itself from the earth.

Richard shifted Barbara's weight and kicked the creature in the jaw so hard, its head snapped back. Another kick snapped the bones in its neck; with a shriek, the thing collapsed on the ground, a jumbled heap of bones and horns. Richard leaped over it and raced on.

Another demon jumped in front of Richard, howling like a banshee. With his free hand, Richard unsheathed a knife with a wicked four-inch blade from his belt. He lunged forward and, in a merciless arc, slashed once at the creature's throat. It staggered to the side. He didn't know if he had actually injured it or just startled it. He didn't stop to look; he kept running.

A roaring sound punctuated by sharp snaps propelled the air behind him. The sap in the burning trees exploded like gunpowder, and Richard ducked as a branch went sailing over his head. It flew smack into the face of another demon, who hurtled itself toward Richard.

He changed directions and kept running.

He didn't know where the others were or if they were even alive. There would be time enough to worry about that later. Behind him he heard another unearthly shriek and felt something swipe at his back. Something like a claw scratched his skin. He did the only thing he could do: He kept running.

Seattle: Michael Deveraux

Holly Cathers was nuts.

As Michael's surprise began to ebb, a malicious wave of joy took its place.

The strongest witch on earth had lost her mind. And she was begging her mortal enemy for help.

It was too delicious. But it was true.

Standing beside him in the ashes of the cabin where the witches had made their stand, his ancestor, Duc Laurent, of the House of Deveraux, gave Holly an appraising once-over, then chuckled and shook his head. He locked gazes with Michael, obviously savoring the moment with the living, titular head of his family dynasty. For six hundred years, Laurent had waited for a moment such as this.

The Duc looked good for a man dead six hundred years. Then again, it helped that he had managed to give himself a new flesh-and-blood body so that he was no longer appearing as a moldering corpse.

"Possession," he intoned in his medieval French accent. "How did you manage it, my boy?"

In wonder, Michael shook his head. "I didn't. The God has smiled on us, Laurent."

Holly burst into pitiful, houndlike howls and clawed wildly at her face. She smacked her bleeding cheeks, yanked at her hair. Then she sank forward and buried her face into the smoking earth that bore the ashes of her coven. Abruptly she jerked up again, sobbing and waving her hands.

"Stay free of contact," Laurent warned him. "It's like a contagion. She could infect you."

Michael took that in; he knelt cautiously beside her, careful not to touch her or get in reach of her flailing hands.

"Make it stop," she whimpered, looking at him out of wild eyes. It was obvious she had no idea who he was. Wisps of hair were plastered to her face by streaks of blood. Saliva dripped from the corners of her mouth. "Make it stop, please." She threw back her head and screamed, "I can't bear this!"

"We can," Michael assured her. "We can make it stop."

She sobbed and began blithering, swaying like a cobra, lacing and unlacing her hands as she whispered to herself, "Make it stop, make it stop, make it stop . . ."

Tears sluiced down her cheeks. She was filthy, and she stank.

"I'm supposed to kill her," Michael said, bemused. "Sir William will be much happier with me once I do." He cocked his head, watching her. "If I *cure* her . . . aren't I aiding and abetting the enemy?" He smiled. "Holly Cathers, begging me for help. Begging me for anything."

"*Oui*. It is a moment," Laurent concurred. "But if you kill her, *mon fils,* the best you will be is Sir William's loyal follower. You will lose this compelling opportunity to raise our House to its rightful place."

Laurent was telling Michael nothing new. And he already knew what he would do. Still, it was so pleasant to have this special time, and to share it across the spans of time and space.

"Make it stop," she hissed, "stop, stop, stop."

Michael nodded at her. "I will," he said slowly and

deliberately, hoping his words could find a way to sink into her boiling brain, "but you have to do everything I tell you. You must obey me without question. Do you understand?"

She nodded fiercely. "Yes, I'll do anything you say, anything. Just make it *stop!*"

"Perhaps something in the Nightmare Dreamtime crawled its way into her mind. Several somethings, by the looks of her," he said to Laurent. "Could that be so?"

"*Vraiment.* I would assume so."

Michael wondered idly if his son, Jeraud Deveraux, was still alive. Jer and Holly had been in the Nightmare Dreamtime, trying to rescue one of Holly's loved ones, when Michael had finally managed to create the Black Fire again. It had been a triumphant moment . . . much like this one.

Michael nudged Holly with the toe of his expensive Italian boot. She didn't even notice, just moaned and kept rocking back and forth faster and faster. He had never seen anything quite like it.

He stood slowly and stared around at the hell that surrounded them. Fire blazed everywhere, escaping into the forest. It was too bad about the trees, really; they had been quite lovely. *More casualties of the Deveraux-Cahors war.* He bowed his head for a moment in the appearance of reverence and muttered a prayer to the God to allow quick rebirth to the trees.

He smirked to himself. *What was it that Treebeard said in* The Lord of the Rings? *Ah yes: A wizard should know better than to destroy the forest.* Unlike Saruman, Michael refused to incur the wrath of the forest gods and guardians.

New trees would spring up, though, from the ashes. That was the beauty of nature, the cycle always continued. He glanced down at Holly, and a smile twisted his lips. For Holly and her friends, though, there would be no renewal, no rebirth—only death.

That's fine by me.

Seattle: Amanda

The new day dawned at last, and the sunrise dripped with ravishing colors—prismatic, jewel-toned hues of tangerine and vermilion refracting on the smoke.

Amanda was surprised. She had thought it would never come, or if it did, that she wouldn't be alive to see it. Yet, the sun was there, shedding watery sunlight on the charred bones of what had once been an exquisite forest. By its light, Amanda could see a little motel, perched just beyond the edge of the trees. Exhausted, bruised, and broken, she began to limp toward it.

Beside her, Tommy shuffled along, dragging himself painfully along. He had stayed with her through-out the night, and she knew she owed him her life for that. Had he not been there she would have lain down and died any number of times. His strength had buoyed her, saved her. Now, as she detected his gasps of pain in every step he took, she knew she must do the same for him.

She clasped his hand and willed her energy to mingle with his, willed her battered body to aid his so that they might share each other's pain and help heal each other. A strangled sob from him was proof that it was working, and tears stung her eyes as his pain washed through her. He, too, was bruised and broken, and her cracked ribs groaned in sympathy with his.

He has borne so much for me, because he loves me. Tommy didn't have to be here, but he was. With a rush of conviction she knew that he would always be there, and that with the last breath he drew he would be call-ing her name.

Somehow that made things a little bit better. Nicole was gone, kidnapped by Eli and James. Holly was insane and perhaps dead by now. Tante Cecile, a woman who had been almost an aunt to Amanda her-self, had died trying to save Holly. The Goddess alone knew where the others were, including her father, and if they were even alive. Still, Tommy was here.

And so was the Goddess. Lying in the dirt for hours, Amanda had heard the still, small voice that so many others had claimed to hear. The soft female voice whispered words of encouragement to Amanda, commanding her not to give up, to keep going.

She had always believed that the Goddess existed. *It's kinda hard to question when you can suddenly levitate stuff and dead ancestors start speaking through your cousin.* Still, despite all the supernatural stuff, the Goddess had never appeared or spoken to her. She had only appeared to Holly. At first, Amanda had been jealous, and then, as things got really crazy, relieved. Sometimes it was just easier not to have so much . . . reality to deal with.

Amanda had never been a leader, but she knew that was going to have to change; the Goddess had told her heart that, had spoken to her and lifted her to her feet back in the forest when all she'd wanted to do was lie in the dirt. She felt like either laughing or crying, and she wasn't sure which. She was an unlikely leader, as the only one who had ever followed her anywhere was Tommy.

Now she turned to look at him. They were in thrall, the Lady to the Lord, and she was so very, very happy about it. Whatever magic and strength each of them had at their command would be shared with the other. He looked like he was going to drop from exhaustion. That was pretty much how she felt. They both needed rest, and soon.

She squeezed his hand. The motel didn't seem so far off; she figured if they could just hold on for five more minutes, they would make it.

He turned to her and said, "Agreed."

Her lips parted. "Did you read my mind?"

Tommy smiled faintly. "I've always been able to read your mind, Amanda. In my own way."

"I was pretty clueless about you," she confessed.

"I know. But now—"

"Now." She leaned toward him for a kiss. It was a very sweet moment.

They trudged on, though she was buoyed as they stumbled the last of the distance in silence. Amanda gradually became preoccupied with willing one foot to step in front of the other, and her thoughts about the Goddess and Tommy faded into the background until they were nothing more than a gentle hum in the back of her mind. A few more steps and they would be there.

She looked up and spied a lone figure staring at them. It was hard to tell through the torn clothing and the burned hair and face, but he looked familiar. They staggered to him, and her heart jumped. It was Pablo, the youngest member of the White Magic Coven. The boy looked wild, and his left eye gazed fiercely at her. His right eye was swollen shut.

Relief flooded through her to find someone else alive. She nearly ran the last couple of feet, dragging Tommy behind her.

At last they stood face-to-face. For a moment, no one spoke.

Then tears welled in Pablo's eyes. "I could feel you," he said, his voice sharp, almost accusing. "Back in the forest I could feel you. I couldn't reach you, but I knew that you would end up here, so I came."

"How long have you been waiting?"

"A few hours."

She stared at him. Pablo had a gift that none of the rest of them did: He could read minds, feel people's thoughts, even track people using them. She felt her throat constrict as she asked, "And the others?"

He shook his head slowly. "I do not know. Once, I thought I felt Philippe, but *duende,* his life force, was flickering." He took a deep breath. "I have felt no one else since the cabin."

She nodded her head slowly.

"We should get cleaned up and try to get some rest," Tommy ventured. His voice was hoarse, barely a whisper, and the sound startled her.

"You're right," she said, looking uneasily toward the lobby. "I don't have anything with me, though—no identification, no credit cards."

"Good." Tommy was grimly satisfied. "We don't want to use anything that can be traced."

"But, I don't have any cash, either. Do you?" she asked.

He shrugged. "Nope."

"Then how will we pay?" she protested, wrapping her arms around herself in an effort to keep her ribs from shifting.

Tommy turned and looked at her fondly. "Ms. Anderson, I've always been a standup guy, right?"

"Yes," she said, somewhat confused.

"You've never known me to steal or cheat or lie?"

"No, never."

"Then take that into account when I tell you this. We don't have any money? Not a problem. You're a witch. Do a damn spell."

She nearly laughed in shocked embarrassment. Of course Tommy was right. They had just survived a war, and the three of them needed shelter. She set her jaw and turned on her heel, leaving the two guys behind.

She marched up to the front desk and looked the startled clerk straight in the eye. "I need a quiet room with two beds."

"I'll need a credit card and some identification," the clerk stuttered.

"I already showed them to you," she told him, her voice dropping lower. She willed her words to wash over him and through him, imbued them with the power to cloud his perceptions of reality.

His eyes glazed over slightly. "I'm sorry, you're right. How long will you be staying?"

"I'll let you know," she assured him.

He nodded absently and handed her a room key. She took it, gave him one last mental push for good measure, and walked out the door. Outside, her knees shook a little, but she kept walking.

She collected Tommy and Pablo, and they all made it to the room. It was clean and much larger than she had expected.

She turned and took her first good look at Tommy since the entire thing had begun. He stared back at her with eyes open wide, and she felt a strange urge to laugh.

Tommy's eyebrows were completely gone, sacrificed to the fire that had tried to consume all of them. Without them, his face looked almost comical. Reflexively she put her hand to her own brows. They felt like they were still there.

With a puzzled look, Tommy mimicked her

motion. His eyes widened when he realized what she had been staring at. He turned and gazed at himself in the bathroom mirror. "Talk about playing with fire," he quipped.

Amanda felt an intense surge of love for him. Tommy had always known how to lighten her mood. She slowly turned her head until she, too, faced the mirror.

She didn't recognize herself. Staring back from the mirror was a young woman with tattered clothes. Dried blood soaked what was left of the material in several places, most noticeably over her ribs on her right side. What wasn't covered with blood was caked with dirt. Her eyes were wild, flashing underneath a mop of burnt hair. The left side of her face was completely covered in blood.

No wonder I freaked out the guy at the front desk.

Silently, Pablo came to join them, and the three stared at their battered reflections. Amanda's throat tightened. *Is this it? Are we all that's left of the coven?* She willed herself not to cry. Her face already had enough gunk on it; the last thing she needed was to wet it all down and have it everywhere.

Reflected in the glass, tears began to slide down Pablo's face. She put an arm around him as she began to lose it too. Tommy put his arm around her. For a moment the trio continued to stare into the mirror. It was like a warped family portrait. A collective shudder went through the group, and then they collapsed on the floor, hugging and crying and screaming.

TWO

HECATE

Thorns twist and pierce the flesh
Keep the wounds nice and fresh
Count the bodies one through ten
Then bleed them all once again

Tears we cry for the dead
With our hearts full of dread
Goddess fill us with your power
Even in our darkest hour

Avalon: Nicole Anderson

The more things change, the more they stay the same, Nicole thought bitterly as she glanced around the bedroom. So much had happened in the last few days and yet here she was, right back in James's bedroom as though nothing had happened. At least this time it was a different bedroom. She didn't know for sure where she was, but she knew it wasn't the headquarters of the Supreme Coven.

Tears of frustration stung her eyes. She had been reunited with her sister and her father, her cousin had been possessed, and she had been put in thrall to Philippe. *Philippe.* Now she didn't even know if he was alive, much less whether she would ever see him again.

Meow!

She glanced down at Astarte. The cat was gazing up at her intently, and her tail was curling and uncurling around Nicole's left ankle. The cat had jumped into the portal after her when James and Eli had kidnapped her from the house in Seattle. She picked the cat up and pressed her to her cheek.

"Last time I left Seattle, I left my cat, Hecate, behind. She died. You are my own sweet cat, now, and you won't let me leave you, will you?"

The cat batted her nose with a paw and purred contentedly. Nicole kissed the top of her head. Astarte had come to her in the Spanish countryside when she had been running from the Deveraux. Philippe had taken care of the cat after Nicole had been kidnapped by Eli and James the first time.

Eli and James. They had pulled her through the portal and they had landed back on the island. Without a word, Eli had left and James had escorted her back to his bedroom before locking her in. This time he had placed magical as well as physical barriers on the door.

It's a new doorjamb, she noticed idly. She had destroyed it when she'd escaped the first time. *Either that or he used magic to fix it. . . .*

Astarte twisted in her arms, and Nicole put her down, before she straightened wearily and sat down on the bed.

There had to be something she could do. *I'm a witch, for goodness sake. I should be able to help myself.* She closed her eyes and forced herself to breathe deeply.

"Goddess, now hear me cry, protect me now, don't let me die, I lift my face to the moon and beg you grant deliverance soon."

The words filled her with power, or, at the very least, a new courage. She turned and opened the hidden compartment in the headboard. It was empty. James was too smart to put his ring and other things back there, given that she had tried to take them before. She turned and spied a small table standing in the corner. She crossed to it and pulled out the single drawer. There was some paper, a pen, and a handful of candles. *At least it's something.*

She picked up the pen and carefully, methodically drew a pentagram upon the ground. "Earth, wind, fire, water, spirit," she blessed each point of the star as she drew it.

She stepped back to observe her handiwork. The

circle around the star looked more like an oval, but given what she had to work with, she figured the Goddess wouldn't mind.

Next she selected five white candles and set each one of them at each point of the star. Once finished, she sat down in the center. She closed her eyes and reached backward in her mind, back past all the pain and terror. When she practiced magic with Amanda and Holly it was so forced, as though she were making everything happen by sheer strength of will.

She fought to remember a different time, one of innocence, before the darkness had come. Back when she hadn't known of her witchly heritage, back when her mother was still alive.

Magic had been so simple then, when she hadn't known what she was doing. She sat quietly, trying not to force the magic, but just to let if flow through her and around her. She felt the warmth of Astarte's body as the cat came to her and curled up in her lap.

She slowly opened her eyes. She placed her finger on the candle before her. Fire jumped into being. Quietly, she moved her finger from candle to candle until all five were ablaze.

"My will is strong, my purpose right, protect me now from evil's sight. I call upon thee, Goddess fair, hearken now to my prayer. Keep me safe from beast and man, I entrust my fate to the Maiden's hand."

A rushing wind filled the room, making the candles' fire dance, though they did not extinguish. She gasped as the wind rushed through her, filling her in a moment with a peace she had never known.

Deep within the castle, on a table in the wizard's workshop, the sorcerer's hat began to glow.

Seattle: Michael Deveraux

Michael placed his scrying stone down with a loud *thump*. He had been trying to use it to find his son, Eli, and James Moore. It had not worked. *They must be blocking me,* he thought angrily. With Holly subservient to him, it was the perfect time to try to claim the Throne of Skulls, leadership of the Supreme Coven. Unfortunately, he needed Eli's and James's help to do so.

"If only I could summon the Black Fire by myself." He sighed, more to himself than to the imp chattering away on the back of the sofa in his living room.

He turned and gazed at Holly for a long moment before shaking his head. The girl was huddled in a corner with her knees tucked under her chin, muttering to herself. Even if he could explain to her how to help him summon the Black Fire, it would be too dangerous with her in this condition. No, he would just have to find his son.

He observed Holly quietly for a moment. Her magic and her potential were nearly boundless. If only he could find a way to merge it with his own. Fortunately the insanity that made her unpredictable and dangerous also kept her unfocused enough to diffuse her power and some of the spells she sent out at random intervals. It was almost safer for him to have her in this state. *Tell that to my lamps,* he thought with a grim laugh. The one thing she seemed hell-bent on avoiding was the light. *Is that the witch in her or the demons?* He didn't know. She had managed to destroy several valuable antique lamps before he had subdued her. He was lucky, though. If the insanity hadn't kept her energy unfocused, she would have destroyed the entire building they were standing in. *And us along with it.*

If I could harness her power, I would be unstoppable. It would be easy enough to place her in thrall; there is no will there to circumvent. He knew that Jer had passed up an opportunity to be put in thrall with Holly. *Fool. He didn't understand the kind of power he was turning away. Together they could have destroyed me.*

He crouched down and approached her slowly, palm extended, as if she were a wild animal. She shrank away from his hand when she saw it, retreating even farther into her corner. He sat quietly, waiting.

He could be very patient when he wanted to be. He had wooed many a wild woodland animal in just such a manner, building trust with them until they would come to him.

The bloodstains on his altar could attest to that.

Mother Coven: Santa Cruz, California

People went to the Santa Cruz Mountains in search of peace and quiet, a deeper communion with nature, or a place to hide. A person could lose themselves on any of the dozens of tiny nameless streets or winding access roads. The mountains were home to executives from Silicon Valley seeking a higher standard of living; old hippies in denial of the fact that the sixties were over or hiding from a government they thought still cared about finding them; and witches.

Up at the very top of Summit Road was a tiny dirt path that led even higher up the mountain. It wound through the trees, hundreds of feet above the last of the Christmas tree lots that covered the mountains. At the end of the dirt path was a driveway, guarded by two giant stone cats. The cats looked Egyptian, with their long necks and alert sitting posture. At the end of the driveway, guarded by cats and wards and the Goddess herself, was a house.

A visitor—if any ever happened to come to the

wild and isolated place—would have an overwhelming sense of peace and life. The spirits of the woods and streams were alive here. Even the very trees seemed to breathe upon one, their breath the silvery mist that draped the land.

The tranquillity without the house was unearthly. The suffering inside it was unreal.

The closest thing to what it was, was a field hospital in a war zone. This hospital was owned and run by the Mother Coven, and the suffering women inside it had fought Michael Deveraux and his family to save Holly Cathers and her coven.

Lying in a bed in an upstairs room of the house, Anne-Louise was lucky she wasn't dead. The same couldn't be said for dozens of her sisters. Yet, as she lay in bed nursing thirty broken bones, she didn't feel lucky. Actually, she felt pissed. The healers of the coven were working overtime, not just on her but on others as well. Still, it would be a couple of weeks before she or the others would regain any semblance of normalcy.

She glared at the High Priestess of the Mother Coven, who was standing at the foot of her bed. The other woman actually looked nervous. She had not been present at the slaughter. In fact, of all the witches of the Mother Coven, only a small percentage had been present, and most of those were the weaker covenates.

Still, the High Priestess was standing before her, murmuring platitudes. "We did the best we could—"

"Really?" Anne-Louise managed to ask, her voice a throaty whisper. Her vocal cords had been badly burned, and there was a chance they might not recover—even with witches for her healers.

"The forces allied against us were too strong. We must conserve our strength now, prepare for battle—"

"While our enemies only grow stronger?"

The High Priestess remained silent, her eyes skittering away toward the door and then back again.

"You want to know what I think?" Anne-Louise asked. She continued, not waiting for an answer. "I think the Mother Coven has no intention of trying to save those three girls or their coven. I think you're just hoping that Michael Deveraux kills them all. Then the Mother Coven can return to 'business as usual.' If the Mother Coven were truly opposed to the Supreme Coven, we would have acted against them years ago."

The High Priestess seemed to bristle at that. "The Mother Coven has always stood against the Supreme Coven," she hissed.

"Really? Then how come the Supreme Coven is still standing? How come both Covens are still around if they are so bent on destroying each other? No, I think that having a visible enemy to point to has been good business for both sides. It keeps us from fighting amongst ourselves, and questioning the leadership of our superiors."

The High Priestess blanched, and if Anne-Louise wasn't mistaken she saw fear creeping into the other woman's eyes. She pressed on.

"If not, then why did you only send the weakest of our coven to fight, or those who held any sympathy for the girls at all, *or those who ever questioned anything you do?*"

Silence, pregnant as the full moon, descended on the room. Anne-Louise stared at her leader. She had probably shocked the other woman. Anne-Louise had been orphaned at a young age and had been raised in the coven. She had always been the good little witch, doing as she was told, going where she was ordered, even studying only that which she was instructed to.

Now she didn't care. Maybe it was the pain, maybe it was the aftereffect of witnessing the slaughter of her friends and sisters, maybe it was a lifetime of unasked questions that finally demanded answers. Whatever it was, she knew that she had hit a nerve with the High Priestess. The woman was in danger of losing her place in the coven. Anne-Louise wasn't the only one questioning her judgment since the battle.

She continued to stare at her, when six days ago she wouldn't even have met her eyes. The world had changed, though. *I have.* She had always viewed the High Priestess as the anointed of the Goddess, almost a deity in her own right. Now she just saw a tired woman, one who looked more frightened than any of the young women who had faced death two nights before.

All Anne-Louise knew was that she would not blink first. The High Priestess lifted her chin slightly, seeming to rally her mystique back around her. Her eyes began to flash with heat and power, *real* power.

The door opened, and three witches glided in, shattering the moment. They closed the door, and the High Priestess turned to formally greet them. They all dipped their heads in acknowledgment.

"You are to come to work some more on Anne-Louise." It was a statement, not a question. The three nodded their heads and moved to the bed.

"I will leave you then to their ministering," the High Priestess informed Anne-Louise. She smiled coolly and left the room, gliding through the closed door. It was a simple show of power, but one that Anne-Louise had to admit was quite effective.

She closed her eyes as the healers laid their hands on her broken body. She could feel heat flashing through her, agonizing in its intensity. Dislocated shards of bone began to right themselves in her body, tearing even more flesh and muscle as they did so. Soon, they would begin to knit back together, but not today. They first had to find all the bone fragments.

Anne-Louise lay quietly. The healers had gone again, for a while at least having done their best to numb her pain. Still, it hurt to move, to even breathe.

Mew!

She opened her eyes just as a gray cat leaped up onto the bed beside her. The cat stared at her with large, unblinking eyes. "Where did you come from?" she asked in a tortured whisper.

The cat began to purr as it continued to stare at her.

"Do you have a name?"

Whisper.

"Whisper, yes, that does suit you," she said, feeling herself grow groggy.

The cat curled up against her side, lending her body heat to her. A feeling of well-being began to spread through Anne-Louise, and she fell asleep with a smile touching her lips.

Tri-Coven: Seattle

Amanda awoke to the sun streaming into her eyes. She rolled onto her side with a groan but quickly sat up as her cracked ribs screamed in protest. She choked back a sob. Next to her, Tommy stirred. She glanced at the clock. It was nine A.M. They had been asleep nearly twenty-four hours.

She glanced over and saw Pablo sitting on the other bed. His face was scrunched up like he was in pain.

"Are you okay?" she asked, her heart starting to pound in fear.

He looked at her and his eyes were glazed over. He nodded slowly. "Someone is close, one of ours. I'm not—" He stopped. "I'm not quite sure who. They don't feel . . . right."

"Then how do you know they're one of ours?" she asked, heart pounding faster.

He shook his head. "That's the only thing I can read clearly."

She nodded. She would just have to accept that. It didn't make her happy, but Pablo's gifts were not hers to understand. At least he was sure that it was a friend. She felt a ray of hope. Maybe it was her father, or maybe Nicole had escaped. *Or it could be Holly.* She shuddered and instantly felt ashamed of herself. She didn't wish any harm to Holly, but in her cousin's possessed state, Amanda also wasn't sure she could face her. *Not just yet.*

"Are they close?" she asked Pablo, praying to the

Goddess that they were. She would rather know soon than spend hours wondering.

"*Sí,* about a mile away." He stood up. "I will go and see."

She stood, too, doing her best to ignore the fire in her side. "I'll go with you." She glanced at Tommy. "We'll let him sleep. He's earned it."

Pablo nodded sympathetically. "We all have, *señora,* we all have."

She was about to correct him, to tell him that since she was not a married woman, she was a *señorita.* Then she glanced at Tommy. They had been placed in thrall, the most sacred ceremony between a man and a woman in Coventry. A lump formed in her throat. Pablo then was correct in a way. In his eyes, those of a young man born and raised in Coventry, she was a *señora.*

She scribbled a note to Tommy on the hotel stationery in case he awoke and she was not there. Then they exited the room, locking the door behind them. She warded the door, something she should have done the night before. *But all the wards in the world didn't save us,* she thought, remembering the cabin and the demons breaking into it.

She shuddered and almost couldn't leave. She began to panic. What if she didn't come back? Or worse, what if she returned to find Tommy dead or gone? She didn't know if she could handle that. In an agony of indecision, with tears sliding down her cheeks, she reached for the doorknob.

Pablo gently grabbed her wrist, stopping her. "If anything is going to happen, it will happen whether you are here or not," he told her. "Perhaps he is even safer without you."

She stared into Pablo's eyes. He was a couple of years younger than she was, but the wisdom of a far older man shone forth from his eyes. She knew that he was right.

Together they turned and headed back to the forest from which they had dragged themselves the day before. When they reached the timber line, they stopped.

"Can you tell where they are?" she asked.

Pablo closed his eyes for a moment, then opened them and nodded. "They're closer. Maybe half a kilometer away."

She tried to ignore the chill that danced up her spine, but she couldn't quite do it. Pablo stepped into the trees and began walking. She squinted for a moment along the direction he was traveling, but couldn't see anything. Heart in her throat, she followed.

Pablo was like a bloodhound, stopping every minute or so as if to pick up the scent. Every line of his body was taut, alert, and she couldn't help but admire him. He was more in touch with his instincts than anyone she had ever seen. Suddenly he stopped, head up, and held his hand up for her to listen.

She couldn't hear anything. She closed her eyes, trying to *feel* something. There was nothing. She opened her eyes. "Where?" she finally whispered.

Pablo shook his head. "Here."

The hairs on the back of her neck stood on end. "Where?"

"Right here," a voice said, nearly in her ear.

She screamed and jumped toward Pablo, twisting in midair.

A massive creature with dull black skin and flashing eyes stood before her. It was over six feet tall, with a hump on its back, and bulging muscles. A loincloth was wrapped around its midsection.

It opened its mouth and spoke again. "Hello, sweetheart."

Amanda blinked. "Daddy?"

The creature nodded, and she took a closer look. It was indeed her father. He had something slung over his back and he was coated in soot and mud from head to toe. Relief flooded through her.

"Daddy!" she cried, flinging herself against his chest. He wrapped an arm around her and hugged her tight. For a moment she was five again. Her daddy was there and he would make everything all right, he would protect her from the world.

"Princess," he said at last, bringing her back to the present. "We need to keep moving."

She pulled away slowly and only then realized that what he had slung over his back was Barbara Davis-Chin. Startled, she looked back to her dad. "Is she—"

"She's alive."

"Come with us—we have a place," Pablo said. He headed off back toward the motel.

They fell into step behind him. Amanda walked beside her father, touching his arm from time to time to assure herself that he was real. Within ten minutes they made it back to the motel.

Inside, Tommy was awake and he broke into a huge grin when he saw them.

Richard slowly lowered his human burden onto a bed and then straightened. He stared Tommy in the eyes, and then reached out to embrace him. "It's good to see you, son."

As they embraced, Amanda began to cry. She moved forward, and they welcomed her into their circle until the three of them were hugging and crying.

Tears flowed along with warmth; the three of them were bonding, becoming a new sort of family.

This is a gift from you, Goddess, Amanda acknowledged. *Thank you.*

Richard finally pulled away, and Amanda and Tommy sank down onto the bed beside Barbara's inert form.

Pablo was already inspecting Barbara. The three looked on while he completed his exam. "She's good. In her soul."

Richard nodded. "A couple of times she came to, and then passed out again about three hours ago. She seems more at ease."

"She needs rest. You, too," Pablo said pointedly.

"I need a shower first, if no one minds," Richard said, already heading for the bathroom.

Amanda sat quietly for the next twenty minutes. Twice she heard the water in the shower turn off only to be turned back on again. At last it turned off and stayed off. After another minute, her father reappeared with a towel wrapped around his waist.

Scars shone on his chest. Some were small, barely visible. Others were larger, some the size of a quarter. One in particular caught her eye. It was a long, jagged scar that stretched from the area above his heart to the middle of his stomach. With a start she realized that she had never seen him with his shirt off. Even when they used to go on vacation when she was little, he had always had a tank top on when he'd gone swimming.

He smiled grimly as though sensing her thoughts. He sat down on the other bed and threw another towel over his shoulder, partly covering his chest. "They're from the war, honey. They're a part of me that I tried for too long to leave behind." He glanced down for a moment and then looked back at her, a faraway look in his eyes. "Maybe if I hadn't, your mom would have—"

He stopped abruptly with a quick shake of his head and plastered a smile on his face. Amanda grimaced. She knew he was talking about her mom's affair with Michael Deveraux, who had later been instrumental in killing her. Back then, her dad had been what could only be described as "boring." Marie-Claire, ever the exciting and flamboyant parent, had sought excitement elsewhere. Amanda herself had often wondered if her mom would still be alive if her dad had only been more exciting—or, at least more vigilant in guarding his wife from other men.

She, too, shook her head. It was too late to change the past. Maybe her mom's death had been inevitable, anyway. She might have died any number of times or a number of ways since, like others had a few days before.

She glanced at Pablo. The others of his coven,

Philippe, Armand, and Alonzo, were still missing. She wondered if he could feel anything from them. If they were dead, he would be alone in the world. *Except for us.* She grimaced. *We might all be dead soon enough.*

Her thoughts drifted to the others who were missing: Sasha, Silvana, Kari, Holly, Dan, and Tante Cecile. *No,* she corrected herself, *Tante Cecile is dead, killed by the demons possessing Holly.* The reality of that hit her hard, but she had to let herself care. *Otherwise I'm no better than Michael Deveraux.*

Then there were the two who were certifiably missing. Jer Deveraux was still trapped in the Dreamtime, where he and Holly had gone to rescue Barbara. The Goddess only knew if he was alive, but Amanda prayed he was. The other, Amanda's twin, Nicole, had been kidnapped by Eli Deveraux and James Moore right before the battle had broken out. Amanda clenched her fists at her side. *I swear I'll find you and get you away from those monsters.*

Richard spoke, interrupting her thoughts. "All right, first thing's first."

He retrieved his wallet from Barbara's pocket. He pulled out several bills. "Tommy, you look more presentable than the rest of us. Go buy some clothes for everyone, including the others. We also need medical supplies and food."

Tommy took the money and saluted. "I'm on it," he said, already heading out the door.

Amanda felt herself starting to panic as he left, but her father's voice snapped her attention back to him. "Amanda, I need you to look after Barbara. See if there's anything you can do to help her, a spell or something. We need her intact, both body and mind. Also, can you set up an alarm, sort of a magic-motion sensor, to let us know if anyone is coming?"

She nodded. "I think I can do something like that." Her stomach started doing flip-flops. She was not at all sure she could do as he asked. Holly was the strongest of them. Still, she would try.

"Good, get started," Richard instructed his daughter. He saw the fear flashing in her eyes, but he saw resolve there as well. That was good. It was best to give her a challenge, something for her to worry about besides Tommy's safety.

He turned to Pablo and sized up the young man. "I understand you can sense others?"

The boy nodded. "That's how I found you."

"That's what I figured. From what I heard Nicole saying, you can also keep others from finding us?"

He nodded. "I can keep them from finding us using magic means, but not ordinary ones."

Richard nodded. "That was our mistake with the cabin. It was an obvious place to look for us. This, at least, is a little less likely. There are dozens of places we could have come out of the forest that were a lot closer to the cabin, in case they're looking for us. We should be safe for a little while, at least."

"I don't think he's looking for us yet."

"Good. Now, have you felt any of the others?"

Pablo shook his head glumly.

Richard reached out and squeezed his shoulder. "Try, Pablo, please."

He didn't tell the boy that he had seen one of his coven die. Until Richard knew who it was, he wasn't going to upset him.

No sooner had the thought entered his mind than Pablo glanced at him sharply, eyes narrowing. He felt pressure, as though, someone were pushing against his brain, trying to get in. He pushed back. *Don't go there, boy.*

Looking startled and guilty, Pablo dropped his eyes. Richard gave his shoulder one last squeeze before standing up. He moved as far away from the others as he could in the cramped quarters.

Tommy returned sooner than Richard had expected. Amanda called out an alert, and a moment later there was a knock on the door. Even as Richard opened it for Tommy he knew they had to have a lot more warning than that in case the next arrival was not so friendly.

The young man dumped his findings out on the bed not occupied by Barbara. He had several sets of sweatshirts and sweatpants all sporting the logo WASHINGTON. He also had socks, a newspaper, a small first-aid kit, and a bag full of groceries. "There's a general store right next to the lobby," he explained.

Richard nodded, grabbing a pair of sweats and some socks and heading to the bathroom to change. Clean and now warm, he emerged feeling like a new man. Amanda headed for the rest room next and while she was in there, Tommy and Pablo also took the opportunity to change clothes.

When Amanda reappeared she gave Tommy a fierce hug, which Richard dutifully appeared not to notice. Amanda had always been his baby. Nicole had been flamboyant, wild, more like her mother. Amanda, though, had always been strong and steady. For years it had been the two of them against the rest of the world. As happy for her as he was, it was still hard to see his little girl as a woman.

Pablo broke into his thoughts. "I feel people!" he said, his voice cracking with excitement.

"How many?" Amanda asked.

"Two. I feel Armand and Kari."

★ ★ ★

Kari stumbled along, Armand's strong arm supporting her. The last thirty-six hours were a blur of pain and confusion. She didn't even remember leaving the cabin. Armand had spoken only a few words to her. All she really knew was that the cabin had caught fire, he had carried her out, and the others might be dead. Several times she fell and thought about staying down, but every time, he picked her back up and spoke a few encouraging words.

So, she marched on, unsure what the future held, or if there would even be a future for her. How had she gotten herself into this mess? She was just a grad student; she studied the occult, she didn't participate in it. That had all changed, though, when Jer Deveraux had introduced his dangerous world into her life. Not like she'd given him much choice.

She didn't dare ask Armand if he knew what had happened to Jer's body when the cabin caught on fire. Jer's spirit was on an astral plane, trapped in the Dreamtime. At least, she hoped he was just trapped and not dead. If his body had been destroyed, though, it was moot. If he had no body to return to, his spirit would wander forever. *Or maybe it would just vanish instantly,* she thought.

She tried banishing such thoughts from her mind, but it wasn't easy. Love was hell and she was the queen of the damned.

Hecate

Seattle, 1904: Peter and Ginny

Ginny stood on the train platform as the tears coursed down her cheeks. Her husband, George Morris, was already on board, waiting for her. In moments they would be steaming their way toward Los Angeles, leaving behind everyone else she loved.

Her father, Peter, wrapped his arms around her. Together they had been through so much: the death of her mother in the Johnstown flood, the journey west to settle in Seattle, and the tears and pain and unexpected joy when he had found dear Jane, who had become his second wife.

She stepped back, wiping the back of her gloved hand against her nose. It was an unladylike gesture, but she didn't care. Peter touched his hand to her cheek, and she closed her eyes, imagining that she was once again small and that he would always be beside her.

"Los Angeles is not that far away," he tried to reassure her, his voice cracking.

It was a lie, and not a very convincing one. Los Angeles was a world away, and the thought of leaving him and her half-sister was overwhelming. As though sensing her thoughts, Veronica spoke up.

"I will come visit you when you are settled, I promise."

Ginny looked to her sister and saw her pain mirrored in the girl's face. She had the eyes of a child and the body of a grown woman. How easy it was to forget that they were a few years apart in age.

Then Veronica flew into her arms, and they embraced tightly, each fearing to let go. At last Ginny whispered in Veronica's ear, "I know you are young, but Father will accept Charles and permit you to wed if you just give him a chance to see how good he is to you."

Veronica's slender form began to shake, racked by sobs that she muffled against Ginny's shoulder. They stood for a moment more until the conductor shouted the last call.

Ginny reluctantly pulled away and quickly kissed her father's cheek before stepping up onto the train. She clasped the rail with one hand and waved fiercely with the other as the train groaned and began to slowly move.

Her father and Veronica waved back, and Ginny kept waving until they were lost from her sight. Tears streaming down her face, she turned and entered the car. Her husband, George, was waiting for her and held out his arms to her. She sank down into the seat beside him and spent her tears upon his breast. He stroked her hair gently, murmuring words of love and comfort that she scarcely heard.

"I am eager to start our new life together in Los Angeles, but I'm afraid that I shall never see Father again," she whispered.

"Nonsense. He can come visit us anytime he likes, and we shall be back soon to see him," George tried to reassure her.

His words brought no comfort, though, for she had seen something when she'd kissed her father's cheek: a gravestone with his name on it. He was going to die soon, she could feel it.

Be at peace, my sister. The gentle words whispered in her brain in Veronica's voice. *All will be well and we'll be together again soon.*

She fervently hoped so, and she felt herself relax slightly. Since she had been born, Ginny had been able to hear Veronica's thoughts. It didn't happen all the time, just when Veronica was concentrating and Ginny's mind was open. It didn't go the other way, though. Veronica had never been able to hear Ginny's thoughts.

She sighed and looked up at her husband. She and George had been married for only four months, but it seemed like they had known each other forever. *I wish*

I could read his thoughts, she fretted. She pressed her hand against her stomach. *I wish I knew what he is going to say when I tell him about the baby.*

"Is everything all right?" he asked suddenly enough to startle her.

She stared into his eyes, searching. Was it possible he had heard her? His eyes were clear and innocent, though, with no mysteries or knowledge hidden within them. No, it was a coincidence. She forced herself to smile. "As long as we are together, it is."

He gave her shoulders a squeeze, and she felt warmth spreading through her. It was good to be in love.

Mother Coven: Santa Cruz

Luna, the High Priestess of the Mother Coven, was in trouble and she knew it. One by one, every woman who had survived the massacre had questioned her *or had thought about it.* Anne-Louise was the most vocal, but everyone was wondering what had gone wrong and beginning to doubt their High Priestess's intentions.

Truth is, they're right to doubt, she thought. *Holly Cathers and her coven are an inconvenience, to say the least. Then, House Cahors has never played by anyone's rules but their own. Still, maybe I've judged them too harshly. Amanda seems like a departure from the rest of her families. She's gentle and eager to please the Goddess and others.* Luna sighed. For Amanda's sake, if nothing else, she should act. Besides, the covenates were restless, and that was never a good thing.

That was why she was sitting alone in her chamber surrounded by purple candles and burning mugwort and wormwood. She had to find Holly Cathers and she was going to need magic to do it.

She sat quietly, a bowl of water before her ringed with even more of the purple candles. She hummed softly to herself as she pricked the tip of her forefinger with a needle and squeezed three drops of blood into the bowl.

"One for Holly, one for me, and one for the Goddess," she murmured as she did so.

She stared at the crimson spot in the water for a moment and then closed her eyes. She breathed deeply.

"Goddess, I come to you seeking that which was lost, that it might be found, a Cahors witch is somewhere around, grant me sight that I may see, where on earth this witch could be."

In her mind's eye, a face appeared and she gasped in surprise. *It was not Holly's.*

THREE

DECHTERE

☾

Within the fire we dance and laugh
We sacrifice on the God's behalf
Light the pyres and ring the bell
Summon all the fiends from hell

Surround us now in cloak of night
Rejecting the Horned God's light
Death we are and death we bring
Striking from the sacred ring

Veronica Cathers Covey: Los Angeles, September 21, 1905, 11:00 P.M.

"Must you really leave in the morning?" Ginny now asked, as she hugged her sister in the lobby of the Coronado Hotel. It was a large, spacious place, and there was an actual cobbled walkway in front of the entrance. Ginny and Veronica had spent their childhoods in much lower-rent neighborhoods in rainy Seattle, where even boardwalks were a rarity . . . making mud a commonplace.

Veronica tried to laugh lightly, but it came out

more as a sob. "If I could stay, you know I would, but I must get home to Charles and the baby."

"But Seattle is so far away!"

Veronica's tears fell on her sister's dark curls. It seemed ages since they had last seen each other, and who knew how long it would be before they were again reunited? "I will see you again soon, I promise."

Ginny nodded and finally pulled away from her. Tearfully, she turned and walked inside. She threw a last look over her shoulder and waved before stepping into the carriage.

Veronica continued to wave until the carriage was out of sight. Then she turned wearily toward the front desk. *At least I will be soon home with Charles and our son, Joshua.* She smiled, buoyed by the thought. She headed for the staircase.

"Ma'am?"

She turned and saw the night manager walking toward her, a telegram in his hand. Puzzled, she took it from him. He nodded briefly and then returned to his duties. Clutching the telegram, she hurried upstairs.

Inside her room, she sat down on the settee across from the lavatory. Her eyes dropped down to the name of the sender: Amy. Her sister-in-law.

With shaking hands and a sinking feeling, she tore open the telegram and began to read it in a whisper.

"DEAR VERONICA. STOP. COME HOME AT ONCE. STOP. CHARLES DROWNED THIS MORNING. STOP. JOSHUA IS SAFE WITH ME. STOP. ALL MY PRAYERS. STOP. AMY."

A cry ripped from the very center of her heart. She got to her feet and flung the telegram across the room. It fluttered like a hapless paper boat and sank to the wooden floor. "No," she whispered.

There was a soft knock on the door, followed by a man's voice. "Madame, are you okay in there?"

Numbly, she opened the door. She stared at him, her mouth working. For a few seconds, no sound would come out. "No," she said. Then she sank to the floor.

Something burned Veronica's eyes and nose; she bolted upright to discover herself reclining on the settee with a small crowd around her. A mustached man with a shock of white hair was tapping her wrist. A stout woman beside him moved a vial of smelling salts from beneath Veronica's nose, once she realized Veronica had been revived.

"My husband," she managed.

The woman nodded kindly. "I read your telegram. Hope you don't mind none."

How can he be dead? There was so much left to do, to experience. We were going to have another child. . . .

"Drink this. It's laudanum. It'll help you sleep," the man with the mustache ordered as he held out a glass of milky liquid. More gently, he added, "I'm a doctor. And permit me to introduce my wife, Mrs. Kelly."

Mrs. Kelly's eyes shone with tears. "You dear girl," she said. "You dear, sweet girl." She gestured to the glass. "Drink up. Get some rest. I'll stay with you until you sleep."

More in shock than anything else, Veronica gulped down the draft. Then she lay numbly against the pillow and closed her eyes.

She woke much later, to discover that the Kellys had left. Groggily, she sat up, then swung her legs over the bed. She found her slippers, slid her feet into them, and rose.

The room tilted and spun, and she grabbed hold of the bedpost. She put on her peignoir, then silently glided to the door.

Something whispered to her to open the door. She frowned, knowing that to walk the halls of a hotel in the dead of night wearing nothing but her sleeping clothes was not something she should do; and yet the little whispers persisted, urging her to act.

Before she realized it, her hand turned the knob. In a daze, she began to walk down the empty hall. It was as if someone walked beside her, guiding her, whispering directions to her in her ear.

After a time, she realized she had found her way somehow to the fourth floor. A chill swept through her, and she turned around, shivering. The door at the end of the hall seemed to shimmer briefly in her sight. She wanted to turn, to run down the hall, but she didn't. Instead, she found herself drifting toward the door, pulled as though against her will. At last she stood before it and she could feel someone, *something,* on the other side.

Of its own accord, her hand lifted. She tried to stop it, but she had lost control. Fear washed over her, leaving her stomach churning and her knees trembling.

Touch the door, a voice inside her mind commanded.

"No," she whispered. But the choice was not hers.

Her fingers brushed against the wood, and the contact sent electricity shooting through her arm. She pressed her palm against the door and felt, for a moment, the thing that was on the other side. There was rage, and hatred and . . . curiosity.

Suddenly it was as if her will was hers again, and she snatched her hand away with a cry. She turned and, picking up her skirts, fled down the hall. As she reached the top of the stairs she heard the door open; the sound lent speed to her feet.

She raced blindly down the stairs until she reached the first floor of the Coronado. She glanced toward the double entrance doors. *No.* It was the middle of the night, and she would be exposed outside.

She needed somewhere to hide. She was terrified, quite overcome; she wondered briefly if it was the laudanum, but she doubted that. Her Cathers intuition had come on full throttle, and every fiber of her being shouted that she was in real danger.

A door caught her eye and she raced to it, yanked it open, and found another set of stairs. Skirts held high, she bounded down the stairs, her heart pounding and lungs burning.

She shot into the basement. The light from a single lantern tried to push back the darkness and failed woefully. She stopped, took a few deep breaths, and looked around. *There must be somewhere to hide.*

But why do you want to do that? It was the soft, insistent voice again, the one that had spoken to her outside the door upstairs . . . only this time so loud, she could hear its timbre. It was a woman's voice.

"Who are you?" she whispered. "Are you angel or demon?"

I am Isabeau.

"Isabeau?" She tasted the name on her tongue. It seemed very familiar to her, although she could never remember hearing it before. "But . . . who are you?"

Before the voice could answer, the door at the top of the stairs opened. Footsteps followed, echoing loud as thunder.

There was a pile of rags on the ground; maybe she could hide in them. Before she had taken a step toward them, though, a voice boomed, "Stop!"

She turned, the hairs on the back of her neck lifting. She was pinned to the spot by a pair of smoldering eyes. The firelight danced across his hair, and his features twisted demonically.

And yet, there was something strangely compelling about this dark, hard-featured man. . . .

"Well, well, looks like I found myself a Cahors witch," he said. "One of two remaining, if I'm not mistaken. And their father, of course."

"Y-you are mistaken, sir," she stammered. "My name is Veronica Cathers, and I am certainly no witch. And . . . and neither is my . . . fath . . . anyone I know."

For a moment a shadow of doubt crossed his face. Then he shook his head. "Your name doesn't mean a thing to me. I am concerned with who you are, not what you call yourself. And, my dear lady, you are a witch."

"I am no witch," she cried again, moving away from him. *I'm a widow,* her mind wailed. *A widow. Oh my God, my family is dead! My true love . . .*

My true love . . .

Jean . . .

The darkly imposing man smiled and lifted his right hand. A ball of fire danced in it, and he lobbed it at her slowly. She opened her mouth to scream, but instead, words strange to her ear came out, and the fireball fizzled, dissolving in midair.

She was so astonished that her legs gave way; she grabbed on to a chair for purchase, panting wildly. A cold sweat burst across her forehead, and she was terribly hot, though she wore only her nightdress and peignoir.

The man chuckled cruelly. "You see? A witch."

Her mind raced. She backed away further. "Go away. Please."

He smiled. "Not for all the tea, sweet lady. Allow me to introduce myself. I am Marc Deveraux, of the House Deveraux, a warlock, and your sworn enemy."

"My . . . enemy?" she said slowly.

Did he have something to do with the drowning? Did he kill . . . did he . . . murder . . .

Non, he is Jean, my love, my enemy, my husband, the voice whispered. *Jean comes to me through him. You will stay. You will allow him to touch you, to kiss you, to make love to you.*

And then . . . you will kill him.

For me.

Marc Deveraux cocked his head to the side, and his eyes took on a faraway look as though, he, too, were hearing something. "Isabeau," he whispered.

"Jean," she answered.

His face softened. He reached out a hand. "My love. *Mon amour, ma femme, tu est ici, avec moi . . .*"

"*Oui,* I am here . . . *je suis ici, mon homme, mon seigneur . . .*"

She moved toward him as if in a dream. Her hands raised toward him.

"No," she whispered. And then again, more fiercely, "No!"

The shout punctuated the air, and Marc's face snapped back into sharp focus. "Then die!" he shouted.

He raised his hand and sent a fireball her way, full-speed this time. She cried out and ducked to the side. The fire landed in the pile of rags that she had thought to hide in. Within moments they were blazing out of control.

From somewhere deep inside of her, Veronica recalled a half-memory, shadowed in the fog of her early childhood. It was of a beautiful woman with flowing hair muttering in a foreign tongue. Veronica opened her mouth, and the same words came pouring out of her, the memory growing stronger. A fireball appeared in the air before her, and she willed it forward.

Marc leaped to the side, but the fireball caught the sleeve of his jacket and the fire began to burn. Raging, he shouted in French as he peeled the jacket off his body.

They faced each other for a long moment, circling warily. Veronica could feel the heat of the fire as it spread to other parts of the basement. It was licking at the roof of the room in the corner. She tried to edge nearer to the stairs and safety. There was a popping sound, and it was followed by a far-off scream.

Maybe someone will find us, she hoped. Suddenly Marc shouted, and the room began to disintegrate around her, turning into a whirling dervish of tools, cans, and wood. She ducked as the lantern whizzed through the air where her head had been.

She took a step backward, and the backs of her ankles hit the stairs. He started toward her. There were more shouts from upstairs.

Part of the ceiling in the corner collapsed in a

shower of sparks. The door to the basement opened, and she heard a man shouting, "The fire's down here!"

She turned and ran up the stairs as fast as she could, with Marc on her heels. He reached out and grabbed the hem of her robe, and she heard the rending of cloth. Part of her skirt ripped free, and she burst past the man at the top of the stairs who had shouted.

He swore under his breath and then yelled, "Lady, what's happening?"

She ignored him and kept running. She hit the front door and burst outside into the fresh air. Her lungs were burning, and she felt like her heart would explode from her chest. More shouts began to come from the hotel behind her, but she didn't look back.

She kept running until the night had swallowed her.

Marc Deveraux tried to fight off the arms of those who were holding him back, asking him questions about the fire. He seethed, ignoring them. The witch had gotten away. He held the piece of skirt that had ripped free in his hand and rubbed it slowly between his thumb and forefinger.

Heat, which had nothing to do with the flames that were beginning to engulf the hotel, filled his being. *Veronica Cathers, we will find you, Isabeau,* the voice in his head sobbed. *Come back, my love. Come back.*

Tri-Coven: Seattle

The band—Kari, Tommy, Amanda, and Nicole—left Barbara behind in the motel to inspect the ruins of the cabin. Though they hoped to discover more survivors, death hung in the charred landscape like a pall. The twilight sucked whatever color might have been left, and they walked in an alien landscape that mirrored Amanda's notion of limbo.

Amanda found Silvana lying at the edge of the trees. Her eyes were fixed wide, her face frozen in terror. She fell to her knees beside her. For years, Silvana had been her best friend. She and her aunt had come to help when all the craziness had started. Now, she was gone—they both were. *They are dead because of me.*

She balled her hands into fists. No, not because of her—because of Michael Deveraux. His evil had brought pain and death upon them all.

She could not tell what had killed Silvana. She reached down and lifted Silvana's head into her lap. Something sticky coated her hands. She began to wretch when she realized the cause. The back of Silvana's head was gone.

Rage ripped through her. Silvana had not deserved to die. A shout from Tommy pierced through her fog of pain and brought her to her feet.

He was standing amid the smoking ruins of the

cabin. He was frozen, staring down at something she could not see. Picking her way carefully across the field of debris, she joined him. He was standing in front of a bookshelf that had been snapped in half and fallen in a tepee shape.

There, wedged between and underneath the two halves, was a person. Amanda reached out to touch the bookshelf, but was painfully repulsed. The space was heavily warded. "Is—it—alive?" she asked, not even sure if it was human, let alone whether "it" was male or female.

"I don't know," Tommy answered quietly. "I couldn't touch it either. We need help."

"Have you found anyone else?"

He shook his head. "You?"

"I found Silvana's body—what was left of it."

He grabbed her hand and gave it a fierce squeeze.

"Has anyone else had any luck?"

"I don't know, let's—"

He was interrupted by a loud, keening wail—as if it were an animal's. Tommy shot her a grim look, and they hurried toward the sound.

They found Pablo a little ways off. He was kneeling by a fresh mound of dirt. Two sticks had been tied together with a strip of cloth to form the shape of a cross. The cross had been driven into the ground at one end of the mound. In the dirt on the mound a pentagram had been drawn along with other symbols unknown to Amanda. She grasped Pablo's shoulder. "Who is it?" she whispered.

"Alonzo."

The oldest member of the Spanish Coven. Tears stung her eyes. Another dead. Pablo bowed his head and sobbed.

A thought struck her: *If Alonzo is buried, who did it?* A ray of hope shone through. *It must have been Philippe.* He alone of the missing covenates would have thought to adorn the grave with both Christian and Wiccan symbols.

"Pablo!"

The boy looked up, startled.

"Can you sense Philippe? He must have buried Alonzo."

The boy closed his eyes. After a moment, a look of frustration crossed his face. He put out his hand, touching the symbols marked into the dirt. His eyes flew open, and he nodded eagerly. "Yes, and he is not far away."

As if on cue, a branch snapped behind them. They whirled around to see Philippe emerging cautiously from the trees. Pablo leaped to his feet and flew to him. Philippe clasped him tight. Amanda approached more slowly. When she had reached them, Pablo released Philippe, who in turn hugged Amanda.

"It is good to see you."

"And you," she told him.

"Armand?" he questioned.

"Safe. He saved Kari as well."

Philippe sighed deeply, as though a burden had been lifted from him. "And the others?"

"Dan, Holly, and Sasha are still missing. Silvana and Alonzo are dead. Everyone else is alive."

"Have you heard anything of Nicole?"

She shook her head. "No, not since James and Eli took her."

Tommy broke in. "We did find someone, or something, in the debris. It's warded, though, and we can't reach it."

"Show me."

Minutes later they were all gathered before the broken bookshelf. Armand, Kari, and Richard had joined them, and they all took turns peering into the recess. Finally Philippe observed, "The wards are strong. It will take all of us to break them."

Amanda agreed. The others, except for Richard, formed a chain with Philippe at one end and Tommy at the other. They began to chant quietly, each in his own way but with a common purpose.

Philippe and Tommy each laid a free hand on one of Amanda's shoulders. She could feel the group's power washing over her and through her.

She took a deep breath and reached through the ward, which had already been weakened by the chanting. She grasped the creature's arms and tugged. The body moved only a little. She tensed all her muscles and yanked. The body flew out and into her arms.

She stumbled backward, and the group caught her. Tommy relieved her of her burden and lowered the body to the ground. It was Sasha.

Everyone pressed forward to look at her. Her eyelids flew open, and everyone jumped back. Sasha gazed up at Amanda and asked, in an eerily normal voice, "What happened?"

Amanda couldn't help herself, she started to laugh. And then, as a portal opened up in front of her and four lumbering gray creatures exited it, she began to scream.

Philippe hurled a fireball in the blink of an eye, but it had no effect on the creature it struck. He threw another and another with no effect. As the group stumbled backward, Amanda threw up a barrier. The first of the creatures hit it, and simply opened a portal on the other side of it.

"What are those things?" Amanda shrieked.

"I don't know, but we have to get away from them!" Philippe answered.

"To the woods, everyone, quickly!" Richard yelled, voice booming.

They turned and fled, the creatures pursuing. Another portal opened in front of Amanda, though, and the creatures just cut them off.

"They're after Amanda!" Tommy shouted, yanking her away from a reaching arm.

"Armand, do something!" Philippe shouted.

The other witch nodded and raised his arms. Suddenly, the creatures stopped. The one closest to Amanda cast its head back and forth as though looking for a scent it had just lost.

"What, what's happening?" she asked in a whisper.

"He's cloaking your energies from the creatures, making it so they can't sense you."

"But they know there are people here—they see us!" she hissed.

"Yes," Tommy whispered. "But I think they're only after you."

"That is correct," Armand said through gritted teeth. "Now, everyone, just move quietly away. Try not to attract undue attention, and don't distract me!"

They did as he said, moving steadily away from the creatures. Amanda could feel her heart pounding in her chest. *They're after me! Why not everyone else?* She turned once to look back and saw the creatures standing around, looking for all the world like lost puppies.

"We had the hotel warded, blocking our presence. When we came out in the open, I think they were able to pick up on you and come to where you were," Philippe said after a brief exchange with Pablo.

Amanda shivered. "Remind me not to go anywhere without Armand again."

She glanced at Tommy, and his eyes were bulging out. "Anywhere?" he asked, sounding forlorn.

She picked up his hand and squeezed it, appreciating him again. "Well, I'm sure he can block my vibes just fine from the next room."

Tommy smiled. "That, I can live with."

"Did anyone see any sign of the cats?" Amanda asked.

"I have not seen them," Philippe answered. "I saw their tracks, though, I believe they escaped."

Goddess, go with them, Amanda prayed. *Lead them to young women who need their strength and guidance.* In her heart she knew she would not see them again, but she also knew, somehow, that they were safe, and that made it a little easier.

The hair on the back of her neck suddenly stood on end, and Amanda swiveled her head to the side. She gasped and stopped in her tracks.

There, his back to a tree, was Dan. He was covered in dried blood, and flies were buzzing around him.

Her father moved quickly to him. "Dead," he announced, without even touching the body.

Tears sprang to her eyes. "Too much death," she murmured.

"He must have put up one heck of a fight," Richard noted.

"It didn't save him, though," she whispered.

"Come on, Amanda, we have to keep moving," Tommy reminded her gently as he wrapped an arm around her shoulders.

When will it all end? she thought in despair. *And how many more of us will die?*

Seattle: Michael Deveraux

Michael Deveraux slammed his fist down on his altar. Bits of broken glass embedded themselves in his flesh. He raised his hand slowly, savoring the pain and the sensation of the blood dripping down his hand to land on the altar. He slowly picked the glass, left over from last night's sacrifice, from his hand.

He knew that members of the Cathers Coven had survived the fire, but his scrying stones, his imp, and all his magic had been unable to locate them yet. That was going to change. What he had planned would not only enhance his power, it would also give him a unique insight into the workings of the Cathers and their pitiful little coven.

Chittering to itself, his imp appeared in the room. Michael watched it silently for a moment. He had still never discovered the creature's motivation for attaching itself to him. Then again, with imps, one rarely knew why they did much of anything.

"Well?" he asked.

"Everything is ready," the imp chortled, clearly pleased with itself.

Michael smiled. Seattle was an interesting town, a hotbed of supernatural activity. It was only natural that the Deveraux and the Cathers had both chosen it as home. There were haunted places that made even his hair stand on end.

One of those places was his destination tonight. A delicious shiver ran up his spine, and he took a moment to savor the sensation.

"Is Holly ready?"

The imp jumped up and down, wagging its head in glee.

Michael nodded. "Let's go."

Holly was in the backseat of the car, heavily tranquilized and drooling slightly. The imp jumped up and down on her, even hopping up to perch on her head, and she took no notice. Michael glanced in the rearview mirror and smiled grimly. The night sky was clear, and the stars shone brightly. The cursed moon was nowhere to be found. Michael had planned to conduct the rite on a moonless night, better not to have that symbol of the Goddess present. He would have preferred to hold the ceremony when the God reigned supreme in the midday sky, but discretion had dictated that the cloak of night hide him. Thus, when he pulled into the parking lot of the Baptist church, there was none around to see.

He got out of the car slowly, almost reverently. His actions had nothing to do with the current function of the church, but with its older uses. It had once been a Masonic church, and rumor had it that sacrifices, both animal and human, had been made there. He had never been able to verify the identity of those making the sacrifices, but he had seen enough in the walls of the church and in hidden rooms beneath to know that far worse things than human sacrifice had occurred there.

He opened the back door and dragged Holly out. She wobbled when he tried to stand her up, so after a moment he just slung her over his shoulder and, with the imp prancing at his side, headed for the side door of the building.

The door was unlocked—*Christians can be so trusting*—and he slipped inside. Once inside the door, he headed for the usher's closet, trying to avoid touching the pews as he passed them. The closet door was unlocked, and the imp held it open while Michael walked inside, Holly still slung over his shoulder.

He set her down, propping her in a corner in the hope that she wouldn't fall. He then knelt carefully by the back wall and ran his fingers under the edge of the carpet. It lifted up, and with a mighty tug he pulled, folding it back onto itself and revealing a bare floor with a trapdoor.

After securing the carpet so that it wouldn't fall back down over the trapdoor, Michael opened it and picked up Holly once more. The imp grabbed a flashlight and staggered down the steps before them, the flashlight beam waving drunkenly from side to side.

Down they descended into a darkness so thick, it made Michael wonder bemusedly if they had reached hell. Violent odors assaulted his nostrils, dank air carried the scent of blood and death. Then the stairs finally ended, and they were standing in a basement the little Baptist church above knew nothing about. Evil coated the walls and seeped up through the floor. Michael shivered as it washed over him, and the hair on the back of his neck stood on end. This was a dark place, an evil place, that had seen worse things than any he had ever done. It frightened him and, since so little did, he reveled in it. He had been here once before when he was a child. His father had brought him, and the entire experience still lived crystal-clear in his memory. How his father had first found the place he had been too afraid to ask.

He stood Holly up once more on her feet and put his arm around her to keep her standing upright. She turned and looked at him with great wild eyes and began to coo softly. It almost sounded as though she were singing a children's nursery rhyme. She laughed, loud and hollowly, and the sound echoed off the walls, coming back wilder and deeper.

He shivered again as he searched her eyes. She looked . . . happy . . . as though whatever had possessed her had found this place to its liking. He was glad it approved. The imp flitted here and there, setting everything up just so. At last he was finished and came to stand beside Michael. The strange little creature pulled itself up to its full height and bowed very slowly and with more dignity than he would have thought it capable. Truly it was a momentous occasion.

An upside-down pentagram had been drawn on the wall opposite of where they stood. The symbol had been inscribed with fresh blood—whose, he did not know. The figure of an old man suddenly appeared, coming from the wall and passing through the pentagram so that blood from the five points rested on his clothes.

Michael had seen him before when he had come with his father. The old man was some sort of dark priest—or, at least, the ghost of one. He performed rituals for those who needed them and haunted the Christians above when he was off duty.

"What do you seek?" he asked, his voice creaking.

"I seek to have this woman placed in thrall to me."

The old man drifted closer, his eyes burning. "To such a one as this?" he questioned, lifting Holly's chin with a long, bony finger.

"Yes."

"Carefully should you do this. She is not of your kind."

Michael smiled thinly. *A ghost and a Yoda wanna-be on top of it.* "Neither is she of her own mind."

"True, true. But you should be wary of the day that that changes. Whatever I bind to you, you are also bound to."

"I accept the risk," Michael told him.

The old man nodded slowly, and Michael could hear the creak of brittle bones. The priest's pale fingers reached inside his ancient robes and pulled out an athame. It glowed wickedly with a light of its own, and Michael could hear the sounds of faraway screams coming from it. *A reminder of sacrifices past,* he thought.

The old man reached out and slashed first Holly's palm, then Michael's. Michael couldn't help but hiss slightly at the pain. He was used to being cut ceremonially, but this pain was somehow different, as though it were amplified by the place, the time, and his intention.

The old man peered at him from beneath bushy brows. "To be in thrall is to share each other's power . . . and pain."

Michael hesitated, wondering fleetingly what that would mean when the time came to kill Holly. He shrugged, though, dismissing the thought. Thousands of witches and warlocks had gone through this ceremony, and it was rarely more lasting for them than marriage was for mortals. He was sure he could find some way to break the contract.

The priest took their bleeding palms and pressed them together until Holly's blood flowed in his veins and his in hers. Next the priest took a black silken cord from the imp and lashed their hands together.

"Blood to blood, magic to magic, in this very hour you double your power. As Eve bound herself to the serpent, so this woman is now bound to you." The priest then walked slowly around each of them, slashing at their clothing with his athame. At last, hands still bound, they both stood naked and bleeding from several shallow cuts from the blade.

Michael stared at Holly and could feel lust spreading throughout his body. He hadn't given much thought to this part of the ceremony, obviously an oversight on his part.

"Take her, for she is yours," the priest commanded.

Michael stepped forward to do just that, but Holly tottered and slumped to the ground, unconscious. The force of her fall undid the black cord binding their hands together, and Michael stood staring down at her.

She was his, and he would have her . . . but he would find no pleasure with her unconscious. He'd learned that the hard way, with Holly's aunt Marie-Claire—the mother of the two other Cahors witches, Nicole and Amanda Anderson.

He sighed. "Bring the change of clothes," he commanded his imp as he turned his back on Holly's inert form.

Seattle: Tri-Coven

Richard paced the floor like a caged animal. He felt as though the walls were closing in on him. He could feel his daughter's eyes on him. The woman, Sasha, was staring at him as well. They three alone were awake, keeping watch in the night while the others slept.

Now that they had accounted for all but Holly and Nicole; the others had started talking about rescue missions. Sasha was particularly insistent that someone should try to go into the Nightmare Dreamtime to find her son, Jer. If he was still alive. His body was, at least. They had found it a few yards away from the ruined cabin. Someone had carried him that far.

Considering that Holly had come back from the Dreamtime insane and possessed, almost everyone was disagreeing with Sasha. He could see her point, though. If he was alive, they needed to at least try to rescue him. If he was dead, then they could all move on and put their energies elsewhere.

Sasha interrupted his thoughts. "You saw a lot of pain during the war."

It was a statement, not a question, and he glanced at her in surprise. "Is it that obvious?"

She smiled slightly. "It is to me. But then, I know something about pain."

He stared at her. Amanda had told him that Sasha had been married to Michael and had had to give up both of her children when she'd fled from him and his evil. He guessed that she did know something about pain . . . and loss.

He pulled up a chair and lowered himself into it deliberately, though he only perched on the edge of it. "Yes, I believe you do."

Amanda glanced from one to the other of them with a bewildered look on her face.

Richard leaned forward. "I spent a year in the jungle. Very little food, less sleep, friends dying every day. Just when we thought we'd gained a couple of hours' peace, a chance to rest, the VC would be there, all around us, and the sounds of gunfire would all but drown out the screams of the dying. And in the night when I didn't know if I'd live to see another sunrise, all I had to hold on to was the hope of making it home and spending the rest of my years in peace and quiet with my wife."

He glanced at Amanda and saw the tears streaking down her face. "I guess we know how well that plan worked out," he said sardonically.

"Mom didn't understand," Amanda whispered brokenly.

"No, she didn't. But I think you do," he said, touching his daughter's cheek. "I'm so sorry, baby. I'd give anything to have spared you this kind of pain and fear."

"I know, Daddy," she choked. And then she flew into his arms, and he was holding his daughter as they cried together, for themselves and each other. Sasha placed a hand on his arm, and he could feel her pain, too, and the grief that she suffered for them as well. In that moment, he knew he was going to find her son.

Santa Cruz: Mother Coven

Luna, High Priestess of the Mother Coven, was stunned. She had asked the Goddess to help her find Holly. Instead, the Goddess had shown her another Cathers witch.

"Goddess, how can this be? Who is this witch I see?"

A gray cat with great yellow eyes scampered into the room and proceeded to sit down before her. Then the cat opened its mouth and a resounding female voice poured forth:

"What you seek has been lost for a century. Two sisters, removed from one another, one to dwell in the City of Devils, and the other to stay with her father. Death came to both, and the menchildren they bore lost their way, so that their descendants forgot who they were. House Cahors was all but lost."

Luna sat, stunned, barely able to breathe, let alone speak. The Goddess had only come to her in this manner twice, long years before. She bowed her head, feelings of unworthiness washing over her.

"My Goddess, I was seeking Holly."

"And to find her you must first find her counterpart. Seek the other witch in that city where darkness dwells. Look for the name changed once again from the ancient. You seek a Carruthers who alone may help to restore Holly's mind."

The cat stood, blinked once, and left the room, leaving Luna shaken and humbled. "To the City of Devils I will go," she vowed.

She could swear she heard the Goddess sigh in answer.

FOUR

ARTEMIS

☾

Triumphant now, Deveraux reign
Nothing will ever be the same
Cahors moan and Cahors cry
In death throes beneath the velvet sky

Everything pure is but a ruse
And love is naught but the excuse
We make for all the things we do
There is little good and nothing true

Seattle: Michael and Holly

Michael thought Holly might actually be looking better. Then again, it was so hard to tell. Her eyes were bright . . . *she could have a fever, or one of the hell-beasts in her could be ascendant.* She wasn't drooling on herself . . . *maybe she's dehydrated.* She had actually managed to eat some food on her own . . . *she got more on her face than in her mouth.* He sighed. There was only one way to know for sure.

She was sitting on the couch, contemplating her

knees. He warily sat beside her. "Holly, do you hear me?" he asked.

She nodded briefly.

"Do you understand me?"

She looked at him and again nodded.

Ah-ha, progress! "Holly, I want you to listen very carefully to me."

Her eyes were still on him. It was a good sign. "Holly, I want you to kill Amanda and Nicole Anderson."

He waited for a moment while she seemed to think about that. "Kill Amanda and Nicole," she said slowly.

He felt like holding his breath. The connection was tenuous, but it seemed to be there. He reached out to her with his mind, gently pushing. *My will to yours.* It was the way of thrall.

Aloud, he asked, "Holly, can you do that?"

She raised her hand. "Kill," she whispered. Every lightbulb in the room exploded at once.

In the sudden darkness, Michael could think of nothing else to say but, "Very, very good."

Luna: Los Angeles

Luna, High Priestess of the Mother Coven, stared out the window as the plane circled over Los Angeles

International Airport. Heavy, poisonous smog hung over the city like a shroud over a decaying corpse. The earth, the sea, the air itself were poison here, and all the people were walking corpses, shells of human beings, hollow and empty. That didn't account for the darkness, though, the darkness that she could see but most could not. There was a pall that lay over the entire area, black and twisting like so many shadows. The evil seething from the buildings, the people, the very earth was overwhelming.

She moved her lips in supplication to the Goddess, for protection and for guidance. Her skin crawled as the plane began its final descent. The teenager sitting next to her shifted uncomfortably in her seat and moved away from Luna. *She thinks I'm crazy,* Luna thought sadly. She looked at the girl's revealing clothes, her soulless stare, and the features perfected by plastic surgery. *In reality she is the crazy one, sacrificing her youth and her soul to this city of evil, which has devoured so many before her and will devour so many after her.*

Luna turned back to the window. The plane hadn't even touched ground, and yet she already felt tired, drained, old. She continued her prayers, fortifying her mind and trying to calm even the cells in her body, which were shrinking from the horrors below.

When the plane landed, she felt sick inside and

out. It took fifteen minutes to reach the gate, and when the FASTEN SEAT BELT sign was finally turned off, the girl beside her leaped from her seat and headed toward the front of the plane. The door opened, and the air from the terminal rushed inward, mixing with the air from the plane, and Luna felt her stomach twisting with nausea. She glanced around her; everyone else seemed unaware of the change as they struggled with their bags. She sighed deeply and closed her eyes. *Sometimes it's hell to be a witch.*

She made her way through the airport as quickly as she could. Even here the seedy underbelly of the city flourished. Beggars walked around selling stickers and other trinkets, pushing their presence into the faces of all. Luna shook her head slowly at one of them. The young woman made more in a year from her begging than most of the families trying to escape on vacation who threw guilty dollars her way.

When the woman pressed up to her, Luna stared into her eyes. "I think you should go home. Stop being a burden on society, work to better it."

Dazed, the young woman nodded slowly and turned to go. The mesmerism would wear off within a few hours, but at least she had purchased a few moments of peace for the young couple from Ohio who would have been the woman's next mark.

Luna continued on to ground transportation, her overnight bag held tightly in her hand. Los Angeles was a dangerous place, even for a witch. And somewhere, amid all the chaos and insanity, was a young man she needed to find. She only prayed that his heart had not been twisted by the evil around him. She prayed that he served the Goddess. She prayed that at least he did not serve the Horned God . . . *or something worse.*

Outside, the tangled cars vied with one another for positions at the curb. The honking horns and shouting voices mingled with the shrill whistles of the parking police to form a cacophony of sound that was deafening.

She hailed a taxi and stepped inside. It took all her powers just to communicate with the driver the name of the hotel she wished to visit. The Wilshire Grand Hotel was one of the most prestigious hotels in Los Angeles. She didn't know why, then, she had such a problem explaining her destination. She sighed and sank back into her seat. It was not going to be an easy trip.

Half an hour later, the taxi pulled up to the hotel and Luna pulled her nails from the seat of the car. *I must have lost ten years of life,* she thought bitterly. The drive had been enough to turn the most hardened warrior green with motion sickness and pale with fright.

She checked in and was shown to her room. She did not have much to unpack. Still, she took the time to ward the room and place various magic arcana around.

She ordered a light dinner from room service and ate it leisurely. Once finished, she dressed for the evening. She donned a simple white gown that she decorated with silver moon-shaped jewelry. She took one look in the mirror before heading for the door. It was time to go the theater.

Within minutes she was at the Ahmanson Theatre. She accepted her program and found her seat about ten minutes before the show was to start. She took the time to read her program.

The historic Ahmanson Theatre had been the site of the West Coast premier of *The Phantom of the Opera*. Now the musical was back, with a fast-rising young star playing the role of the Phantom. She read his bio with an amused grin. Alex Carruthers had been mesmerizing audiences across the country with his portrayal of the tortured Phantom. Alex had been acting since the age of seven, when he played Winthrop Wallace in a local theater's performance of *The Music Man*. He had attended a prestigious acting school in Los Angeles after high school. At twenty-three, he was the youngest actor to star in *The Phantom of the Opera*.

The lights in the theater dimmed briefly, signaling theater patrons to take their seats. Five minutes later, the curtain lifted. By the time the first act ended, Christine, the beautiful heroine of the story, was not the only one under the Phantom's spell.

Alex Carruthers had mesmerized the entire audience.

Alex Carruthers played the crowd and they ate it up. Luna watched him as the Phantom. By the time he was singing "The Point of No Return," trying to seduce the young actress playing Christine, the sexual energy flowing off every woman in the room was overpowering. And at the end of the final act, even the grown men were weeping.

Five curtain calls later, the house lights came up and the rush to leave the theater began. Luna sat for a moment, waiting for her row to empty out.

The young man was powerful. If he had any other skills that could match his ability of mesmerism, he would be a formidable force indeed. *Now it's time to find out whom he serves.*

She rose and made her way toward the stage. "Cloak my passing from all eyes, make invisibility my guise," she murmured. She smiled at herself. When she had become High Priestess, she had ceased needing to speak her spells aloud. All of the upheaval in the coven must be upsetting her more than she'd realized.

She took the stage and slid behind the curtain, walking past stagehands already putting things away for the next evening's performance. As she drifted by one of the dressing rooms, the actress playing Carlotta glanced up suspiciously. *She's a witch and she can feel me. She does well to be worried; she has a lot to hide*. In a twist of irony, the actress playing the diva that the Phantom despised couldn't actually sing well. She glamoured her voice so that it would appear passable. Luna paused for a moment as a new thought occurred to her: *Or perhaps someone glamoured her voice for her*.

She moved on; the woman was not the one she sought. When she stopped outside the men's dressing room, Alex was waiting for her. He rose from his seat and glided toward her. He alone saw her; the rest were still blinded to her presence. *Walk with me*.

She fell into step beside him. Within moments they had reached his private dressing room and entered. Once in the room, she allowed her invisibility to drop from her, so that he could see her clearly.

He was tall, just over six feet. He had white-blond hair, and blue eyes that crackled with energy. *He looks nothing like a Cahors, and yet I can feel their blood coursing through his veins*. There might not be a physical resemblance, but the psychic one was undeniable.

He sat down and motioned her to a seat as well. She took it and began probing his mind even as he was probing hers. She freely opened areas of her mind where she wanted him to go, and reinforced her mental blocks around the things she was not ready to share with him. He did the same, and they danced back and forth, thrusting into each other's minds and parrying the other's attacks.

At last, a truce was called, and just in time; he had nearly torn down her defenses. *By the Goddess, he is strong!*

"Why have you come?" he asked simply.

"To see you."

"Whom do you serve?" he asked.

"I belong to the Goddess. I am Luna, High Priestess of the Mother Coven." She lifted her chin. "And you?"

"I am Alex Carruthers, of the Coven of the Air. I serve the Goddess as well."

She narrowed her eyes as she studied him. Somehow, she didn't think that that was entirely true; it didn't feel like the first response that had come to his mind. She glanced around the room. On the back of a door hung a dark blue silk robe with a large moon on the back. A small statue of Aphrodite rested on the dressing table. Other than that, the room was bare of magic symbols.

She forced herself to relax slightly. *These are both Goddess symbols. If he has not benefited from formal instruction, there might be some slight variations in the way he worships, and that might be what disturbs me.*

She smiled grimly. Just as the Goddess had many forms, there were many ways to worship her, different ones adopted by different cultures. In the end they were more alike than different, and they worshiped the same being. *It's like Protestants arguing over whether they're Lutheran or Methodist.*

Alex smiled disarmingly at her. "I believe we worship the same Lady?"

She nodded. "The others in the troupe—they are your coven?"

"Some of them," he admitted. "We of the Craft must stick together."

"And the actress playing Carlotta—you were the one to glamour her voice?"

He sighed in a frustrated manner. "Yes. She's a marvelous actress, and she's always been like an aunt to me. She just can't sing."

"No one in the audience would know that."

"Except for you," he pointed out.

"Except for me," she admitted.

He gazed at her for a long moment. "You said you

came to see me, Luna of the Mother Coven. What is it that you wanted?"

She smiled and leaned forward. "I want to reacquaint you with your roots."

He frowned, and she could tell that she had truly surprised him. After a moment, he spoke: "I discovered at the age of five that I was different, that I could make things happen. When I was ten I realized I was a witch and that my mother had been one. I joined my first coven a year later, and by the time I was fifteen I was the head of my own. I am a witch and have had to hide this fact from a society that really has not moved much past where it was during the Salem witch trials. What more could you possibly have to tell me?"

She chuckled softly. "Everything."

Tri-Coven: Seattle

Holly, or what was left of her, stood outside the hotel room where the others were hiding. She cocked her head to the side, listening to the multitude of voices within. Something was being said about death.

There were barriers around the hotel, but they were weak—at least they *felt* weak. She raised her hands, whispering, "Kill them, kill them all."

Fireballs appeared in the air before her, hundreds of them, shining and pulsing with deadly energy. They quivered, eager to be unleashed upon their target. *"Aggredior!"* she cried, and the fireballs whizzed through the air like flights of arrows.

The first wave exploded against the wards, weakening them. The second wave punched holes through the wards, and they shimmered briefly before vanishing. The third wave assaulted the building, setting it instantly ablaze.

There were shouts from within and doors flew open, the covenates burst from the building, lobbing fireballs of their own as they scrambled for some kind of cover. Holly laughed and raised her arms to send another volley their way.

Before she could, something tackled her from behind and knocked the breath from her. She lay on the ground for a moment, stunned. *Get up, get up,* a voice hissed in her mind. Was it hers? She didn't know. *Run quickly. No! Stand and fight, destroy!*

She clamped her hands over her ears and screamed. The voices were arguing, urging her to do one thing, then another.

"What do you want from me?" she shrieked. "Leave me alone!"

"Holly!" she heard a voice cry, far away and muffled, as though it were underwater. "Holly, look out!"

What do they want from me? she thought, angrily

raising her head and turning to look. What she saw made no sense. A giant man-beast of gray hovered over her.

She rolled to the side as a massive fist crushed the earth where she had lain. She breathed, and fire exploded from her fingertips, engulfing the creature.

The fire didn't phase it, and it just reached for her again. It picked her up and began to squeeze, crushing her ribs. She let her head fall to the side as her vision dimmed.

The end at last . . . thank the Goddess.

No! Kill it. Destroy it.

I don't know what it is.

Golem. Erase the first symbol on its forehead.

Holly reached up with her hand and jabbed her thumb into the *e* of the word *emet* on the thing's forehead. She ground at it. It howled in anguish and dropped her, hands flying to its head.

She scrambled to her feet, ready to finish what she had started. Another voice inside, more insistent, screamed, *Run!*

She did.

Amanda stood panting, watching helplessly as Holly ran off, pursued by four great lumbering creatures.

"What, what are those things?" she gasped.

"Golems," Sasha answered solemnly. "Creatures made of clay and imbued with the will of their creator."

"Who made them? Michael?" Philippe questioned.

Sasha shook her head slowly. "To make one of those takes years of serious study in the Kabalistic teachings. It is one of the most difficult and dangerous pieces of magic one could ever do. Michael doesn't possess the knowledge of such teachings to have done it."

"You're sure of that?" Richard questioned sharply.

Sasha nodded. "His magic isn't based on that, and from all that I know, he has never reached into other religions with enough zealousness to learn such things."

"If not Michael, then who?" Philippe asked.

"I don't know, and that's what frightens me."

"The leader of the Supreme Coven," Pablo whispered, so softly that they barely heard him.

Armand nodded. "You said these Golems were imbued with the will of their creator?"

Sasha nodded.

Armand turned to Pablo. "And it was the leader of the Supreme Coven that you felt when they were here."

Pablo shuddered lightly. "Yes. And they were searching for Amanda."

"If they were after me, there are probably more

looking for Holly and Nicole," Amanda groaned.

Sasha put an arm around Amanda's shoulders. "We'll look after you, sweetheart. Your father is right, though: We're not safe now; we have to go."

"Where?" Amanda asked, her heart heavy with worry.

There was silence for a long minute. It was finally broken by Kari, who had said nothing since the attack. "I know a place."

Alex and Luna: En route to Seattle

Alex sat beside Luna on the plane to Sacramento. A call from one of her covenates before they left L.A. had redirected them here. The plane was nearly empty, and they were the only ones flying first class. Alex looked . . . nervous. *I would be, too, if I were about to meet a long-lost branch of my family and join them in combat against evil.* He turned and smiled at her.

The rest of his coven had stayed behind in Los Angeles, though with extreme objections. In the end, Alex had not ordered them but persuaded them. They had agreed to stay behind at last, not because what he was doing was dangerous, not because he should meet his family alone, not even because he wished it. They stayed because the show had to go on. They had an understudy who could play the Phantom for a few days, but they did not have enough understudies to allow them all to leave. So, with much sighing and ritual blessings, they let him go, bidding the Goddess speed his way back. The bond between the members of the group had astounded her.

It made her nervous that his coven had been operating for several years beneath the Mother Coven's radar. *How is that possible when we both worship the Goddess?* It was a mystery, and she knew she would get no answers from Alex. There would be time enough for the priestesses to puzzle over this. Now she just had to join Alex with his cousins.

They hadn't even been on the plane yet a half hour and it was already painfully clear that one of the flight attendants found Alex irresistible. He seemed to have an energy that radiated from him, and his face shone with an unnatural light. She was not surprised that young women were drawn to him.

To his credit, he did not encourage the young lady. In fact, he barely seemed to notice her at all, as though she didn't even exist. Luna's eyes narrowed as she watched him.

"Would you like something to drink?" the attendant asked, at last turning her eyes to Luna.

"Ginger ale," she said, and under her breath she added, "forget him, child."

The woman blinked and stared at her for a moment blankly before regaining her perky no-one-on-this-flight-has-annoyed-me-yet smile.

The flight seemed interminable, but at last the plane landed. They made their way to baggage claim. Luna pulled out her cell phone and called a member of the Mother Coven who had stayed behind in Seattle when the rest had withdrawn to Santa Cruz. The other woman answered on the first ring. She spoke only three words: *moving, cabin,* and *Winters*.

Luna pressed "end" on her phone and hung up without even saying a word. After retrieving Alex's luggage, they walked outside and hailed a taxi.

"Where to?" the driver asked, looking them over.

"Winters."

"What country you from?" the driver asked, speaking around the gum in his mouth.

"Canada," she said briefly.

"Ah, Canada. Pretty country. You here on vacation or what?"

With a flick of her wrist, Luna dispelled the driver's interest in them and sat back to enjoy the ride. Given the luck of the Cathers Coven, she would need her energies when they met up.

Tri-Coven: Winters, California

Richard had won the argument: Of all those present, he had been selected to enter the Dreamtime and go after Jer Deveraux. He had argued that he was in excellent physical condition, and thus more able to withstand the rigors of the place. Armand had wanted to go, but Richard had vetoed that: If those Golems showed up, he wanted him protecting his little girl.

Now, in the cabin Kari had shown them—it belonged to her family—Richard could feel his pulse accelerating, as though he were preparing for battle. *Which I might well be,* he thought. He wished they had been able to get something from Holly about the Dreamtime, but she had only babbled about fire. That and, of course, demons. He grimaced. Barbara had not been much more help. All she had really been able to tell him was that she had been trapped in some sort of cave. Or so she thought.

He stood and accepted the markings as the shaman placed them on his body. He had been warned that, in the Dreamtime, his mind was his most powerful weapon. That worked. He had no magic abilities whatsoever, but he could certainly imagine carnage. Quite a lot of it.

He had mixed feelings about going in to find Jer, but then everyone around him seemed to also have mixed feelings about it. All except for Sasha and Barbara, that is. Barbara had insisted they could not leave him there. She herself had spent more than a year there before Jer and Holly had rescued her. She couldn't stand the thought of someone else being trapped and suffering the hell she had.

In his gut, he had to agree with her. He had been a Ranger, after all. *Rangers never leave anyone behind. We can't afford to have the bodies identified.*

He took a deep breath and lay down in the circle. He exhaled slowly, allowing his mind to become acutely focused while at the same time emptying it of all exterior distractions.

He closed his eyes and opened them in another place. The earth beneath his feet was scorched. A hot wind whipped past him, causing his hackles to rise. Evil was afoot; it permeated the air like moisture until he was afraid it was coating his skin in its dank decay.

He shook his head to remove the fanciful thoughts buzzing there. He had a job to do. He turned slowly in a circle, taking in his environment. He smiled. Not too far away was a huge mountain of rock. That had to be where Barbara had been trapped and therefore was the last place that he knew Jer had been.

He walked toward it slowly, senses alert. In his mind he cast barriers about himself, impenetrable walls. And beyond those he placed alarms that would warn him of the approach of any creature. A year in the jungle had taught him how to put up barriers in his mind, to be master of his thoughts when he chose. He had never dreamed that he would have to go back to that.

He knew Marie-Claire had hated that control. She often complained when he first returned from the war that he wouldn't "let her in." God knew he had tried. She had grown tired of waiting. He had often wondered of late if she would have been pleased to know that his barriers had crumbled around him once she had died, leaving his mind exposed to all.

Those thoughts had no part of him now, though. He had picked up the pieces of his life, and it was time to embrace his instinct for survival.

He reached the mountain quickly. Even the stone had been burned by whatever fire had swept through. Slowly, deliberately, he began to walk clockwise around the mountain, looking for an opening, a fissure, anything.

He had been walking for several minutes before he saw it. It was an outcrop of rock that was shaped like a human hand. Scalp tingling, he stepped in for a better look.

It didn't just look like a hand, it *was* a hand. It was

as though it were pressing out against the rock, trapped inside and seeking to break through. He lifted his fingers to touch the hand and closed his eyes. He reached with his mind, past the layer of stone and inside.

He felt pain, rage, and . . . surprise. He smiled, knowing that he had found Jer. He pushed his thoughts from his head, down his arm to his fingers, through the rock and into Jer's hand, up his arm and to his mind. He connected, he felt it.

Are you all right?

The answer came, faint but clear. *Not hurt, but going a little nuts.*

Good, I'm here to help.

Who are you?

Amanda and Nicole's father.

The sense of surprise became almost overwhelming, and he couldn't help but chuckle. *Never count the old man out.*

I won't make that mistake again, Jer answered.

So, what happened here?

Didn't Holly tell you?

She didn't make much sense.

There was silence for a moment, and he could tell Jer was wondering what to make of that. He didn't ask, though.

Well, the rock turned into two snakes who were battling

each other. One of them swallowed me, and then they froze back into stone.

Richard stepped back for a moment and took another look at the stone. It looked like any mountain. He was looking with his eyes, though. He closed his eyes and saw the image again in his mind. Slowly he began to make out two different forms, serpents, biting each other. Jer was trapped in one of them, only a few feet down from its mouth.

He stepped back to touch Jer's hand and felt the other's panic at having been left suddenly alone again.

It is all right. I will not leave you, he reassured him.

The Fire . . .

It is not burning here now. I'm going to disconnect for a moment, but I am not going anywhere.

Jer didn't respond, but Richard could feel his reluctant acceptance. He pulled his hand back again and studied the mountain.

He could see the serpents now with his eyes. He studied them, the position of Jer in the throat of the one. He focused his gaze on the rock around Jer's hand. He imagined the snake's skin stretching, growing thinner, and at last rupturing, spilling forth its prize.

The rock groaned in anguish, and then with a sharp scream began to part around Jer's hand. Slowly, as though it were being born, the hand pushed its way through a tear in the rock. It was horribly scarred, barely human. The tear widened and was followed by the rest of the arm. Then a second hand appeared, and then the arm.

At last the head burst through, and Jer let out a strangled gasp. He looked hideous, but Richard had prepared himself for that. The kid had been burned by the Black Fire, and Sasha had told Richard that it was only because of incredibly strong magic that he was still alive. After gulping in several breaths of air, he yelped, "Help!"

"Help me help you," Richard said calmly. "Imagine the rock parting, imagine the neck of the serpent rupturing and freeing you."

Jer closed his eyes, and Richard could *feel* him helping. He could feel the stone parting faster. In moments, Jer was spilling onto the ground, retching.

Richard gave him a moment to collect himself before moving forward to help him stand. The young man stood slowly, on shaking legs.

"How long have I been trapped in there?"

"Just a few days," Richard assured him.

"It felt like an eternity."

"I'm sure it did. Can you move? We should get out of here," Richard said. As though on cue, one of his trip alarms went off. Something was coming.

Part Two
Fire

☾

Some in fire go to their death
Some by water are bereft
Air may bring death, not birth
But they all return to Earth

So of these three I choose the fire
To dance aflame in death's desire
And as the flesh melts from my bone
You will hear me blissfully moan

FIVE

MAGOG

Witches now are on the run
Beaten by the great god, the sun
They scream and die from the fright
Fading now into the night

Cahors dancing shall return
As we make the Deveraux burn
Someone new within our sight
Hails the watchfires of the night

Tri-Coven: Winters

I hate waiting, Amanda thought as she sat, keeping watch over her father's still form. *That's all I seem to do is wait.*

"Then maybe it's time to stop," said a male voice she didn't recognize. She jumped as the High Priestess of the Mother Coven appeared on the inside of the door accompanied by a gorgeous guy.

"We have to get better wards," Tommy muttered.

Amanda rose hastily to her feet. "High Priestess, blessed be."

"Blessed be," the older woman said solemnly.

Everyone else chorused in.

"Amanda, may I introduce Alex Carruthers, your cousin."

Amanda blinked twice. "My what?"

"Your cousin."

"I never knew you had so many relatives," Tommy quipped. "Cousins have just been popping out everywhere."

Amanda just stood staring. *Another cousin? Did my mother know about him?*

Alex stepped forward, hand extended. Amanda shook herself and stepped forward to clasp his hand. The contact sent electricity through her arm, and her palm burned. It felt like the first time she and Holly had clasped hands, when they had propelled each other across the room.

She broke the contact, stepping back. "Well, Alex, welcome to our little corner of the world. These are the other members of my coven: Tommy, Kari, Philippe, Pablo, Sasha, Armand. Barbara, and my father, over there," she said, waving toward his prone body, "are not covenates, but they do fight with us."

"I thought there would be more of you," Alex commented.

"There were," Philippe spoke up. "However, several were recently killed, and a couple of others are missing."

"My condolences," Alex said, dropping his eyes briefly in a show of respect.

"They are welcome, as are you," Amanda said. "Please, take a seat. We are waiting for my father; he is in the Australian Dreamtime trying to rescue another of our number."

He nodded as he sat in a chair across from the cabin's stone fireplace. "My two other cousins—Holly and Nicole?"

"Both missing," Tommy said.

"Ah, it looks like I have a lot of catching up to do."

"First, we want to know about you," Armand spoke.

Amanda was startled. Armand, the member of the Spanish Coven who had studied to be a priest, rarely spoke up and almost never questioned anyone. It was a good warning for them all.

"Yes," she said, raising her defenses back up. "Tell us all about you."

He smiled in a way that sent shivers down her spine. *He* can *read my mind. His comment when he appeared wasn't just a fluke!*

"I'm an actor by trade, a witch by practice and belief. I serve the Goddess."

"And you just happen to show up right when we could use another person?" Armand questioned.

Alex raised his hands defensively. "Until a few hours ago I had never even heard of you guys. Then Luna sought me out and told me I had cousins and that they needed my help."

"It's true," Luna said. "I asked the Goddess to show me the lost Cahors witch; I was hoping to find Holly. Instead, she showed me Alex. His branch split off from yours at the beginning of the twentieth century. His family, like yours, forgot their ancestry. Like you, Amanda, and your sister and cousin, he discovered his magical abilities on his own."

"I've been in a coven since I was quite young," he confessed. "I'm the head of my coven now."

"Well, you don't need to do a spell to find Holly anymore," Kari said, her voice trembling.

"You found her?" Luna asked.

"More like she found us," Philippe said ruefully. "She came after us."

"She attacked you?"

Pablo cleared his throat. "I have something to tell you. All of you. I have been communing with . . . the forces that tell me what goes on in the ethers and vapors."

"Holly is in thrall to Michael Deveraux."

A stunned silence fell over the company. The High Priestess visibly paled. The other woman shifted her weight uncomfortably before she finally asked, "You know this for sure?"

Philippe glanced at Pablo and then nodded.

He had already told Philippe. But Philippe doesn't trust Alex, else he would have told her before what Pablo felt. Amanda quickly banished the thoughts from her mind. If Philippe didn't want to share some information, then the last thing she needed was to start thinking about it and have Alex read her mind.

Suddenly Pablo lurched to his feet, wild-eyed. "She's here."

Kari scrambled to her feet. "How did she find us? I never even told Jer about this cabin!"

Ignoring her, Amanda turned to Alex. "Welcome to hell. I hope you're ready."

"What can she do?"

No sooner were the words out of his mouth than a skeletal warrior on a ghost-horse crashed through the wall. The beast's shoulder hit Luna, sending the High Priestess spinning into Amanda and they both fell in a heap.

From the floor, Amanda could stare out of the hole in the wall. She saw Holly, surrounded by a ghost army of dozens, her arms lifted in the air and her hair swirling around her head.

Then the ghost soldiers were charging, heading straight for them. Then a voice cried out, deep as thunder, and the walls of the house shook. She looked up and saw Alex standing with his arms open wide.

"Ego diastellomai anemos o apekteina eneka!" he cried.

"What?" she asked. Her words were snatched from her lips by a wind that seemed to spring from nowhere.

"It's Greek," Armand shouted. "He's commanding the wind to fight on our behalf."

Amanda watched in awe as warriors flew apart, tiny tornadoes exploding upon them. At last only Holly was left. She opened her mouth as though she were shouting something, but a blast of wind picked her up and hurled her through the air.

She lay still, unmoving, for a long minute, and Amanda's heart caught in her throat. *Is she—?*

Slowly, Holly stood up. She stared for a moment, and Amanda realized she was making eye contact with Alex. Suddenly Holly turned and melted into the shadows.

The winds died instantly, and Alex seemed to slump a little. Amanda shakily rose to her feet and brushed herself off. "Is everyone okay?"

"Fine," Philippe answered. He turned to stare at Alex. "How did you do that?"

Alex shrugged. "Air—it's one of the basic elements. Everyone in my coven gravitates toward one more than the others. I've always been good with wind."

"And apparently Holly is not. I think we've found a weakness," Luna noted as she, too, stood up. "We can't stay here, though. We need to move someplace safer, where she can't find us."

"We can't go until my father comes out of the Dreamtime," Amanda protested, panic rising in her.

"You say he went in to rescue someone, a witch?" Alex asked.

Amanda hesitated. "Actually, he's more of a warlock . . . it's . . . complicated."

Alex raised an eyebrow. "It must be. I could go in and try to get them out."

"We've already sent too many people there," Philippe protested.

"Ah, but did any of them have experience with astral traveling?" Alex asked with a smile.

Amanda shook her head ruefully. "No. None of us has experience with that."

Alex's smile broadened. "Well, then, it's a good thing I'm here, because it just so happens that I do. It's one of the attributes of those who claim air as their element."

"Of course it is," Tommy muttered under his breath for Amanda's ears alone. She had to agree with him. It was awfully convenient. Still, anything was worth a try if it could bring her father back.

"All right, you're hired," she said, forcing a smile that she knew didn't reach her eyes.

Richard and Jer: The Dreamtime

The fire was burning all around, rushing toward them faster than Richard could push it back. The wicked black flames writhed like something alive, and he could feel their heat upon his cheek. He pushed and the flames pushed back, inching closer until his skin began to blister. Beside him, Jer was chanting, but the roar of the fire was drowning out the words.

A man approached them, his body seeming to cut a path through the flames. Within a moment he was in front of them. "Uncle Richard?"

Richard hesitated only a moment before nodding. There was something familiar about the young man, though he didn't think he'd ever seen him before.

The stranger lifted his arms and shouted in a strange tongue. Suddenly wind was everywhere, so strong that Richard and Jer began to stagger. The stranger, though, seemed to remain unaffected. Then, as though the flames were from a thousand birthday candles, the fire was snuffed out.

The silence was almost deafening, and into it the stranger spoke: "I am your nephew."

Heaven help us all, he thought as he stood blinking in disbelief.

"I am Alex. Let's go. Your daughter is waiting for us."

Then, within a minute, Richard was opening his eyes and staring up into his daughter's face. "Baby," he gasped.

"Daddy," his Amanda cried as she threw her arms around him.

"Jer?" he said.

A voice croaked from beside him, "I'm here."

"And—your cousin?"

"Well, thank you, Uncle." The young man came into his range of vision, a pleased smile plastered on his face.

Richard slowly sat up, all the images of the Dreamtime flooding him at once. "No one's possessed, right?" he asked.

"Doesn't look like it," Amanda assured him.

"Good." He turned to look at Jer. Someone must have tossed him a towel, because he had it wrapped around his head and face.

"Anything happen while I was away?"

"Holly attacked us again."

"Holly . . . attacked you?" Jer asked, sounding dazed.

Amanda knelt down and placed a hand on Jer's shoulder. "When she came back from the Dreamtime, she wasn't alone. Demons or something are possessing her."

"No!" Jer gasped.

"There is more that you should know," Philippe said, also placing a hand on his shoulder. "She is in thrall . . . to your father."

The cry of anguish that came from Jer was like no sound Richard had ever heard from a human being. Out of respect, he ducked his eyes, the only gesture of privacy he could offer him.

When Jer finally spoke, though, Richard heard the steel in his voice. "I will find her and free her, if I have to kill my father and myself to do it."

Let us all pray it doesn't come to that.

San Francisco: April 17, 1906 8:00 P.M.

Veronica Cathers waited in the hotel room at the Valencia for Marc Deveraux. She could feel him coming; it was a fever in her blood. It was a trap, it had to be, but still, she waited. She had not seen Marc in the six months since they had battled in the basement of the Coronado Hotel in Los Angeles.

Veronica had been visiting her sister, Ginny, in Los Angeles and had been staying at the hotel. Marc Deveraux had been another guest at the hotel, and it had not taken them long to find each other. She shuddered at the memory.

The hotel had burned down completely, she had heard, though she had never returned to see the wreckage. She had fled into the night to return home in time to bury her husband, who had died that same day.

Veronica, her son, Joshua, and her friend Amy were in San Francisco now. Amy had insisted Veronica needed a holiday, a chance to get away from all the pain present in her little house in Seattle, which was haunted by the memories of her dead spouse. *Some holiday it's turning out to be!*

Marc Deveraux had called for this meeting, claiming a kind of truce so they could talk—about what, he did not say, but she could guess. His telegram had arrived this morning and had rocked her to her very foundation. *How did he find me?* She nervously smoothed down the skirt of her pale pink dress. The lace covering the upper part of her chest and throat scratched painfully. The thin, clinging sleeves restricted her movement, and she cursed her choice of garment.

Anxiety filling her, she lifted her hand to stroke the

locket she wore around her neck. Inside the small piece of jewelry she kept a lock of Joshua's hair. He would be one in another month. He was with Amy now, and the other woman knew not to wait up for her. She had promised Joshua that she would see him in the morning. She only hoped it was a promise she could keep.

There was a knock on the door. She crossed and opened it quickly, before she could lose her nerve.

He strode into the room, and she closed the door. When he turned and faced her, her heart flew into her throat, choking the words of a protection spell that she had been about to utter. He stared at her with his coal-black eyes burning into her. He looked like a panther, muscles coiled and ready to spring upon its helpless prey.

And inside her head she could hear Isabeau whispering, *Jean.*

She couldn't look away from his eyes; they pinned her to the spot and probed her soul. The air between them became charged with electricity until she could feel the skin on her hands and cheeks tingling. *Does he feel it too?*

Then he pounced. She threw up her hands to ward him off, but it was too late. They were crushed against his body as he wrapped his arms around her and kissed her. "*Moi*, Isabeau, how I hate you," he breathed in between kisses.

As she looked at him it was no longer Marc's face she saw, but another's, wilder and fiercer. *Jean!*

From her mouth poured words strange to her. Still, she tried to keep herself; she struggled not to let Isabeau consume her completely even as Jean seemed to be consuming Marc.

He swooped her up in his arms and carried her to the bed, whispering words that were both fierce and tender. He laid her down and sat beside her. He picked up her hand and began to kiss her fingers, then froze at the sight of her wedding ring.

It was Marc who looked at her and asked, "You are someone's wife?"

Veronica shook her head. "I am someone's widow."

Then he was crushing his lips to hers. She heard the ripping of fabric as he tore her dress away from her body. She, in turn, tore at his clothes. At last he lay down on top of her, their flesh touching.

"*Mon* Jean," Isabeau murmured.

But it was Veronica who took Marc into herself.

When their passion was spent, they lay in each other's arms. Veronica had never felt so alive and so complete.

"You are my only love," he whispered.

"Isabeau is Jean's only love. You and I are just the pawns in their game."

"No," he denied it. "I love you and hate you as Jean did Isabeau, but it is not his emotion alone that I feel, it is mine as well. In Los Angeles, I wanted you then. I have spent every night since thinking of you, searching for you."

She stroked his hair, damp from perspiration. "I feel the same for you," she confessed. "I have tried to stop, but I cannot. I do not know much about my family. All I know has come from Isabeau. She spoke to me first on the night that we met."

"As Jean did for me."

"I know that our families have battled."

"And still do," he affirmed.

"I don't believe it has to continue," she breathed.

"Nor I. I pledge to you, Veronica Cathers, that my feud with you and yours ends here. I will do everything in my power to turn the Deveraux from their vengeance."

"And I will work for peace between our two families for the rest of my life."

They kissed, biting each other's lips until their blood mingled together and sealed the bargain.

"For the rest of my life," she repeated.

"For the rest of my life," he answered, whispering.

And as they began to make love again, neither had any idea how short those lives would be.

The earth groaned in anguish as though in the pangs of labor. And as a tremor passed through it, it did give birth to pain, anguish, and loss.

The earthquake struck without warning, jarring Veronica from sleep. Her limbs were tangled with Marc's and he, too, sat upright. Before she could shout a spell, there was the sound of screams and explosions. A mighty groaning ripped through the room, and then the floor collapsed.

Fire had raged through the city following the earthquake. Thousands were dead or dying, and the city was under martial law. It was a high price to pay, but well worth it.

Duc Laurent and Gregory Deveraux stood, looking at the ruins of the Valencia Hotel. All four floors had collapsed into the basement. Gregory stood, not offering even a tear for his brother. The ghostly Duc smiled. "There were no survivors?"

"None," Gregory intoned.

"Excellent. You have done well."

Los Angeles: April 18, 1906, 11:50 A.M.

Ginny Cathers stood with thousands of others, reading the huge bulletin boards that proclaimed the latest news from San Francisco. *God protect her,* she thought. She'd had a telegram from Veronica the day before, telling her that she was going to be in San Francisco and was thinking of coming to Los Angeles for a few days when her business in the city was done.

Names of the dead and missing were posted every few minutes. As more buildings collapsed from aftershocks or the fires raging through the city, their names were listed on the board. *So much death, so many lost,* Ginny thought. Her mind turned toward her husband and infant son safe at home several miles away from where she stood. *God protect them.*

This is useless. I don't even know which hotel she was staying at, she thought. Suddenly the earth shifted beneath her feet. Screams rippled throughout the crowd as the earthquake hit. It was small, not large enough to cause any damage, but those who were waiting for word of the final death toll in San Francisco did not know that.

The crowd turned, running away, *as though they could actually escape, somehow.* Ginny was caught up in the tide of stampeding people. She ran because she could do no differently. A screaming man careened wildly through the crowd, and bounced off Ginny. He kept running, but Ginny stumbled. Someone else slammed into her from behind and she fell, landing hard on her wrist. She tried to push herself up, but someone stepped on her back, shoving her down into the dirt. Suddenly the mob was running over her. She tried to scream, but her cries were lost in the crowd.

Someone kicked her as they rushed by, and she felt her ribs cracking. Pain knifed through her lungs, and she began to cough. Someone else stepped on her back, and another on her good arm.

She tried to get up, but it was no use—bones cracked, and muscle gave out as they trampled her. *I'm going to die,* she realized in horror. She lifted her eyes, blood dripping into them from a wound in her head. Before her, she saw a woman in white standing serene in the throng. People seemed to pass by her, and Ginny blinked fiercely as she saw a couple pass *through* her.

"*Ma petite,* I shall watch over your child," the woman said.

I believe you, Ginny thought, with her dying breath.

SIX

FREYA

))

Playing now our deadly game
The evil that you know by name
Decisions at last must be made
Betrayal is our stock-in-trade

Goddess hear us in the night
Help us now to choose the right
Give Cahors strength to persevere
And banish now our every fear

Avalon: Nicole

Nicole sobbed as pain ripped through her. She was chained to a dungeon wall, not far from the spot where James had once attempted to place her in thrall.

James was attempting now to break the thrall between Nicole and Philippe, her beloved. The two men could not have been any different. James was evil and had married Nicole against her will and kidnapped her twice now. Philippe was good and kind and had entered with respect and reverence in thrall with her in a ceremony that was a marked difference to the dark wedding James had orchestrated. *Rescue me, Philippe,* she begged mentally, wishing he could hear her.

Thoughts of him calmed her, steadying her nerves and helping her fight the pain. Still, she could feel parts of her mind slipping away. She let part of it go, the part that was horrified at what James was doing to her. The rest of it she tried to keep intact, knowing she would need it when her moment came. *Came. Came, game, same. Same game different name,* she thought to herself.

In front of her, James was cursing. Eli was there, too, standing back in the shadows and watching the proceedings.

Eli was staring at her through narrowed eyes, and she could all but see the wheels in his head turning. *Turning, burning, churning,* she thought, trying to distract herself from the pain.

James cut a thin line across her abdomen. She could feel the blood spilling out and running down into her jeans and underwear. *Yearning, spurning, learning.*

James next cut a line in her forehead; blood rolled down her face and she tasted it on her lips. *Earning, concerning, kerning . . . is* kerning *even a word?*

"Witch!" James shrieked, and cut a circle around her heart. *Witch, hitch, ditch.*

"I cut him from your mind, heart, and your organs," James crowed.

Pitch, rich.

"I shall cut him from your loins as well."

Her eyes narrowed, and she focused her sight on the knife he held in his hand.

Bitch.

She kicked, and the knife went flying in a wide arc, landing at Eli's feet. She stepped away from the wall. *"Libero!"* she said in a singsong voice, and the chains fell from her wrists.

Eli stared at the knife where it lay at his feet. He bent and picked it up, brushing his thumb slowly along the blade. It was stained with blood, Nicole's blood. Before Nicole had belonged to Philippe or James, she had belonged to him. *She was my girlfriend and she adored me.* He stared at James as he grappled with Nicole. *He took her because I was intimidated by him. He had no claim to her but he took her, anyway. He is arrogant, proud, and he doesn't care whom he crushes, just like my father. Just like me.*

Nicole fought back tooth and nail, like a wildcat, and he couldn't help but feel a stirring of pride. *I remember when she couldn't have hoped to defend herself with magic or with fists. She has learned so much the last two years . . .*

. . . and I wasn't the one to teach her.

I should have been. Back when she was starting to dabble in magic. I should have shown her. Maybe then she would be in thrall to me . . . maybe she would be my wife. . . .

He shook his head fiercely. *I don't want her.* It was a lie, though, and he knew it. He had never really stopped wanting her.

Maybe I should help her, he thought, as James threw Nicole into a wall. He took a step forward before he could stop himself. *Fool, she's probably put a spell on you.*

He forced himself to breathe deeply as he crossed his arms over his chest. *She means nothing to me,* he told himself as James knocked her unconscious.

Nicole's body slid down the wall to the ground. He stared at her crumpled, battered form. James stood panting, blood streaming down his face from scratches around his eyes.

"Hellcat," James spat. "She's useless now. We'll sacrifice her tonight, a gift to the Horned God."

Eli blinked, not entirely sure what he thought of that.

Supreme Coven: London

Every corner of the Supreme Coven shook as a roar of rage ripped through it. Every creature residing within, from the most powerful demon to the tiniest mouse, trembled with fear. Sir William's wrath had no bounds.

The skull throne cracked from top to bottom, shards of bone flying through the air and impaling the warlock who trembled before it. He died as his organs ruptured. His companion fell to her knees before Sir William, her head bowed. "My lord, I am, as always, yours to command."

Sir William stared at the young woman. She was one of the female members of the Supreme Coven. Outnumbered by their male brothers, they often worked harder to gain power and recognition. This young warlock had proven herself time and again in his service.

"Rise, my child," he commanded her.

Eve rose to her feet but kept her head down. He probed her mind. A myriad of emotions washed over him. Women, be they witch, warlock, or mere mortal, all had a complicated emotional makeup. He slowly peeled back the layers of anger, lust, sorrow, and joy. At last he reached her core, and she shuddered slightly. He pulled back out of her mind, satisfied. The one emotion he had been looking for was absent. She was not afraid of him or of what he had done to her companion.

He smiled slowly, a wicked grin that he knew made him look even more the fiend. Then he rose to his feet and made his proclamation, projecting his voice throughout every room and cavern.

"Michael Deveraux has broken faith with the Supreme Coven. From this moment forth he is to be hunted by all. Whoever brings me his head will receive my favor and riches beyond his—or her—wildest dreams."

Eve met his eyes and nodded.

He lifted his hand to her slowly, as in benediction. "Happy hunting, my dear."

She turned and vanished from sight.

Sir William sat back down on the throne. Michael Deveraux was persona non grata now. Every warlock in the Supreme Coven would be seeking him.

"Michael Deveraux has betrayed us," a voice hissed from the shadows.

Sir William sighed. "Yes, no surprise there. We should have destroyed House Deveraux years ago."

"But they alone know the secret of the Black Fire."

"We've been holding out for it too long already," Sir William growled.

"So surely a little more time cannot hurt."

"Unless he brings me Holly Cathers's head, I will have Michael Deveraux's."

As the voice from the shadows began cackling, Sir William stood. "Guard!"

A warlock swiftly entered the room, eyes probing the darkness. The laughter continued and it visibly unnerved the man. Sir William allowed himself to smile at the other's fear. "Bring James to me. I shall brook no delays."

The man nodded and disappeared.

"James, your son," the shadow whispered.

Sir William nodded. "We will soon find where his loyalties truly lie."

Nicole: Avalon

Nicole woke with a gasp. The last thing she remembered was fighting James. She had been about to try to crack his skull open when he had hit her. She tried to sit up but found that she was tied to her bed. A feeling of dread rose in her. *What has James done?* She managed to turn her head slightly to look at the chains anchoring her left wrist. *Or what is he about to do?*

She shivered as she gave the chains a tug. The clanking metal grated upon her ears, and she winced. She raised her head and noticed that her legs were similarly manacled. *Great.* She exhaled slowly. *Goddess, come to me, be with me.*

She closed her eyes and tried to center herself, to focus her energy. She concentrated on making a small ball of heat in the center of her being. Her mind cleared, and she focused. *First the chains around my right wrist.* The metal around the lock groaned and creaked as she willed the pins to start moving. *Eli once taught me to pick a lock the old-fashioned way. I wish instead he had taught me to do it the magical way.* The process was agonizingly slow, but one by one the pins moved into place until only the last remained. She pushed, pouring more energy into the stubborn metal until the entire band about her wrist grew hot and started burning her.

Ignore the pain, she coached herself as she kept working at the lock. She wrinkled up her nose as she began to smell her flesh burning. *Ignore the smell.* Then suddenly the pin moved, clicking into place, and the metal cuff sprang open. Gasping, she shook her hand and it fell off.

She stared at the burn marks around her wrist. The skin was beginning to blister. *Not good.* She closed her eyes and prayed. *Goddess, take this wounded arm and repair all its harm, heal the flesh and numb the pain, renew that which now is lame.*

She watched in awe as the blisters dissipated. The pain subsided as well. After a minute there was only a slight red ring around her wrist. *Scar?* she wondered. She couldn't help but think suddenly of Jer and the scarring that the Fire had done to him.

It's a miracle he lives, she thought. *I wonder what dark force kept him alive and healed him enough to function as a human being?* She shuddered. *Whatever it is, I hope I never have to meet it.*

Then, out of the darkness, a voice whispered, "Too late."

Mother Coven: Santa Cruz

Anne-Louise Montrachet was uneasy in her skin. *Something is coming. I can feel it in the earth, in the water, but, most especially, in the air.*

Thanks be to the Goddess, and the healers of her coven, she was well again. The pain of healing had nearly killed her, but now she could move with little effort and only slight pain. She stretched out her legs as she walked the wooded paths and breathed in the rich air.

This was her first time at the Mother Coven retreat in the hills of Santa Cruz, California, though she had heard many things about it. For five years now the coven had owned the property and used it. Behind her, Whisper, a gray cat that had mysteriously appeared and adopted her, scampered after a lizard in the undergrowth.

Santa Cruz was a strange place, with a natural, mystical energy unlike any she had ever felt. Strange happenings were also being attributed to the area. There was the famous "Mystery Spot," where gravity seemed to work in reverse. It was but one of several spots like it on Earth, but it had seemed to draw the most attention. Alfred Hitchcock was inspired by a flock of birds that seemingly went mad and flew into houses, killing themselves, and attacking the people caught outside. The incident that became the basis for *The Birds* was just one of the strange things that had happened in the area.

More than any of these stories, though, Anne-Louise had always been fascinated and disturbed by the stories of the Satanic rituals performed in the very hills she was walking. Every year, ignorant, bored, rebellious college students from UC Santa Cruz and elsewhere gathered to perform bizarre rituals and sacrifice untold numbers of animals. She glanced protectively at Whisper.

The cat paused to look at her, half a lizard in her mouth, and cocked her head questioningly to the side. In almost every instance the children involved in such events knew nothing of magic—white, black, or gray. The "rituals" were just an outlet for their own twisted, sadistic natures. A very few of them, though, were worshipers of the Horned God who used the rest as cover for their activities. Since the Mother Coven had

taken property in these hills, they had worked to erad-
icate such horrors. *True witches don't kill cats,* Anne-
Louise told herself. *All the more reason to fear Holly.*

The younger witch had scared her from the first.
She had too much power, especially for one so young
in years and young in the Craft. *They all do.* Anne-
Louise herself had had to work and study for years to
accomplish even some of the most minor magics,
except for wards. Wards were her specialty—her "gift,"
as the High Priestess called it. Every witch had a special gift, the thing at which she excelled. What made
Holly dangerous was the fact that she excelled at everything and had never had to learn discipline to do so.

The trees moaned as the wind picked up, and Anne-
Louise glanced around self-consciously. *Yes, something is
coming,* she thought. *And when it gets here, we're all going to
be in a lot of trouble.*

Nicole: Avalon

Nicole trembled. "Who's there?" she called.

A low, mocking laugh was all the answer she
received.

She saw something move out of the corner of her
eye, a whisper of something not quite there. She twisted
her head, and it was gone. "Goddess?" she whispered,
praying that it was but knowing that it wasn't.

"No."

She twisted her head back to where the sound came from, but there was nothing. "The Horned God?" she asked, swallowing around the lump in her throat.

Another laugh. "No."

"Then, who, what are you?" she demanded, pulse thundering in her ears.

"Something . . . else."

"What?" she gasped.

"Something you can't understand," it roared, and then suddenly it was on top of her, pressing against her, moving through her.

"And now—I'm not alone."

As it merged with her mind, she felt evil, ancient and mysterious. She felt rage, lust, and deceit. And there was something else . . .

. . . there were two.

Kari: California

Kari sped down Interstate 5, leaving the town of Winters behind as fast as she could. "Come on, come on," she shouted, punching her horn to punctuate it. She swerved around the car in front of her and hit the accelerator as she looked at the clock on the dashboard.

Any minute now they would know she was missing,

that she wasn't coming back. She had to get as far away as she could before they sicced the bloodhound Pablo on her—or, worse, the mysterious new cousin, Alex.

They had all been hiding in her family cabin near the town of Winters, which was situated next to the university town of Davis. While everyone got used to Alex and began magical and physical preparations for the evening, she had volunteered to go get food. Somehow, miraculously, they had let her go alone.

She had bypassed the general store, speeding toward the freeway as fast as she could. *I can't handle this anymore. I'm sick of waiting around to be killed like the others. And Alex . . . Alex terrifies me.*

She didn't know why, but there was something about him that made her uneasy. She pushed her foot down harder on the gas pedal. She had to get clear, she had to think. Despair filled her, though, with a sinking feeling that even if she escaped the coven, she wouldn't be safe. Into the blackness of her thoughts, a single small light appeared.

What if I can get the two sides to stop fighting? What if I can get them to call a truce? There must be a way we can all live together in peace.

She narrowed her eyes. Jer had once said his father had a place in the desert, sort of a spiritual retreat. It was in New Mexico. *If they won't listen, he might.*

Nicole: Avalon

Nicole woke up and began to vomit. She tried to curl on her side, but the chains still binding her ankles and right wrist wouldn't let her move too far.

From behind her, a familiar, hated voice commented, "You look like hell."

James! She turned her head slowly and stared at him. "What is on this island?"

"What?" he said, sounding puzzled.

"You heard me," she spat. "What is on this island? There is something here."

He hesitated for a moment, and in that moment he almost seemed human to her, frail and filled with uncertainty. "Once, when I was young, I thought—"

"Thought what?" she pressed.

"Nothing," he snapped, his veneer sliding back into place.

"Tell me!"

He shrugged, an evil grin spreading across his face. "I guess you'll just have to ask the ghosts, once I turn you into one." He threw a dress down on the bed beside her. "Be dressed in that when I return in five minutes."

"Or what?"

"Or, I'll dress you," he said, bending down to give her the full effect of his leer.

Sickened, she turned her face away. She heard him move to the door and open it. Then, with a great clanking, her chains fell from her wrist and ankles. She heard the door shut behind him as she sat up.

He intends to sacrifice me, she thought as she stared at the dress. *Well, he's going to find out I'm not that easy to kill.*

Astarte leaped up into her lap with a soft *mew,* and Nicole stroked her soft fur for a moment before moving her aside so she could begin dressing. Astarte had the most uncanny ability to make herself scarce when James was around.

"That's because I have not chosen him," the cat opened its mouth, and a strong yet feminine voice spoke.

"Goddess," Nicole gasped.

"Yes, child, I have been watching you, guiding you. Your time is not yet over. It has only just begun."

"Those things that attacked me?"

"The betrayer and his apprentice."

"What did they want from me?" she asked while pulling her shirt off over her head.

"What they always want—to corrupt, to pervert."

"Why me?" she asked, as she stepped into the dress.

"Because you are the future."

Nicole zipped up the dress and was about to ask what that meant when there was a sound at the door.

Freya

The cat disappeared, and Nicole turned to face James as he entered.

He looked her up and down appreciatively. "You'll make a lovely sacrifice for the Horned God tonight." He sidled close and grasped her upper arm. He pulled her close, so that they were inches from each other. "Too bad we both know you're not a virgin."

She smirked. "Yeah, remind me to thank Eli for that."

"Slut!" he hissed as he raised his other hand to slap her. She just looked up at him, a smile twisting her lips. She had gotten to him. *That's it, James. I win.*

He knew it too. She could see it in his eyes. With a snarl, he turned and started dragging her toward the door. Instead of fighting him, she shook her arm free—*How did I do that?*—and walked beside him.

When they reached the dungeon he locked her in a cell. "I'll be back for you in a little while."

"Do you really think this cage can hold me, James, if I will it not to?" she asked mockingly. The tides had turned and, somehow, despite the fact that she was the prisoner, she had all the power.

James nearly killed the messenger. "What do you mean, my father wants to see me right away?

The man kneeling at his feet didn't lift his eyes.

"Your presence is wanted at once, no delays."

James felt his blood boiling with frustration. The sacrifice of his bride would have to wait. He was still playing his father's game, pretending to be the dutiful son, and he wasn't ready yet to end the charade.

As James got in the boat to cross the waters back to England, he didn't notice another boat that was docking a hundred yards away. The thick fog obscured its occupants from sight. The island had been heavily warded for centuries, even more so since Nicole's escape. As soon as she'd left they had installed barriers that made it impossible to open a portal on the island.

That was why the four huge, lumbering beasts were crawling out of the boat they'd had to steal to attain the island. Because they landed at the same time that James's boat was leaving, no sensor alarms went off. They were lucky, but then the Golems knew nothing of luck. All they knew was the task that they were assigned, and they had been trying for a couple of days to find and kill Nicole Anderson.

SEVEN

MORDON

☾

We waver now in our quest
Green Man tell us what is best
Shall we kill or shall we bleed
And where shall we plant our seed

Betrayal now all around
Weeping is the only sound
We shall die with Wind Moon rise
Victims of warlock lies

Kari: New Mexico

As Kari swerved around the orange barrels rerouting
her path across the freeway lanes, the torrential rain
pummeled the top of the car like fists in metal
gauntlets. She wasn't sure why the barrels were there,
but they made her progress even harder . . . and it was
difficult enough already.

Her windshield wipers could do nothing against
the onslaught; water rushed down the glass with the

speed and power of a waterfall. Fanning across the highway, the rising waters sent her hydroplaning, and she cried out and grabbed the steering wheel hard.

Kari was struggling across high desert country. Her neck and upper back were knotted with fear; when she had awakened in her motel room, she had listened intently to the news reports about tonight's flash floods. But something told her to drive, anyway, and to keep driving, and she didn't know if the demanding voice inside her head was that of friend or foe. Now that she had bolted, it could be one of the coven members trying to catch up with her; or one of those hideous Golems . . . or Holly herself.

Her stomach clenched. She was scared to death of what Holly had become. What would Jer think of his precious "soul mate" now that she had practically no soul at all? She, Kari, could almost forgive him for dumping her in favor of Holly. Hell, she was the strongest witch alive, and he was a warlock. But she was also the one who'd left him to die in the Black Fire in the gymnasium. His terrible scars were evidence of her "love" for him.

Maybe Kari wasn't as exciting as Holly, but she sure as hell was more loyal. She'd stayed in the coven even though it had meant risking her life, and had offered her apartment as the place to hold Circle until things got too dicey. She hadn't signed up for any of that, but she'd stayed on board when the others needed her. All she had wanted to do was go to grad school, be Jeraud Deveraux's lover, and learn a few bits and pieces of his magical tradition.

How was I to know his family was into Black Magic?

It was as if she were being punished for having ambition. Wanting to learn about things that would stretch her limits; needing to explore beyond the mundane world. . . .

You knew, she told herself harshly. *You knew about his family. Somewhere deep down, you accepted how bad they were.*

No . . .

And you always felt guilty about your relationship with him. He's so much younger than you. You were using him, because it was always a bargain between you and him—pleasure for magic.

Hey, not a bad trade for either of us, and he was old enough to know what he was doing . . .

. . . and then you fell in love with him, for real.

Tears welled.

Now Holly's gone completely dark. If I don't stop her and Michael Deveraux, they'll kill us all.

The car suddenly hydroplaned; she felt the water lift the wheels from the road and rush it forward. It teetered and threatened to carom in a circle, and she cried out, swerving, riding the current until, miraculously, the wheels found the road again.

She had ignored dozens of warnings on TV. A number of people died in New Mexico's flash floods every year, many of them while driving. It appeared that everyone else had stayed home; she could see no other lights in the darkness, though for a time, strange, fiery plumes had bellowed from the tops of concrete towers way off in the distance, as if from some kind of refinery.

There they are again, she thought, squinting through the windshield. Then she gasped.

They weren't like the plumes she'd seen before. These three towered much higher in the sky, and they glowed with the radiant blue of magical energy.

As she watched, they flickered, vanished, and reappeared again, more brightly this time.

They're closer, she realized.

They went out again, reappeared again.

And closer.

She stopped the car.

The three plumes rushed into being about ten feet away from her car, illuminating the black highway, casting the interior of the vehicle in blue light.

"Oh, God," she whispered. Her breath caught in her throat.

Then the flames extinguished. Before she had time to react, fire banks erupted on either side of the car, at ground level, their blue fire geysering past her line of sight and piercing the rain-soaked heavens.

Kari screamed aloud, inadvertently jerking the steering wheel to the left and pushing her foot down on the gas. She kept screaming as she headed straight for the wall of blue flame, pulling her hands off the wheel and raising them above her face. She shut her eyes tightly, screaming for all she was worth.

Then the car began to hydroplane again; or at least that was the sensation she felt. She dropped her hands back onto the wheel and opened her eyes.

Although still pelted by the rain, her Honda was now entirely surrounded by the blue glow. As the individual flames whipped and undulated, she had a clear view of blackness outside her window; she craned her neck and looked down.

Tinted a dull yellow, a thin stretch of highway was visible, and beyond it, the twinkling lights of a town.

Oh, my God, I'm flying, she thought, throwing herself away from the window. She whimpered and stared out the front window, then the other side. Without realizing what she was doing, she raised her feet off the floor.

Huddling behind the wheel, she murmured a

protection spell. The car dipped, and she shrieked. Then it righted itself and kept going.

As the flames separated, she saw again the pinpoint lights of the town through the driver's side window. The car was gliding away from them, and toward the vast expanses of the uninhabited desert.

What if it drops me? What if I land in the desert and the car gets swept down an arroyo, and I drown?

"Goddess, help me," she murmured, clenching her hands as one did in Christian prayer. She felt no reply, no comfort. She never had. She wasn't certain there was a Goddess. She didn't know who made the Coven's spells work. Or who answered the summons of the Deveraux. She had begun her exploration of magic as a folklorist, and she was aware that, despite popular assumption, the religious varieties of Wicca, paganism, shamanism, and other magic-using traditions employed slightly different interpretations of their supreme deities. One witch's Goddess was not necessarily the same as another's.

On impulse she reached forward and turned on the radio. The noise of the heavy rains had made it nearly impossible to listen to the faint signals she had managed to pick up.

There was nothing, not even static.

She pushed the horn. It, too, was dead.

"Help!" she shouted. "I'm sorry!"

And she *was* sorry. She felt a flood of guilt and remorse, although for what, precisely, she wasn't certain. But she knew deep in her soul that leaving the coven and trying to find Michael Deveraux had been wrong, no matter what her reasoning had been.

No matter what lies I told myself. And now I'm going to pay. Now he's found me and he's going to kill me, because that's what he is, an evil killer, and . . . and . . . what the hell was I thinking?

Batted by the rain, the car glided along. Kari began to cry—huge, heavy sobs that forced her stomach to contract. Bile rushed up into the back of her throat, making it burn; when she tried to swallow it down, she found she couldn't. She sat with her teeth clenched, crying harder and harder, until she was wailing like a crazy person.

Next she heard herself reciting the Lord's Prayer by rote, without a thought as to the words and what they meant. It was simply a reflex from childhood, and although once she realized what she was doing she listened carefully to the words, she found no comfort.

All the gods and Goddesses have left me, she thought bitterly. *These are demons I have to face alone.*

Literally.

She had no idea how long she floated along,

buoyed by the magical glow, but she gradually grew exhausted from all the crying, and her head began to bob forward. Fuzzy images drifted across her closed eyelids—happier times with Jer, holding hands and smiling at each other; getting slick and dizzy in the sweat lodge. Kialish and Eddie were there, and now they were both dead. . . .

Oh, God! I'm so tired of all the dying! I'm so scared!

Then she heard the screech of birds and opened her eyes. She caught her breath and swallowed hard, balling her hands into fists in her lap, then gripping the steering wheel—as if doing so made any sense at all.

Surrounding the car, their bodies sheened with moonlight, dozens of falcons flew on either side of the car. One ticked its head in her direction; its eyes glowed bloodred, and it opened and shut its beak like an automaton. She shrank back, blinking at it. It continued to stare at her, then shut its beak and straightened its head.

Next, she heard a strange sound that she took to be her own heartbeat, a rhythmic *whum-whum, whum-whum*. She listened, pressing her palm against her chest. The two sounds were out of sync. Her heart was beating much faster, and she realized the sound was coming from outside of herself.

She stared at the vast flying field of birds. *It's their*

wings, she realized, terrified. The birds were soaring in unison, each one's wings undulating up and down, up and down, in the rain; as she stared, a picture formed in her head of galley slaves chained to tiny benches below the decks of a great barque, raising and lowering massive oars to the steady beat of the oar master.

Whum-whum, whum-whum . . . and then the sound slowed and blurred; she felt her head fall back against the seat. Though her eyes remained open, she no longer saw birds and night sky and the moonlight. Her field of vision shimmered; colors ran like rain on a chalk painting, and then a new place burst into her reality; and a new . . . or very old . . . time.

A very old time.

France, the 13th Century

"Allons-y!" cried the splendid man on horseback. It was the heir of the House of Deveraux, Jean, and this was the Great Hunt that would provision his wedding feast. He was to be married this very night to Isabeau of Cahors, daughter of the Deverauxs' witchly rival in the region.

And then he will think of me no longer, Karienne thought dismally. She rode her horse astride like a man, at a discreet distance. Though most in the Hunt retinue knew her to be his mistress, they also knew that she was being cast aside. He must save his manly virtues for the marriage bed, and get a child on Isabeau as soon as possible. It was the unspoken bargain between the families.

As always, Jean was astonishingly handsome. His ermine-tipped cloak fanned over his saddle and the cropped tail of his warhorse. The rider raised his left gauntlet into the air, and the magnificent falcon, Fantasme, which had been perched there, hurled himself into the golden sky and flew toward the dense thicket just ahead.

A cheer rose from the hunters, mixing with the steady rhythm of the drummers who walked ahead. *Whum-whum-whum,* their measures bold and merciless. *Catch and kill, catch and kill* . . . For the moment, they sought birds, and hares, and bucks.

But soon they would begin to flush out the serfs who would be sacrificed to the Horned God this very night.

Whum . . . whum . . .

Karienne lifted her chin and sternly denied tears from welling in her eyes.

I have pride. I am still beautiful.

But had I the chance, I would kill that bitch of the Cahors, and magick him into taking me to wife . . .

Had I the chance . . .

Had I the chance . . .
Whum-whum . . . whum . . .

With a sharp gasp, Kari opened her eyes and raised her head off the back of the seat.

Whoa, was that a dream? It was so real. Did I actually go back in time? Was I . . . was some part of me actually Jean's mistress? Because, in a very weird way, that would make sense given what's been going on with all of us these days. . . .

She had no time to consider it further. The car tipped downward, floating at an angle toward the ground. The birds' wings continued to flap steadily, and the car was surrounded with the same blue glow as before.

Frightened, she put her foot on the break, then realized how silly that was, and took it back off. She forced her breathing to slow down—she had begun to hyperventilate—and whispered to herself, "Karienne."

With that, the rain stopped abruptly, as if someone had turned off a faucet. One moment the sky was clashing with the storm, the next . . . peace.

The metal of the car *ticked-ticked-ticked* as the engine cooled down. Kari caught her breath again, and slowly exhaled. Her heart was throbbing in her chest; she could hear it roaring in her ears.

The car continued to descend. To her right, a soft yellow light glowed through the darkness, and she made out the low-slung angles of a New Mexican–style adobe building. A path wound its way toward the structure. Otherwise, the landscape was barren.

As she gazed at the building, she saw over its silhouette the gauzy images of trees and lush undergrowth. It was the forest of her dream.

The wings of the birds echoed the drumbeats of the Hunt.

Slowly, one by one, the birds began to fade, and then disappear. The forest vanished as well. Soon, only the car and she remained in the sky, and the dimly lit building below.

It appeared to be the front entrance to a house. The ends of large logs extended from either side of the entrance, and there were three steps leading up to a front door, which appeared to be made of wood.

It's got to be Michael's house, she thought. *He's brought me to him.*

She made no sound, only stared hard at the door, bracing herself for it to open. On impulse she made sure all her car doors were locked—they were—and then she smiled grimly at how ridiculous that was. The futility of it. Whoever was behind that door had made her car *fly,* for heaven's sake.

Her unhappy smile had not yet faded when the lock on her door unclicked by itself.

Then it swung open.

"No way," she murmured. She didn't touch it, didn't move. Her heartbeat grew even more rapid, and she began to breathe so shallowly that she began to get dizzy.

The door remained as it was, insistent that she get out.

Fresh tears welled in her eyes, and her face prickled with fear. A dizzying wave washed over her; she hadn't realized how exhausted she was from fighting the storm, and she had no reserves to deal with her terror.

After a few more seconds, she tried to move, but she remained strapped in place. She still had on her seat belt. It took a supreme act of will to unfasten it, her shaking fingers pressing uselessly until she grimaced and pulled herself together, jabbing it so hard, she broke her nail. The belt slithered back into the retractor like a serpent.

The lights on the porch glowed. A cold wind whipped sand against her thigh, and Kari finally stirred. As if leaping from the car, she swung her left leg out, found her footing on loose gravel, and scooted the rest of the way out of the car.

Unsteadily, she straightened up. Her gaze fixed on the house, she shut her door and made her way around the front of the car, her hand extended as if she were admonishing it not to turn itself on and run her down.

Then the rain started again, drenching her from head to toe. She cried out and shielded her head. In the frigid torrent, she felt her makeup sluice down her face, all in one piece, as if it had been a mask.

Despite the rain, she didn't hurry her pace—she couldn't—but walked unsteadily across the gravel, inching toward the three steps that led to the porch.

She climbed them, remembering that, back in Seattle, there had also been three stairs to the porch of the Deveraux home. *Three* was a magical number, and Michael Deveraux was an architect. If he had built this house, he put those stairs there for a reason.

On the porch, she stepped onto a hemp welcome mat decorated in red and green—the Deveraux Coven colors—featuring a silhouette of a black bird, a falcon, in the center. She was careful not to step on the bird, and then she thought better of it and ground her boot heel hard into its face.

I won't let him intimidate me, she promised herself, then nearly laughed out loud. *Okay, I will let him intimidate me.*

I just won't let him kill me.

She reached forward toward the door. The moonlight cast a glimmer on a door knocker in the center of the carved door, which was a brass rendition of the Green Man, an aspect of the God as a nature deity.

She took a breath, and knocked.

She wasn't surprised when the door swung open.

Summoning every last vestige of her courage, she took a step across the transom. She was standing inside now, in the pitch-black darkness, in a cocoon that muffled the steady patter of the rain on the gravel.

I'm going to betray them all to their worst enemy: Michael Deveraux. The man who's been trying to destroy all of us.

Yes, and he's going to succeed . . . if I don't find a way to stop him. I didn't want this. I didn't want any of this. From day one, they bullied me and made me go along with them.

Cold and fear penetrated her bones. She was trembling, and her knees were beginning to give way; her tears of frustration ran down her cheeks, salty and warmer than the icy rain.

Then a soft golden light bobbed in front of her eyes, and she blinked, startled.

Michael Deveraux stood less than a foot away from her. His palm was outstretched, and above it, a ball of fire the size of a golf ball floated, casting shadows from beneath his chin onto his features, giving him an incredibly sinister aspect. He had long black hair, a black beard, and heavy lashes. His eyes were quite deep set, and his brows were angled slightly back from his nose. When he smiled, she shrank back involuntarily.

He reminded her of the Devil.

"Come on in," Michael Deveraux said jauntily, taking a step back to allow her entry. His heel rang on the stone floor. "Kari, isn't it? We've never formally met, even though you've been sleeping with my son for years."

Her lips parted, but she didn't know what to say in response, so she kept silent.

He was dressed all in black—black sweater, black jeans, black boots—and in his other hand he held out a heavy earthen goblet. She didn't remember it being there before. "Hot buttered rum," he said, smiling. "It'll warm you up. Nasty night out." He raised one brow. "Not fit weather for warlock or witch."

She hesitated. "I'm not a witch. I just know a few spells."

His chuckle alarmed her. "Oh, I know what you are, Kari, and what you're not." He gestured at her with the rum. "Come. Drink." When she still hesitated, he added slyly, "It won't kill you." As if to prove his point, he took a sip, sighing contentedly before he lowered it from his mouth.

She said unsteadily, "I-I made a mistake coming here."

"No. You did exactly the right thing. Believe me."

He turned and glanced at her, indicating that she should accompany him. When she stepped toward him, the area around them suddenly lit up and she stumbled, startled. There was track lighting overhead, and on the wall in front of her, a mirror framed in beaten silver. She winced at her own reflection. Her makeup had collected under her eyes. She looked like a zombie.

"No magic," he said airily. "Just motion detectors."

He led her through the hallway, the soles of their shoes noisy on the hard surface. The walls were crowded with images of fantastic, swirling birds of red and green flying through a verdant forest, the designs painted directly on the white plaster walls. Even the low ceiling above her had been painted with heavy foliage and crazed, vicious birds. Their dark beady eyes seemed to follow her as she walked past them.

At the end of the hallway, Michael opened a set of wooden double doors, revealing a shadowed room illuminated by the glow of flame inside the distended belly of a stone statue of the Horned God. The God's goat-face gleamed cruel and lusty, its taloned hands raised and extended slightly forward as if it were about to pounce on the next hapless person who dared to walk into the room. It sat back on haunches that ended in goat hooves. Kari shivered, looking away.

Other statues stood in the flickering darkness, none of them very distinguishable. All she saw was a vast array of fangs, talons, and horns. Everything sharp, everything ready to cut and wound.

The room was as cold as a meat locker. Her soaked clothes wrapped around her like ice packs.

"Warm yourself," he invited, gesturing to the statue.

She wished she could refuse, but there was no other source of warmth. She edged uneasily toward the figure, stretching forth her left hand as she took another sip of the rum. This time it tasted good, its alcoholic heat spreading through her chilled veins.

"Where are they?" he asked without further pre-amble.

She licked her lips. *What was I thinking?*

"W-who?" she managed to say.

"Kari, dear," he said kindly, "there's no other rea-son you would come to me than to strike some sort of bargain. From what I know of you, I'm guessing that you want to give me the Coven in exchange for my saving my son."

"You . . . should save him, anyway," she replied. She bit her lip and stared into the fire. "He's your child."

"Did you come here to argue with me?" He

sounded amused. "I don't think I've met anyone as brash as you since my wife left me."

She licked her lips. "You might be able to turn him, make him be . . . like you."

He shook his head. "Years of trying puts the lie to that, Miss Hardwicke. Jer's bound and determined to make my life difficult. Trust me: I'd be much, much better without him."

He came up beside her and watched the fire. She was aware of how closely he stood next to her; she could smell expensive soap and aftershave, and his body heat mingled with her own. She was shocked to realize that she was becoming aroused.

He's making it happen, she told herself. *Because I would never . . . he's so evil.*

So powerful, another voice whispered in her head.

"Talk to me," he invited. "It'll only be difficult at first."

Still, she kept her silence. Her heart was pounding again, and she was beginning to worry about having a heart attack. Or that she would faint and he would . . . would do something that he shouldn't. . . .

I'm getting really excited. She glared at him. "Leave me alone," she blurted.

He burst into laughter. "It's a little late for that." He grinned at her and added, "Kari, you made the right decision." He grabbed her hand and wrapped both his hands around it, blowing gently on her knuckles.

"Just tell me," he urged. "Tell me where they are. I'll save Jer—if he can be saved."

She took a breath. "They're in Winters."

He nodded. "Tell me about this new male witch from the missing Cahors line. Alex Carruthers."

Her eyes widened. She felt the blood draining from her face and she wished she could stop feeling his skin against her own. "You know about him?" She didn't know why she was surprised. She cocked her head and looked at him. "If you know he exists, you should know everything else about him." Her fear emboldened her, and she added, "Don't you have scrying stones? Haven't you been spying on us?"

A careless shrug was the only answer he gave her. He took her goblet from her and raised the rim to her lips. Then he tipped it forward, forcing her to take a sip or let the rum and butter splash down her chin.

She let the alcohol warm her veins and give her a measure of courage. Then she cleared her throat and said, "He's very powerful."

"Really." He sounded intrigued. "He's their cousin, correct?"

She wondered then if he had tricked her, making

her assume he knew more than he did. It was too late to go back and repair the damage, if she had caused any.

"If"? I'm destroying them all.

"He's a distant cousin, at best. I'm not sure exactly how they're related." She moved her shoulders. "It's all so complicated."

He looked unconvinced. "And yet, you're getting a PhD in anthropology. I would think you'd be extremely well-versed on kinship systems."

"I'm getting a doctorate in folklore," she corrected.

"Ah. My mistake." He eased her goblet of rum from her hand and took a hefty swallow. Sighing with contentment, he handed it back to her. "You came here of your own free will," he reminded her.

Did I? she wanted to ask him. Now she wasn't so certain. . . . "His powers are strong," she continued.

"They would have to be, to defeat Holly."

There was a strange clattering on the stone floor, like the nails of a dog, followed by a high-pitched cackle. The cackling echoed around the room as the clattering skittered toward Kari; she whirled around, glancing at the floor, then cried out when something flashed past her and landed on Michael's shoulder.

It was an ugly, troll-like creature, almost reptilian in appearance, with long, pointed ears and sharp features. It was unclothed, and leathery-skinned, and it hissed merrily at Kari, then cocked its head and began to babble at Michael.

"She'ssss trying to break free, free she issss," it announced, jabbing a long finger over its shoulder. "Going crazzzzzy."

"Thank you. It's not a problem," Michael said, patting the thing on its head. "Go find a dead rodent to eat, will you?" He swept the thing off his shoulder. It soared through the air and landed on the floor, then scrabbled away into the darkness.

Kari's knees buckled.

"Oh here, here, how thoughtless of me. You must be exhausted."

Michael snapped his fingers. An overstuffed chair upholstered in brilliant crimson materialized behind Kari, bumping against her calves. She fell backward into it, sinking into the softness, which was also very warm. Her drink sloshed onto her wrist, sending the scent of nutmeg into the air.

She took a drink to steady herself and leaned back. To her amazement she realized she was about to fall asleep. *He must be casting a spell on me. I was a fool to come here. I was so scared. . . .*

"You did the right thing," he assured her. "This is really the only reasonable choice you could make. I'm going to kill the rest of them. And I'm going to begin with Holly." He looked pleased with himself.

"Jer . . . ," she murmured.

"I haven't decided." He leaned over her, smoothing her wet hair away from her forehead. His eyes were compelling; his smile, a terrible thing.

"I have Holly here," he told her. "Did you realize that? And in two nights, I'm going to kill her. On the Wind Moon, and when I do it, I'll absorb her power. No one in the history of Coventry will be stronger than I will become."

He lifted his chin and focused his eyes toward the ceiling. "Your timing couldn't have been more perfect, Kari. For coming to me, I'll spare you. By that, I mean that I won't kill you." After a beat he added, "That's a good thing, honey."

She followed his line of sight, and her blood ran cold.

Painted onto the ceiling was an enormous black falcon, its wings stretching into the dark recesses of the room. In its massive, wicked-looking beak it clutched a human heart, and from that heart, blood dripped onto the breast of the huge creature itself. Its eyes—enormous, even for a creature its size—glared down at her, seeming to follow her.

"Fantasme, the spirit of the Great Falcon." Michael made a motion with his hand. "He lives in the spiritual Greenwood, and there he hunts Pandion."

Kari heard again the thrumming of the drums of the Great Hunt, a counterpoint to the quicktime wingbeats of the birds that had flown beside her car. She was incredibly dizzy; the room was spinning. She held on to the arms of the chair and began to gasp. Her lids fluttered, and she heard herself moan.

The evil bird lifted its head and screeched. The cry was ear-piercing, shaking her brain inside her skull. The heart in its mouth dropped from the painting, erupting into the real world, and tumbled in a slow-motion float toward Kari.

She lurched to her feet, knocking over the chair, then whirled on her heel and raced awkwardly for the doorway. Michael's laughter trailed behind her.

At the doorway, a wraithlike figure stepped from the darkened hall and blocked her escape. Shorter than she, it was wrapped in a glowing blue gauze, which it slowly lifted as its maniacal laughter trilled from beneath the layers, like the echo of the bird.

Seeing who it was, Kari gasped. Her knees buckled, and she fell hard against the stone floor.

"*Bonsoir, ma belle,*" said the figure.

It was Holly, her eyes spinning with madness.

But inside those eyes, cloaked more deeply, were another set of eyes, and they glared at Kari with fury.

Get me out of here! they demanded. *Maintenant!*

"Isabeau," Kari whispered. "Isabeau, are you trying to communicate with me?"

Holly herself made no response. Kari wasn't sure she had even heard her. But the eyes said, *Oui! Get me out! He will destroy us all!*

Behind Kari, Michael Deveraux said, "Put her somewhere safe, Holly. We'll make good use of her later."

Holly's face cracked into a mad, bewitched smile.

The Tri-Coven: Santa Cruz

The others drew around the fire as Alex stood with his hands spread for warmth. The dual scents of smoke and wood reminded Jer of the old sweat lodge on the University of Washington campus—the one he, Kialish, and Eddie had built together. Of the three of them, he was the only survivor.

And God only knows where Kari's gone off to. . . .

"It's nearly Wind Moon," Alex said, looking up at the pearly orb in the sky. He looked across the fire at Jer, who wore his hooded robe low over his face. Now that Holly was gone, he saved his magickal reserve for things other than creating a glamour of his former appearance. Still, it bothered him when the others glimpsed his features, then grimaced and looked away. He knew they didn't even realize they were doing it, and that Amanda, especially, would be mortified to know how much her revulsion wounded him.

But it's not about me now. It's about all of us surviving long enough to defeat my father.

Alex looked at Jer and said, "You know what that means, right, Deveraux?"

Aware that Alex continued to use Jer's hated last name even though he had asked him repeatedly not to, Jer nodded grimly. The Wind Moon would be ascendant when his father struck hardest. When Michael Deveraux tried to bring Hell to Earth.

He stared into the fire as if he could will it skyward. Witches spoke of drawing down the moon; if only they could, so he could set it ablaze and throw it back up into space and watch it burn. Then Wind Moon would never come.

The ensuing silence made the others nervous. Jer could feel the tension in the air. He took a sip of his coffee and found it bitter. But to him, all of life was bitter.

I'm staying alive to bring him down. And then . . .

Amanda frowned and drew closer to Philippe, saying to him, "What? What does Wind Moon mean?"

"I don't know," Philippe replied, shrugging. He gazed first at Alex, and then at Jer.

Jer looked up at him. Amanda flinched, but Philippe did not.

"It's the Horned God's moon. Any witch or warlock who dies during the next full moon becomes the damned servant of the God for all eternity."

"Well put," Alex said. "Accurate."

"Dios mio," Pablo murmured, crossing himself.

"Why didn't you two bring this up before now?" Armand demanded, looking angry. "We have hardly any time to prepare."

"I wasn't sure," Alex said. "I threw the runes."

The others turned to Jer. "Not every Wind Moon is charged with the same energy. But Alex is right about this one: This is a bad moon."

Amanda sighed heavily. "It never ends," she murmured. "It just gets worse and worse."

Pablo said to Jer, "What do we have to do?"

Before Jer had a chance to reply, Alex cut in and said, "We should kill a warlock to get his power, just like Michael Deveraux is planning to do."

He stared straight at Jer . . . who gazed steadily back.

"A witch serves the same purpose," Jer replied.

The two glared at each other.

One of us is going to die on Wind Moon, Jer thought. *And it sure as hell isn't going to be me.*

"That's enough," Richard snapped. "The two of you, back off, now," he said. He stepped between them, giving them both the benefit of his eyes, which were threatening.

Alex dropped his gaze, but Jer could still feel his threat lingering in the air, a promise for him alone. For his part, Jer unclenched his fists and turned his attention to Richard. He owed Holly's uncle his life, and it was a debt he would not soon forget. Alex might have come along and beat down the Black Fire, but Richard had been the one to free Jer from the rock, and Jer secretly believed that they would have escaped without Alex's help. *In fact, the fire didn't even appear again until after he entered the Dreamtime.*

He had no proof, though, and if Alex could help them defeat his father, then he would be grateful for the assistance. *My father . . . I wonder where he is, what he's up to.* Jer clenched his fists again reflexively. *It's like I can feel him, his presence. He's coming for us, and we're not ready. We need some intel, and we're not going to get it sitting around here. I could find him, though, discover what he's up to . . . see if he knows what happened to Holly. . . .*

He waited for the others to sleep. He rose from his bed, slipped on his shoes, and snuck quietly outside. As he passed Pablo, the young man twitched, a frown clouding his features. He held his breath, but the young witch didn't waken.

He eased the door open and made it outside, closing it behind him. He took three steps away and let out the breath he had been holding. Something moved in the corner of his eye and, he jumped, startled.

Richard was standing there, his gaze almost kind. Jer didn't know what to say. He had thought the older man asleep in the cabin with the others.

"I know where you're going and I just wanted to wish you good luck."

"Thank you," Jer said.

Richard clapped his hand on his shoulder. "Be careful. If you find Holly or Kari, get them out if you can."

"I will."

"We won't be here when you get back, I hope you understand. If you need us, though, try to call to Pablo. That boy's got incredible abilities."

Jer nodded. He knew the Mother Coven safe house was somewhere close by, but he didn't know where, and he wouldn't be likely to find it. After a moment, Richard reached out and hugged him. Surprised, Jer hugged him back. Tears stung the back of his eyes. "Take care, son," Richard whispered.

They broke contact, and Richard smiled before stepping back and disappearing into the darkness.

★ ★ ★

The day dawned clear and cool. Amanda stood with the two men she cared most about: her father and Tommy.

"It is good that he left," Tommy said. "It was not working with both of them here." He wrinkled his nose. "Testosterone poisoning for both of them."

Her father chuckled as he nodded agreement, but Amanda still felt bereft. It wasn't bad enough that so many had died or been kidnapped; people were now leaving willingly. Strange as it sounded, Jer had been her last solid link to Holly.

"Time to go," Amanda said as she saw Luna walking toward them. Her voice was raw from fighting to hold back tears for so long.

Within minutes they were all piled back into cars, Luna driving the lead car and Richard driving the other. Sooner than she would have thought, they were pulling up to a large house on a hill. Standing outside, her arms crossed and a large gray cat wrapping itself around her ankles, was Anne-Louise Montrachet.

Amanda got out of the car with a feeling of relief upon seeing a familiar face. She walked up to Anne-Louise and, almost without thinking, hugged the other woman. Amanda could sense her surprise as she returned the embrace.

"You are safe here," Anne-Louise whispered.

Amanda began to sob, unable to contain it any longer. "I haven't felt safe in so long."

"I know, I know."

Amanda felt rather than heard someone walk up behind her, and when he placed a hand on her shoulder, she knew it was Tommy. Anne-Louise pulled back, and Amanda turned, collapsing into Tommy's arms.

She heard Anne-Louise address the others in a strong, clear voice, "Welcome, all of you. We offer safe refuge and a place to heal. Blessed be."

"Blessed be," the others chorused.

"Blessed be," Amanda whispered against Tommy's shoulder.

EIGHT

EPONA

☾

Cahors fall into our hands
Victims of Deveraux plans
We do with them what we will
Savor it now as we kill

Goddess deliver us we pray
Help us live beyond this day
Twist our hearts away from pain
Keep us now safe and sane

Eli: Avalon

Despite the fact that he had had an easy time sneaking into the dungeon where Nicole had been imprisoned, Eli wasn't happy.

It's been too easy, he told himself as he snuck along, slipping on the wet stone floor. He had exchanged his usual 'kickers for a pair of soft-soled high-tops, and they were getting soggy. His feet were icy. *It's got to be a trap.*

The back of his cloak—and beneath that, his black leather jacket—were both soaked with foul moisture from the dripping, moldy wall. The castle was said to predate Arthur's Merlin, and the ancient Druid wizard was also said to inhabit it to this day. The mere thought made Eli's chest tighten with fear. If Merlin was helping Sir William, he, Eli, could be a pile of ashes by the time this day was over.

Or a warty old toad, like Laurent . . .

He meant it as a joke, but he shivered nonetheless. He was terrified, and that was not something a Deveraux warlock should ever admit to, not even to himself. Too much had happened to shake his faith in his family's power. It had been said that Deveraux magic was the strongest there was, at least on the side of the shadows, and that the Moores had usurped Eli's family's rightful place as the head of the Supreme Coven. After all, no other House could conjure the prize of the Black Fire . . . and many had tried.

This dungeon is nothing to me. It's for sure no threat to somebody as powerful as me.

But now, slinking along in the dark, smelling the stench of death and filth, hearing distant shrieks of agony as torturers practiced their art on various enemies of Sir William, Eli wished himself away. He wouldn't do that; even if the new wards on the island would have allowed it, he couldn't go through with that impulse—wouldn't transport himself—but the temptation to do so rose inside him like a hunger.

Nicole doesn't even like me anymore. Why should I bother saving her?

Because she's valuable, he told himself, frowning at his own wimpiness. *She's a Cahors descendant, and she and her sister and Holly make an unbeatable triumvirate. And besides, James took her from me.*

No man, warlock, or mere ungifted human takes what's mine.

With a seething grimace of jealousy, he continued on, mincing his way down the narrow tunnel that his finder's spell had led him to. Using his left hand to shield the light from potential onlookers, he examined the iridescent green glow in the center of his palm. The glow, in the tiny image of a Deveraux falcon, had "flown" slightly forward toward his middle finger, which indicated he should continue moving directly forward. There was always the chance that someone had managed to tamper with it, and was using it to misdirect him. He could unknowingly be walking straight into a trap.

But his magical compass appeared to be clean, and the tiny falcon was an image only a Deveraux could conjure.

Epona

There were other Deveraux alive in the world.

Jer's stuck in the Dreamtime, he thought, *and he's probably dead by now. I don't think Dad would go through all this to work some scheme he hasn't shared.*

But it's been too easy, he told himself again.

He tugged at his cloak of invisibility, slung over the black leather jacket. He had placed dozens of wards and amulets all over his body, but he had expected at least a few obstacles—a threshold guardian or two, perhaps an invisible demon force that detected the presence of an intruder. But thus far, sneaking around the cliffs above the shoreline, then snaking his way through a field of heather to the cavelike entrance of the dungeon, had proven to be uneventful. Even boring.

Then a silhouette rose against the dark wall—blackness on black—and Eli knew he had relaxed his guard too soon.

The shape was that of a round, bulbous creature with an ax slung over its shoulder. Its head was disproportionately large, giving it an almost apelike appearance.

It was a Golem, a creature fashioned of mud, whose mind was not its own. It would obey the commands of its creator; it could not be reasoned with or turned from its path. And they were very difficult to kill. Not impossible, but if Eli could accomplish it, he would have to make a lot of noise.

Eli turned his head, expecting to see the Golem standing on the other side of the tunnel. But nothing was there. Alarm prickled up his spine, bone-cold fingers skittering up the center of his back. Golems were very solid creatures. They could not cast apparition silhouettes, like ghosts or wraiths.

Damn it. Where the hell is it?

He closed his fist over his scrying stone to hide the glow and melted into the shadows himself. Narrowing his eyes, he tried to breathe as quietly as he could while he studied the shape. What he was seeing made no sense, unless some form of magic he was unfamiliar with was being employed.

Then, as he stared, the silhouette disappeared.

He blinked. Then he understood: The shadow had not been projected across the tunnel; rather, he had seen through the wall. One of his wards must have empowered that ability.

The Golem shambled along on the other side.

It's been sent after Nicole.

Then all I have to do to find her, is follow it.

He murmured spells, trying to remember which amulets he had put where—he'd been in a hurry—and finally clasped his hand around the sun disc that hung from a leather band around his neck. Its warmth told him he had picked the correct token. He murmured a spell of seeing, and sure enough, the wall thinned again. Again, he saw the Golem, lurching implacably along, a stone-mud monster as relentless as the Terminator.

He trailed slightly behind it on his side of the wall. The thing stumbled, stopped, and then began to recede from Eli's line of sight.

It's turning to the right, he realized.

He hesitated for a moment, then waved his hands and whispered words that melted the wall. He hoped that, with its back turned, the Golem would be heedless; but there was always the possibility that other beings in the same tunnel—if there were any— would notice what Eli was doing.

Soon, a hole big enough to crawl through materialized at waist height; Eli bent down and climbed through, his fist still tight around the scrying stone. He had not forgotten that his purpose was rescuing Nicole, and he knew that he might have to wait for the proper moment to battle the Golem. Where there was one Golem there could easily be another. And another.

As soon as he got through the hole, he trailed the massive stone construct. He was still on alert for guards, and still baffled that none advanced on him.

Then all hell broke loose, and he realized he'd been right: It was a trap.

As the Golem whirled around and began swinging

its ax at him, what had looked to be crumbling pieces of the stone had now detached from the walls and flung themselves at him. They were misshapen creatures made up of gelatinous bodies and long, taloned arms. They slashed at him as they catapulted themselves toward him.

Skilled warlock that he was, he immediately protected himself with a spherical barrier, aiming fireballs at the projectiles and deflecting the swinging ax of the Golem. He was aware of a blur of larger shapes racing around the sphere; and when he had a moment to look at them, he almost lost his rhythm: Three more Golems had joined the first. One had an ax, one a mace, and one a net of chain mail, such as Roman gladiators had once used. All of them were battering at the sphere; and he realized his only chance to survive would be to keep the sphere intact. That was made more difficult by the fireballs he was lobbing at the enemy.

More of the wall-creatures pushed off from the walls and slammed against the sphere, flattening and collapsing into heaps of gelatinous goo as they slid down the sides of the sphere to the floor. There were perhaps a dozen of them now. The four Golems continued to hack and batter the sphere, and its integrity began to give way. It wobbled and began to crack.

Then the Golem with the mace raised the weapon high over its head. The spiked ball of metal crashed down with a bone-jarring impact, and the force of the blow sheered off the topmost section of the sphere. Eli was now trapped inside like an animal in a burrow.

An animal . . . he thought, as he dropped to his knees. *An animal.*

Keeping his calm, he closed his eyes and focused his magical strength, seeing each feather clearly, each shining talon, the beady eyes and greedy beak:

Fantasme, he called. *I summon you across the faceless void. . . .*

Now the Golem with the broadsword arced his blade into the side of the sphere. Cracks like lightning flashes jagged all over the surface, obscuring Eli's vision.

Fantasme . . .

Three of the strange gelatinous creatures scrabbled to the top of the sphere, rose on their haunches, and dive-bombed inside. One of them landed on Eli's head and immediately began digging into his scalp with his long, sharp fingers. Eli roared with pain and grabbed the creature with both his hands; its body squirted between his fingers, and he flung it away from himself, disgusted.

The second one took up where the first one had left off, and Eli smashed that one too. The third had landed inside the sphere at his feet and was trying to crawl up his pant leg; with a grunt, he pushed it off with the sole of his high-top and stomped on it.

Two of the Golems rammed the sphere with their shoulders, trying to roll it onto its side. Eli was tossed to his knees; he spread his arms to prevent himself from slipping forward along the curved surface like a hamster in a wheel.

Fantasme! he commanded.

"There he is!" someone shouted in English, and Eli was aware that human troops had just entered the tunnel.

As if they need reinforcements, he thought. He took the opportunity of the rolling sphere's condition to lob fireballs out of what had once been the top, and now was an open side. He caught the first two human soldiers, who were wearing what looked to be black leather jackets and trousers. The men burst into flame and fell shrieking to the ground.

Damn you, Fantasme, come!

None of the men bothered to help the two who were burning to death. One was blocked by the Golems; it was almost humorous to watch him struggle to bully them out of his way. They paid him absolutely no mind, only kept on taking chunks out of the sphere.

And that is not funny.

The Golem with the mace reached inside, grabbing Eli around the neck. It began to squeeze. The rough dirt of the creature's flesh sanded Eli's neck. Eli grabbed his hands around the thing's thick wrists and fought for air. In another moment or two, the Golem would crush his windpipe . . . and he would be dead.

Bird, he thought, his brain a roar of words he could no longer bring to mind. *My servant . . .*

An explosion rocked the tunnel. The Golem with its hands around Eli's neck was thrown backward. Eli was yanked out of the sphere and onto its chest. The impact loosened its grip, and Eli savagely lobbed a fireball directly into its face.

It made no noise, simply went limp, letting go of its weapon. Eli was surprised—he'd had no idea fire could harm Golems; the fireball had been a reflexive attempt to protect himself—and then he saw a small piece of paper curling into ash inside the Golem's mouth. Of course. As creations of ancient Jewish magic, one activated a Golem by writing a magic spell on a piece of paper and placing it inside its mouth. His fireball had destroyed the spell.

Seizing the moment to gather his wits, he caused a great wall of flame to ignite, sealing off the majority of the guards and the monsters as they raced into the tunnel. Left with a small band to fight, he poured on the aggression and started taking them out one by one by one, as fast as he could.

There was another explosion. Eli mentally took note of it but otherwise spared no attention. The battle at hand took all his focus . . . but he knew that if he lived through it, he would have to deal with whatever was coming next.

There was a third explosion, and the ceiling of the tunnel began to shake apart into huge chunks of stone, crashing down on the gelatinous creatures and the Golem with the broadsword, which had just been about to lunge forward toward Eli. Eli immediately shielded himself with a spell, yet the barrage was so incredible that he rolled into a ball and covered his head with his hands. Then, realizing how vulnerable to attack he was allowing himself to be, he rolled onto his side and staggered to his feet as the floor beneath him cracked apart. One huge jagged mass of it collided with another, forcing both pieces upward like a mountain.

His wall of flame held; yet, incredibly, something so massive rose up behind it that Eli saw its silhouette through the rippling tongues of flame. Then it strode through the fiery curtain, sending the third Golem flying with a punch of its gigantic fist.

It was a hideous creature, leathery and black, approximately ten feet high. As it shambled toward Eli, it had to duck to avoid hitting the top of the tunnel. Its face was an elongated rectangle ending in a strange triangular configuration of flesh and feathers. Its eyes were huge, and there were no irises, only pupils at least half a foot across. Instead of arms, large, fleshy appendages were covered with quills. Its feet were clawed, resembling those of a hawk.

The thing opened its mouth and made a high-pitched, eerie wail. With a start, Eli realized who and what it was: It was the spirit of the falcon, Fantasme, materialized in some bizarre manifestation he had never seen before. "You heard me," he blurted.

The bird-creature reached forward with its arm-parts, scooped up Eli against its chest, and whirled around, lunging forward and opening an enormous mouth at the end of its snout. Its jaws cracked open and expanded; another set of jaws extended forward and ripped open the throat of a gelatinous creature that was sailing through the air in an attempt to land on its back.

Bits of goo flew everywhere. Then Fantasme turned back around and began to lope through the tunnel.

The two remaining Golems took off after it. Craning his neck to see, Eli watched them draw near, then recede as Fantasme picked up speed. The tunnel was filling with smoke and a horrible burnt odor. The acrid, oily smoke poured into Eli's throat before he had a chance to protect himself. He began to cough, his eyes watered. Fantasme gazed down at him and squawked in its incomprehensible speech. Then it jerked toward him and, before Eli could respond, it had engulfed his head inside its beak. It inhaled, exhaled; Eli understood. Fantasme was giving him fresher air to breathe.

The act probably saved Eli's life, and he kept his head inside Fantasme's beak as the bird-creature raced faster, and faster still, hunched protectively around Eli like a quarterback around a football.

He didn't know how long Fantasme ran—it seemed like hours—but the hot, moist breath of the bird grew stale and smoky, as it undoubtedly drew in the poisonous air around itself, filtering as best it could before offering it to Eli. Weakening and feeling ill, he could feel his grip around Fantasme loosening, but the creature held him tightly, and Eli felt a rush of gratitude as they loped along. Throughout the centuries, Fantasme had been a good and faithful servant of his family, in whatever incarnation the bird presented itself.

Of course, that faithfulness had been dearly purchased . . . with the blood of many, many virgins. . . .

But now, he was growing fainter. The air was too polluted; he was suffocating inside Fantasme's mouth. His fingers went limp, and his arm dangled at his side, jangling like a spring as the bird carried him through the dungeon of the castle on Avalon.

I'm not going to die, he thought angrily. *I'm a Deveraux. We don't do that.*

Then everything faded, and his soul screamed in terror, for fear that the Horned God would devour it, and gray and spiritless oblivion would be its final reward.

When he woke up, Nicole was bent over him with her mouth over his. He smelled a delicious fragrance of cloves and roses and inhaled greedily. Witch breath. Magic breath. She was apparently unaware that he had regained consciousness, and he made his lungs rise with the air that she was breathing into his mouth. She was giving him mouth-to-mouth, and he loved it.

She was so intent on what she was doing that when he gently touched his tongue to hers, she continued to work on him.

Then her dark, deep-set eyes gazed directly into his own, and she broke contact.

With a grunt, she sat up and narrowed her eyes, on guard. He made a show of coughing and rolling onto his side, spasming and clenching and unclenching his fists.

She pounded on his back. He grinned to himself and made himself cough a few more times.

"Eli, wake up. Get me the hell out of here," she demanded harshly. "The water's rising."

The water?

Dropping his act, he sat up, realizing that it wasn't so much of an act after all—he was incredibly weak, and the cave—*the cave?*—was spinning around him like a crazed merry-go-round.

"That thing broke me out and brought us both to this cave," she said, pointing to a place behind. He turned. Sure enough, Fantasme loomed protectively over him, its beady eyes reflecting back nothing but the darkness. There was a source of light somewhere in the cave, and Eli glanced around in search of it. A small globe bobbled beside Nicole.

She must have created it, he thought, and reminded himself sternly that she was a Cahors witch and, as such, still his enemy. The old days of high school and her having the hots for him belonged to two inhabitants of a past, foreign country.

"If this is a plan to deliver me to your father or James, I'll kill you," she said. As if to prove that she had the moxie to do it, she pulled a dagger on him and held it to his throat.

Fantasme lunged toward her, but Eli held up a restraining hand and said, "Back."

He recognized the dagger from rituals he had performed with James. It was one of his athames. Wicked-sharp, it had sliced through the breast of a goat with one easy stroke—but he doubted Nicole knew that.

"I'm not here to give you to James or my father," he said. "I'm here to rescue you. Period."

"Why?" she demanded.

He thought about telling her that he loved her, but she would never believe that. Or that he wanted her, which she would probably find offensive. So he told her the truth. "You're powerful, and you're valuable. I need some bargaining chips. You're good in my back pocket." He chuckled at his nonsensical but vaguely sexual turn of phrase.

"Don't you touch me," she said savagely, showing her teeth like a feral cat. That turned him on. "Don't you so much as get near me."

"No worries." He held up his hands. "Down, Sheba." Then he smiled and said, "But if I need mouth-to-mouth again, I'll be sure to let you know."

"I saved your life," she hissed. "But not out of any

compassion for you, Eli. I need you to get me out of here. But if you try anything, I'll kill you."

Fantasme took another step forward. Again, Eli motioned to it to stay put.

"Fair enough, babe," he tossed off. "Same here. Let's agree to a truce until we're out of this mess."

"And then . . . ?"

"Then we'll see where we're at. As we used to say back when we were kids."

She scowled at him. "I never talked like that. Neither did you. Your father did, maybe. He was always trying so hard to be 'cool.'" She tossed her hair, and it was hard for him not to grab her and kiss her. He loved sassy, bitchy chicks.

"My dad is cool," he retorted.

"You know what, Eli? I really don't care," she said.

She was dressed in a shapeless rustling gown of satin and black lace, which was quite fetching on her. It was richly embroidered with Cahors silver at the low-cut bodice and long sleeves, which half-covered the backs of her hands. Though she had been a prisoner slated for death, she was also the bride of a Moore—until such time as she was the dead bride of a Moore. Her dark, curly hair had grown since they'd been together, and it was twisted at the sides and hung long down her back. She was incredibly beautiful.

For a moment he imagined what it must have been like for her, with James. James had shared some of the brutal details with him, and Eli had been angry, jealous that another man touched her. Until now, though, he had never stopped to think what it must have been like for her. He shook his head.

Fantasme made a strange scrying noise, and for a moment Eli had the ridiculous, giddy thought that they were in a *Scooby-Doo* episode and Fantasme was the guy in the suit. Then he sobered as icy, brackish water sloshed over his already-sodden track shoes. "All right, so where are we? I'll skip the Kansas cliché."

"We're at sea level," Nicole informed him. "It brought us to a cave. The water's been coming in steadily. I think the tide is rising."

"Are we still being hunted?" he asked her.

She snorted. "Of course. There are a couple of these icky guys made out of mud—"

"Golems," he informed her.

"Whatever. And demons and goo monsters. All kinds of things. Your birdman outran them and then I put a glamour on this cave so they couldn't see the entrance. But I don't know how good of a spell it was, and I don't know when they'll break down my wards and stuff. I used your cloak of invisibility," she added. "It's a good one." That sounded like a difficult admission for her to make, so he didn't reply.

"So. Did you have a plan?" she demanded.

"Of course," he shot back. "It was based entirely on stealth," he added, so she wouldn't press him for details he did not have. "James knows this entire island. He spent most of his childhood here. He'll figure out where we are." He frowned. "If he hasn't already."

Nicole cast an anxious glance over her shoulder. All he saw was rock, but he guessed that that was where his cloak was shielding the entrance. For all either of them knew, an army of Supreme Coven minions, human or otherwise, was massed on the other side, waiting for them to come out.

He could have taken the knife from her then, but he liked her cute little show of power, so he gave up the chance. Maybe she sensed his thoughts, because she whipped her head back at him and pressed a little harder on the knife. He doubted that she realized that it turned him on even more.

It was too much for Fantasme. The creature arced back an . . . appendage . . . and whacked the knife out of Nicole's grasp. She screamed in agony and crumpled onto the cave floor. "My wrist!" she managed, her voice a raspy shriek.

Eli smoothly picked up the athame and slipped it

inside his black leather jacket. Then he roughly covered her mouth to muffle her screams. That made her scream harder, so he murmured a spell of silence, which rendered her mute.

And for old times' sake, he took away the pain and told her wrist to start healing itself.

Jer, Gorman, California

Jer had stopped to gas up the car on the top of the Grapevine before starting the descent into the L.A. basin. From there he would head east toward New Mexico. The night was dark, clouds covering the face of the moon as he glanced anxiously skyward. *Wind Moon is coming,* he thought with a shudder. *There's a good chance none of us are going to survive it.*

"Not if I can help it," he vowed out loud, startling a woman pumping gas into a red minivan five feet away. He narrowed his eyes; there was something about the woman that didn't seem . . . right.

Her short hair was plastered to her head, and there was something distinctly European about her features. He stared at her hand as it replaced the gas nozzle. She was gripping it tight, the muscles in her forearm knotting. Impressive muscles they were, too. He narrowed his eyes and tried to make out more details in the fluorescent light.

There was scarring on her arm, a long, straight line consistent with self-mutilation. It was on the top of her arm, so it couldn't have been a suicide attempt. No, it looked familiar, like something one would inflict doing a ritual—

She lunged at him, throwing him to the ground and landing on top of him. His head hit the concrete with a dull thud, and a roaring sound filled his ears. His vision blurred, but he felt a sudden stabbing pain in the area of his throat.

"Tell me where your father is," the woman hissed.

His vision snapped back into focus as he realized she was pressing a knife to his throat.

"I'm not entirely sure," he answered honestly. There was no need to lie to a woman who could and would kill him for doing so.

He could tell by the way she pursed her lips that she knew he was telling the truth.

"Don't tell me, he jilted you and you're looking for revenge?" he joked, not knowing what else to do. She had him, and could slit his throat before he could do a thing, magical or otherwise, to try to escape.

She laughed soullessly. "Nothing so exciting. But I am going to kill him."

Jer swallowed hard, trying to ignore the feeling of

the blade cutting his skin. "You'll have to stand in line, then."

"Why should I believe you? Why should I believe you are going to kill your own father?"

"You know who I am and who my father is and yet you have to ask?"

She nodded, seemingly satisfied, and stood up in one fluid motion. She extended her hand, and he took it. As he scrambled back to his feet, he put a few feet between them with a sense of relief.

"Sir William has ordered your father executed. You, however, he said nothing about."

"I never thought being ignored could have such advantages," he quipped lamely as he touched his hand gingerly to his neck. Spots of blood came back on his fingertips, and he cursed under his breath.

"Trust me, he's not ignoring you, he never ignores anyone, which is why he's still alive."

"Sounds like you speak from personal experience."

She glanced up at him with a shake of her head. "I've seen what he can do. I'm not anxious to have him do it to me."

Jer smiled at the double entendre. It was a grim testament to the world that the woman had chosen to live in, the side she had aligned herself with.

"Leave the car. You're riding with me," the woman ordered.

He looked at her warily. "So, I'm your prisoner?"

"Think of yourself more as an accomplice. As I see it, we're both pursuing the same goal."

"If you don't mind, I'll just meet you there," he said, backing toward his car and preparing to erect a barrier between them.

"I wouldn't do that if I were you," she warned as he touched the handle on the car.

"And why is that?"

She smiled, a little wicked smile that felt like daggers of ice being showered at him. "Because while you were inside buying soda, I rigged your car to explode."

He froze, his hand still on the handle. With his mind he began to probe the car, looking for something, anything. It was his eyes that saw it, though. There, lying on the passenger side seat, was a tiny black box with wires running out of it. *It could be a fake,* he thought.

"Are you willing to risk it?" she asked. "Not only your life, and my life, but also the life of the poor slob behind the counter, and theirs," she said with a nod. He turned to watch as a family poured out of a station wagon that had just parked at a nearby pump. They were all wearing matching Mickey Mouse shirts, and it was clear from their exhausted yet happy faces where they had just come from.

A bead of sweat trickled down the middle of his back as he instinctually turned his face away so that the children wouldn't see his scars. *Strange,* he thought, as he stared again at the woman. *I didn't care at all what she thought of them, even before she attacked me.*

"If I go with you, you'll defuse the car so that no one will be injured after we leave?"

She hesitated for a moment before nodding.

"All right," he agreed.

"Take your hand off the handle, gently," she instructed.

He did as he was told and then stepped back away from the car.

"Good boy," she crooned. "Now, get in the van."

He gave her a wide berth as he did so. As soon as he closed the door, she headed for his car. The mirrors in the van were angled to let him see what she was doing, and before she could adjust them she had appeared at the van's driver-side door. She opened it and hopped in.

"Finished?" he asked, surprised.

"Sure," she answered as she started the engine and put the van into gear. As they merged back onto Interstate 5, she added, "There was no bomb."

He put his head back against the headrest and sighed. She was clearly not to be trusted. "So, do you have a name or shall I just call you Deceiver?"

"How about Temptress instead?" she asked in a coy voice. "My name is Eve."

It was going to be a long trip.

June Cathers: Santa Paula, California, March 12, 1928 11:57 P.M.

Four-year-old June Cathers lay awake, too excited to sleep. In the morning it would be her birthday and she would be five. In the bed next to June, her twin brothers, Timmy and Tommy, were sound asleep. She held her breath so she could listen to them breathing for a moment. They were younger than she was, and when they had been born her daddy had told her that she had to look out for them.

She let out her breath with a *whoosh*. There was going to be a party tomorrow, with cake. Her grandmother was going to be there, and both her grandfathers. She only had the one grandmother. Her daddy's mommy had died when he was younger than June. It always made her sad for her daddy when she thought about it.

She rolled onto her side, squeezing her eyes tightly shut as she did so. She had forgotten to shut the closet door when she went to bed; she had been too excited, thinking about her birthday. The closet frightened her; there were things that moved in at night. Once, she had opened her eyes and seen shadows in her closet, shadows that stared at her.

She had screamed and screamed, and when her mommy came she had told her she was just imagining things. She hadn't been, though, she knew it. There were monsters in the world. She saw them sometimes and she knew they wanted to hurt her and her brothers.

The grandfather clock began to chime midnight. She jumped and then forced herself to breathe deeply, calming herself down. She slowly began to drift off to sleep. From somewhere far off she heard something . . . a deep, low sound. She pulled the blankets over her head, but the sound grew louder, increasing to a dull roar. She clamped her hands over her ears, but it just got louder. At last it was deafening, and she sat up. She turned and looked at the closet just as a wall of water came rushing out of it.

She screamed just as the water washed over her. Suddenly, a light appeared, shining brighter than anything she had ever seen. A woman stood in it, with long, flowing hair. She picked June up and held her close. The water passed around them, but did not touch them. June coughed out the water she had already swallowed as she clung to the dark-haired lady. "What's happening?" June wailed.

"The St. Francis Dam broke," the lady answered, holding her closer.

The house collapsed around them, and they remained untouched. The water washed away the debris, and they stayed where they were. At last the deluge passed, and the shining lady set her down on her feet. The mud sucked at her legs, and her night-dress was wet and dirty.

"Be safe, *ma petite* June of the Cahors," the lady said, and then she disappeared.

June Cathers looked around at the destruction of her home and her town. Her family, her parents, and her little brothers were gone, they were dead. She was five years old, and it was her birthday.

NINE

BAST

☾

Something now in the wind
Reveals to us all our sin
We meet this darkness with more hate
This alone a Deveraux's fate

Cahors watch and Cahors pray
Wish away the light of day
For in the night alone we sing
Dancing in a silver ring

Tri-Coven: Santa Cruz

"Goddess, how I miss Nicole," Philippe prayed, as he lay in his narrow bed. "Let me find her well and safe."

He rolled onto his side, preparing for another sleepless night. He couldn't rest since Nicole had been taken—*again by James and Eli!*

He found Pablo staring at him. "What is it, *hijo?*"

"We will find her," Pablo whispered.

"Thanks, Pablo," Philippe answered. "I only pray that it is sooner rather than later."

Pablo nodded at that. The other surviving member of their coven, Armand, snored quietly from his cot. Philippe raised a head to look at him.

Leadership is a difficult burden. I do not know how José Luís bore it so long, he thought.

"He was able to bear it so long because you were there to encourage him," Pablo answered, reading his thoughts.

Philippe reached out and touched Pablo's shoulder briefly. *Thank you,* he thought.

"You're welcome," Pablo answered.

"Any luck in finding any of the others?"

"*Sí,*" Pablo admitted. "Holly is with Michael Deveraux."

"Where?"

"A place called New Mexico."

"And Kari and Jer?"

"Kari is there, too, and Jer is traveling there to kill his father."

"Goddess grant him success," Philippe half-said, half-prayed. "And Nicole?" he asked after a moment, afraid to hear the answer.

Pablo shook his head, clearly frustrated. "Nothing, still."

"Is it possible they took her back to Avalon?"

"I do not know, but I would guess there or London."

"Thank you for trying."

"I will not give up hope, as you must not."

Philippe sighed. There were days that was easier said than done. With thoughts of his missing covenates allayed for the moment, his mind turned to the other concern that had been weighing on him. "Have you sensed anything from Alex?"

"No, he is very closed. It is hard to feel anything from him—and he is always watching, like he knows I am watching him."

"That makes me nervous," Philippe confessed.

"The High Priestess, too," Pablo told him.

Interesting. Maybe she and I should talk, he thought.

"That would be good," Pablo said. "I have worked on it so that he will not be able to read us three," he said. "I will work on the others, as well."

"Thank you, again."

After lying awake for another hour trying to meditate, Philippe drifted off into a fitful sleep. He was awakened in what seemed like minutes but was really hours, by Pablo's excited exclamation.

"I found her!"

Philippe sat up, instantly alert. "Where is she?" he demanded, knowing exactly who Pablo was talking about.

"She is on the island of Avalon. She contacted me briefly. She was trying to reach you, but couldn't quite," Pablo said, suddenly sounding embarrassed.

"It is all right, Pablo," Philippe said gently. The younger man was clearly embarrassed at having intercepted a signal meant for him from his beloved.

"She said that she is fine and that Eli is helping her escape."

Philippe sighed deeply. "Goddess be praised that she is safe. I do not like that Eli is with her, but if he is to become a friend to us, I will welcome him gladly."

"Shall I wake the others?"

Philippe glanced at the clock on the nightstand. "They should be up in another hour. Let them sleep. We will all need what sleep we can get. You should try to rest more too."

Pablo nodded and lay back down slowly. He closed his eyes, and after a moment his breathing began to even out. Philippe sat for a moment until he was sure Pablo was asleep, and then he rose and went downstairs. He found Sasha making breakfast.

"Pablo has found Nicole," he offered by way of greeting. "She is alive and safe on Avalon. Eli is helping her to escape."

A look of relief passed across her face, and she lit up like the sun. A cloud soon obscured the radiance, though, as she asked, "And what of Jer?"

Philippe nodded. "He is on his way to confront his father."

She sagged against the counter, a stricken look crossing her face. "I knew in my heart that that was where he was going," she admitted.

"It doesn't make it any less hard to hear it," he said sympathetically.

"True," she said, forcing a smile. She visibly shook herself. "It is good to hear that Eli is helping Nicole. I wonder what has brought my son to that?"

Philippe shrugged. "Maybe he has realized that he has been serving the master when he should have looked to the mistress."

Sasha smiled. "More likely it has something to do with Nicole."

"Yes, she can be quite persuasive when she wants to be. If he ever did love her, I am sure she can turn him to her will," Philippe said, hating to admit even to himself that the words stung.

The others began to straggle in slowly until everyone was present. They all looked tired, but everyone took renewed courage from the news about Nicole. Her sister, Amanda, was especially relieved.

Last to arrive was Alex, and he, in contrast, looked fresh and rested. Philippe envied him that. Members

of the Mother Coven, some of them having already
been up for hours, seemed to be avoiding the kitchen.
Even Luna was absent, and she had spent much time
with them in the last couple of days.

Philippe looked around at the few of them who
were left. Sasha and Richard stood together. They were
the parents whose children played some of the key roles
in the battle that was being fought. He knew that they
had taken great solace in each other's presence of late.
Barbara Davis-Chin sat at a table, sipping tea and staring
around at the others. He knew Armand and Pablo were
standing slightly behind him and had been engaged in
earnest conversation in Spanish about everything Pablo
had told him in the middle of the night. In a corner, also
having their own private conversation, were Tommy
and Amanda. He had his arm around her, and Philippe
didn't need Pablo's psychic abilities to see that Amanda
was both excited and upset with the news about her sister. Alex Carruthers made ten in the group.

At last everyone had heard the news about all their
missing comrades. Alex cleared his throat, and they all
turned their attention to him.

"I have spoken with Luna, and she has graciously
offered us the use of the Mother Coven's private jet
and whatever they can spare in the way of equipment
and people.

"We need to rescue Nicole, and we need to take the fight to the enemy. The leader of this coven is gone, and we have to face the fact that she might not ever return. If she does, we shall welcome her back with open arms. Until that day, though, this coven needs a leader. I am the leader of my coven back home, and I propose to lead this coven into battle. To that end I pledge to you my life, my allegiance, my skill, and my knowledge."

There were murmurs, but no one said anything. Of all those present, Philippe was the only one who had led a coven. He had never liked leading—he was always more comfortable as the lieutenant—still, it was his place to speak for the other two coven leaders who were not present.

Can we trust him? he asked Pablo silently.

I do not know, but I do know that we need him, could really use his help, the boy answered in his mind.

Which he's not likely to give us if we oppose him in this?

I cannot tell.

Philippe nodded slowly. *I guess we will have to take a chance. If he can help us rescue Nicole, we must.* Out loud, he said, "I would consent to your taking leadership temporarily while our other two coven leaders are absent."

"Is it agreed, then?" Alex asked.

"It is agreed," Amanda answered, her bright eyes on Philippe.

"Good. We should do the proper rituals and then we all need to rest up. Tomorrow we fly to England. Half of us will go to Avalon to rescue Nicole, and the other half will attack the Supreme Coven."

As the others gasped, Philippe thought, *By the Goddess, what did you just do?*

That night, Philippe could again not find rest. He relived the events of the day, from the decision he had made in the kitchen, to the ceremony installing Alex as leader of the coven. All of them were to have spent the rest of the day resting and meditating, but Philippe had not been able to do either.

Alex had retired before the rest. The others were just too worn out and too shell-shocked to rest. He glanced at Pablo. The boy was dreaming, and for a while Philippe watched him. Joy and pain passed in rapid succession across his youthful face, and Philippe wondered what his dreams were and if they were true visions of the future or fanciful flights of the mind.

He flipped back onto his back and stared up at the ceiling. He had never felt as out of sorts as he had since Nicole had been taken. *She is a part of me as I am a part of her. It is as though a chunk of my soul has been taken as well,* he thought. *I don't think I'll ever know rest again unless she is at my side.*

From Nicole, his mind drifted to her newly discovered cousin. *I wonder what she would say about everything that has happened?* He smiled. The what-would-Nicole-say game was quickly becoming one of his favorite distractions.

He heard gentle snoring from Armand, and more snores from the room beyond. *Alex, are you asleep? If so what are you dreaming? If not, what are you doing?*

June Cathers: Santa Paula, California, March 12, 1928 11:57 P.M.

Four-year-old June Cathers lay awake, too excited to sleep. In the morning it would be her birthday and she would be five. In the bed next to June, her twin brothers, Timmy and Tommy, were sound asleep. She rolled onto her side, squeezing her eyes tightly shut as she did so. Her closet door was open, and it was bothering her.

It was growling and rumbling, louder and louder. She was trying not to listen to it, but it was getting so loud, she wondered why the others didn't wake up.

She turned and screamed.

A wall of water rushed out of it: A river was gushing right out of her closet!

Then suddenly, it stopped, frozen as though in

midair. A light appeared, shining brighter than any-thing she had ever seen. A woman with beautiful, long flowing hair stood inside the light. She picked June up and held her close.

Then a man appeared, also shining with a brilliant light. His hair was light-colored, and he was beautiful.

He picked up Timmy and Tommy, one in each arm, and all of them huddled close together. Then the water began moving again, flowing around them. But the shining people held June and her brothers in their arms, standing easily in the water.

"What's happening?" June wailed.

"The St. Francis Dam broke," the man told her. "There is a curse on your family, that they will die by water. But we have saved you. You are our future."

"Are you an angel?" she asked, touching his face in awe.

"No," he said, with a faint smile. "My name is Alex, and I'm not an angel. I am someone, though, who owes his very life to you."

He leaned over and kissed her. "Happy Birthday, June."

Then he and the lady disappeared.

And June woke up to a lovely day . . . and she was five years old.

Bast

Mother Coven: Santa Cruz

Anne-Louise sat up in bed with a gasp. "Something is wrong," she whispered out loud.

Whisper stared at her, her head cocked to the side and her yellow eyes boring through her.

"Something is different—changed, somehow," Anne-Louise said, looking at the cat and praying for answers.

The cat spoke. "The time line has shifted around you."

"What has caused such a thing?" Anne-Louise asked, horrified.

"Someone has changed the past. Look to House Cahors for answers."

A chill shot up her spine. It was serious business to change the past. In the Mother Coven, it was an act that demanded the death of the one who had performed the powerful magic to accomplish it.

She argued, "But if the time line has shifted, how come I'm aware of it?"

The cat blinked at her. "Because I have allowed you to remain an observer of both."

Anne-Louise felt her mouth go completely dry. "What has changed?"

"Much."

Eli and Nicole: Avalon

Within minutes, Nicole's wrist was healed. Eli had taken the time to think about how they were going to get off the island. So far he had come up with nothing, but he wasn't willing to admit that. He looked at her. *She is so beautiful, and she glows so bright.* He swallowed hard. He had to know. The question had tormented him, and now it had to be asked. "Is—is the baby mine?"

Nicole flushed scarlet as she placed a hand over her extended abdomen. "I don't know," she whispered.

"When are you due?"

"The night of the Wind Moon."

"That's just a few days from now!" he exclaimed, beginning to panic slightly.

She gave him the sweetest smile he had ever seen, and he began to calm. *It could be my child,* he thought, a sense of wonder filling him. Almost before he could stop himself, he started to stretch out his hand. He stopped, though, and stared her in the eyes.

She nodded ever so slightly and took his hand, pressing it to her belly. He could feel movement within, life stirring in her, and something more: a slight tingle of electricity.

"The baby has power," he breathed.

"Yes, he does."

"You know it's a boy?"

She nodded. "I can feel it."

"And he might be mine."

"He might be."

He began to shake uncontrollably. Nicole wrapped her arms around him and held him close as he began to cry.

Nicole felt like crying herself. She was moved by the softening in Eli. *He's been changing, right before my eyes,* she thought. *I used to think I could tame him, maybe I was right.*

What she had told him was true: Eli could be the father; she really didn't know who was. She hoped it was Philippe, though they hadn't been together very long. *The funny thing is, I don't remember much about being pregnant. I know it's a boy and when it's due, but other than that, there's not much there.* She shuddered. *What if it's James's child?* She suddenly felt sick to the bottom of her soul. The truth was, there was magic of some kind being done. Nine months ago she hadn't been with anyone in order to become pregnant. She and Eli had broken up before that. She and Philippe had been together only a short while, and James had—done what he had done to her—relatively recently as well.

Another thought whispered through her mind:

What about the thing in my room? Could it have done this to me? She began to cry as well, her tears mingling with Eli's. The truth was that neither of them was likely to make it out of this alive. She had loved him once, and if it brought him comfort to think he was the father—and she really didn't know if he was or not, then it could not hurt to let him think he was.

Jer and Eve: New Mexico

They had stopped across the border at an all-night truck stop for food. Jer's attempts to get more information out of Eve had been met with resistance. They had eaten in silence, and Jer didn't even remember what he had ordered. All he knew was that the food was tasteless and that he didn't care. There was too much to worry about to care.

He waited in the van while Eve used the rest room. He could sense his father's presence, feel his stench even from here. *He's like a plague. His evil spreads, infecting those near him, even the land around him and the sky above. He has to be stopped while there's still some light in the world, some good that is as yet untouched by his hand.*

He turned to look at Eve as she climbed into the minivan. She had changed into black jeans, a black turtleneck, and a black leather vest. The vest looked thick, more like something he would have expected to see used as a bulletproof vest by a police officer rather than used as a wardrobe accessory for the occult-minded. She also wore black leather boots that came up to her knees.

"I feel underdressed," he commented dryly.

"Isn't that like a man," she tossed back at him. "Forever wearing the wrong thing."

He was about to make a snappy retort when something crashed into the windshield, or rather, crashed *through* the windshield. It was an imp and it chortled wildly before stabbing at Jer's eyes with its wicked nails. With a shout, he twisted his head to the side just in time. Eve backhanded the creature, sending it flying back through the windshield.

She started the engine and threw the car into reverse in a single motion. She hit a car parked in a stall behind her and threw the car into drive. Anguished tires screamed as she peeled out.

"I guess they'll be taking away my international driver's license," she noted grimly.

Jer braced himself as she made a hard turn to exit the parking lot. He flew forward, though, when she came to a screeching halt. There, lined up in front of the car, was a row of demons standing shoulder-to-shoulder. They ranged in type and size.

Eve gunned the engine as Jer stared at the demons.

One extended a casual arm, waving them forward. *Red Rover, Red Rover, send Jer on over,* he thought. *If we break the line, we live, if not, we get to join the dead.*

Eve pulled her foot off the brake, and the minivan leaped forward. He wanted to close his eyes, to look away, but something wouldn't let him. Together, he and Eve shouted as the minivan hit the line of demons. Body parts went flying everywhere. A hand came soaring through the broken windshield and landed in Jer's lap. With a scream of revulsion, he picked up the twitching appendage and threw it in the backseat. Meanwhile, demons had leaped onto the van, clinging by hands and feet and tentacles.

One put his fist through the passenger-side window, and a shower of glass flew into Jer's face. He instinctively squeezed his eyes shut. The shards of glass almost felt like rain pelting his skin until the pain began to register.

The demon suddenly demanded his full attention by wrapping his hand around Jer's throat. He desperately grabbed the creature's head with both of his hands and started banging it against the frame of the door. The creature tightened his grip, and as Jer's lungs became oxygen-starved, his actions became more frantic. At last he headbutted the creature. Pain exploded along his temples, but the demon's grip loosened for a moment.

Jer grabbed the creature's fingers and tore them from his throat. It was momentarily off balance, and he took advantage of that to push it backward. It fell to the ground, and the minivan bounced as a rear tire drove over it. An unearthly scream ripped through the night air, and Jer clamped his hands over his ears, gritting his teeth in pain.

It passed in a second, and the van swerved wildly to the right. He turned his attention to Eve. She was fighting a small, scaly red demon for control of the steering wheel. Another demon was hanging half inside the door, clawing at her head.

Jer lobbed a fireball at it that whipped right past Eve's head. It exploded in the demon's face, toppling it backward with a cry. Jer could smell the stench of burning hair and realized that he must have clipped Eve.

"Depart!" he roared at the little red demon, too agitated to think of the Latin word for it.

The creature turned and cackled toothlessly at him, bouncing up and down on the dashboard. It ceased laughing, though, when Eve hit the brakes and it went sailing through the air to land on the ground several feet in front of them. She floored the van, and it ran over the demon with a sickening crunch. Bits of yellow blood and goo sprayed in through the open windows, covering them both.

Eve got on the freeway doing ninety and didn't slow down for half an hour. Jer charmed their passage so that the three police cars they passed didn't see them. They were only an unexplained blip on the radar. At last she pulled off the road at a small town and parked in front of a motel. "Someone knows you're in town," she remarked.

"It would seem so," was all he could say, trying not to vomit as he tasted the demon blood on his lips.

Kari and Michael: New Mexico

The imp jumped up and down in front of Michael, in a state of great agitation. "We tried to kill him, but he had someone with him, a girl," the thing hissed.

It was so upset, Kari could barely understand what it was saying.

"Die, die, he wouldn't die, and neither would she. Warlock she is, powerful one."

"He has a warlock with him?" Michael mused. "That can't be a good thing. Let me guess, that weakling Sir William has finally decided it's bad PR to keep me around?"

"She is strong, stronger than he."

"That wouldn't take much, would it?" he asked with a dismissive wave of his hand.

Kari stood up slowly, her knees shaking. She didn't

remember much about the last twenty-four hours. Everything was hazy. It still felt that way, but she needed to know who they were talking about. "Who?" she asked, her throat dry and her voice barely a whisper.

Michael and the imp ignored her. Instead, the creature just continued to jump up and down, blathering on and on about something. Michael was stroking his chin and looking thoughtful.

"Who?" she asked, her voice cracking but sounding slightly stronger.

They continued to ignore her, and for one wild moment she thought she might be a ghost. *Michael Deveraux has killed me, and now I'm trapped here, seeing but unseen, hearing but unheard.* She picked up a lamp and hurled it to the ground. It crashed and broke.

Michael turned and stared at her. "What's with your coven and breaking lamps?" he asked in an almost amiable tone. "That's all Holly wanted to do at first too."

"Who?" she shouted.

He lifted an eyebrow. "The woman, I don't know— though there are very few female warlocks in the Supreme Coven, so it shouldn't be too hard to figure that out."

"The man, who is the man?" she asked, speaking slowly and enunciating each word.

He smiled bemusedly. "Oh, it's just Jeraud."

"Jer?" she asked, afraid she hadn't heard him right. He nodded.

"He's alive?"

"Apparently so. He seems to have made it back from the Dreamtime, and now he's on the way here."

She grabbed a chair and sat down before she could faint. *He's alive!* Her heart lifted for one glorious moment before crashing back down again. "You're trying to kill Jer," she accused.

"Why so surprised?" he asked with an evil smirk.

"He's your *son!*"

"And I've tolerated his antics long enough. Every parent hopes that their children will grow up to make them proud, to do better than they did, to be a glorious branch on the family tree."

"But?"

"Well, as any good gardener knows, every tree needs pruning from time to time. Jer, unfortunately, is just an unproductive limb that I'm going to trim."

"But you promised."

"No, my dear," he said, moving closer to her. "If you think back, you'll remember that I never did promise you anything. That's one thing my son and I share in common," he ended with a sneer.

"He's coming here?" she asked, her head still fuzzy.

"Yes."

She lifted her chin high. "Then he's coming to rescue me. You'll be sorry."

Michael laughed, an honest, surprised-sounding laugh. He knelt down next to her so that his face was on a level with hers, and stared deeply into her eyes. "My dear, are you so deluded as to think that he's coming here to rescue you?" He clucked his tongue. "Let's be real, pet. He's on his way to rescue Holly."

His words cut her to the quick. He stood slowly as he drove the final nails into the coffin that contained all her dreams. "Not you. It was never you." He turned and walked away, his imp trotting beside him.

Kari sat on the chair, overwhelmed with grief. *Jer is alive and he is coming here to die.*

Let him die, another voice inside her head whispered. *Look what he's done to you.*

He hasn't done it. It's Holly, it's all her fault. Jer would still love me but for her.

Holly should die in his place. After all, you would die for him. If she loves him, she'll sacrifice herself. Or, you could kill her and then Jer wouldn't have to risk himself, and you could have him back.

You deserve more.

With that, she crumbled and began to sob. "No, I

don't!" she cried aloud. "I don't, I don't deserve anything. I've betrayed them all."

Mother Coven: Santa Cruz

Anne-Louise had spent hours on the Internet doing genealogy research. Every time she had thought she was about to break through, though, she had come upon another dead end. Sometimes you just had to do things the old-fashioned way.

She locked her room and set wards up at the door and window. She burned some incense and lay down on her bed. She had taken a herbal mixture, potent, the equivalent of what a shaman would take when preparing to embark on a vision-quest.

That was what Anne-Louise was on. She had a special quest in mind, though, and she would need the Goddess's help. Whisper jumped up and lay beside her, purring.

Anne-Louise breathed deeply and closed her eyes. *Show me all of the Cahors family.*

Part Three
Water

I drown in thee which gave me birth
From within my mother's girth
The tides alone we all must bear
Witness of the Goddess fair

Within the tides, within their flow
We learn to breathe and then to slow
To savor that which we now claim
For tomorrow is never the same

TEN

RHIANNON

Round and round the sun wheel goes
As we vanquish anew all our foes
We revel and dance while they mourn
Cursing the day that they were born

In visions now we seek the truth
Secrets that were lost in youth
For there is evil we cannot hide
Lurking now deep inside

Holly: New Mexico

In a small corner of her mind she sat upon a little stool and watched all the commotion. *There are demons big and small and creatures I don't know at all. They're making such a mess, jumping all around and breaking things, so many things. If I sit very still, though, they won't notice me. They won't look. They won't see. But I've been sitting so very still for so very long, and it is hard to sit up so straight.*

She wiggled a toe, just a toe, and the pinkie one at

that. *This little piggy cries wee*—and a big, hairy demon with bloody stumps for hands slapped her with one of his bloody stumps. And there was blood on her dress. *Is it my blood or his?* It didn't matter, nothing did, except for sitting very, very quiet and not moving, not even a toe.

And now the dark-haired man was moving outside of her mind. He was there, in another room and he was talking. She really should pay attention; he liked that. When she paid attention she could hear him and for a moment no one else, not even the beautiful woman demon with the long hair who brushed it a thousand times every day but had the face of a snake when she was angry.

What is he saying? She grew even more still, listened even harder, stopped her heart so that it wouldn't roar and drown out the sound of his voice. Pesky demons kept restarting the heart, though. *How am I supposed to hear if they keep doing that?*

" . . . Jer . . . kill . . . London . . . good Holly."

Does Holly get a biscuit? He wants something, now. I'm supposed to do something. Maybe talk. I'll try.

She opened her mouth, and they all turned to look at her. An old imp with wrinkled gray skin who smelled like formaldehyde limped over to her. He held out a bullhorn for her to shout into. She leaned, spoke. "Kill." She could hear herself, it echoed around in her head.

And the dark-haired man smiled.

I got the right answer. A plus, gold star.

Then the imp took away the bullhorn, and they all went back to talking among themselves. *And I'll sit really quietly and they won't know I'm here.*

Michael straightened. He wasn't entirely sure that Holly had understood what he had asked of her. She had at least repeated "kill," so that was a good sign.

He had spent the past hour in contact with his demonic spies and using his scrying stones. Sir William had indeed ordered him killed, and New Mexico was soon going to become a lot hotter than it already was.

He had thought briefly of appearing before the Supreme Coven with Holly's head on a silver tray, but had quickly rejected the idea. It may or may not have served to appease the leader of the Supreme Coven, but appeasement was no longer Michael's goal.

It's time the Deveraux took back what is rightfully ours, he thought. He had learned that Eli was on the island of Avalon, trying to rescue Nicole Anderson. *He always did have a soft spot for that witch.* It was something Michael could use to his advantage.

He went about packing his bags. Jer and his war-lock friend would arrive in the morning, but he would be long gone. Instead, they would find Holly. If his luck held, the three of them would kill one another. If it didn't, well, at least one of them would die, and that was good news for him.

If Holly was the one left standing, Sir William's Golems would make short work of her. When he had realized that the Golems had been sent to find and kill her, he had worked to cover her psychic signature. Like bloodhounds, Golems could be thrown off the scent if you knew how.

It had not been easy, though. Her aura was normally so powerful that it would have been impossible to conceal her had it not been for the possession. Yes, Holly definitely wasn't herself.

What to do with the Judas, Kari, was another question. Normally his first instinct would have been to kill her, but he had a feeling she had not outlived her usefulness. He made a decision quickly: She would be coming along.

Finished, he shut off the light in his bedroom with a twinge of sadness. It was a shame, really. It was a beautiful place. He was also more than a little sorry that he'd miss the fireworks. He had pressing business, though, overseas, and now was the time to go.

He found Kari huddled in a chair in the living room. For a moment he thought the girl had gone catatonic. He waved his hand in front of her face and snapped his fingers, but she didn't flinch. He picked up a suitcase and dropped it with a thud and she turned her eyes. *Good.*

She looked at him. "I killed all of them."

"Yes, sweetie, I'm afraid you did. We have to go now, so be a good girl and help me out."

She stood listlessly. *Ah, the quandary of those who like to think themselves moral! How it hurts them when they discover the truth about themselves.*

"Where are we going?"

"To the airport."

As he closed the door he called out, "Holly, remember what we talked about."

Like a wraith, she appeared from one of the shadows. "Kill," she whispered.

He smiled. He was going to miss her on some level. It was too bad he had never truly gotten to enjoy the fruits of their bond. "Good-bye, Holly."

"Good-bye."

And after the dark-haired man shut the door, she added, "Michael." And then she was alone again in the darkness.

Jer and Eve: New Mexico

"So, what is the game plan?" Jer asked as he finished washing up.

"You know your father best, you tell me," she answered.

"Yeah, I know him." He winced as he touched the scars on his face. "He has a witch in thrall, a special witch. I don't want her hurt," he said, quickly changing the subject.

"Holly Cathers," Eve said. "She's more than 'special,' I would say."

"Yeah well, I want her alive," he said.

Eve smirked. "There's a reward on her head, too."

"If you want my help, you'll leave her alone," he warned.

"I don't need your help. I could just as easily kill you."

"That isn't true or you would have done so at the gas station."

He could see the wheels in her head turning as she looked at him. At last she nodded. "Help me get your father, I'll leave you your precious witch."

"Agreed."

"Good. Now, do you have a plan?"

Three hours later all their plans were worthless. As they pulled up to the cabin Jer could tell that his father was gone. Still, they got out and circled around the building. Everything was dark, silent.

"I don't feel anyone," Eve said.

He was about to agree with her, when a fireball clipped his shoulder. With a shout, he dropped to the ground as a hailstorm of them passed through the air where they had been standing. He rolled onto the shoulder that had been hit, extinguishing the fire.

Eve had jumped behind the minivan and erected a barrier. Jer rose to his feet and, ducking, ran to get behind it.

"Who is it?" Eve shouted.

"I don't know," Jer admitted. The fireballs had come from inside the cabin, through an open window next to the door. They suddenly ceased. A minute later the door creaked open, and a slight figure stepped outside into the light.

"Holly!" he shouted.

Holly cocked her head to the side as though she was listening to him.

"Holly, it's me, Jer!" he called.

"What's wrong with her?" Eve hissed.

"She's in thrall to my father . . . and possessed," Jer admitted.

"You couldn't have mentioned this earlier?"

Someone was shouting at her, calling her name. Who was it? She strained to see, but the others were in the way, their big heads blocking her view. *I want to see the picture too,* she thought. *If only I were a little taller, I could see around them.* She wanted to try to sit up just a little higher, but then they would notice and they would yell at her, and hurt her.

The voice was shouting again. ". . . Jer."

Jer, Jer, where do I know that name? It seemed familiar. Why couldn't the devils sit lower, so she could see? *Maybe if I could pull myself up just a little taller, an inch or so, they wouldn't notice, would they?*

But they would, she knew it. They noticed everything, and they had told her not to move. They had said if she moved, they would hurt her and the Golems would come, whoever they were. The Golems were beasties who would kill her.

The voice kept talking to her, and it was familiar. *I should know it. Who's there?*

They said to hold still because of the beasties. Beasties without, beasties within.

"Holly!" the voice shouted.

And she stood up off her little stool and yelled, "What?"

Holly shouted something back, and almost instantly Golems appeared from thin air. Jer shouted a warning, but she didn't move until the first one grabbed her. Jer ran out from behind the shield, with Eve on his heels.

"How do we stop them?" she shouted.

"Either destroy the paper in their mouths or rub out the first letter on their foreheads!"

"Which is easier?"

"Your guess is as good as mine," Jer answered as he tried to grab the nearest Golem's head. The thing brushed him off as though he were no more than a fly. He landed in the dirt and tried kicking at the creature, but to no avail.

He turned just in time to see Eve jump on the back of one and reach around and rub out the first *e* on the thing's forehead. It fell headlong to the ground, and she leaped off at the last moment.

Meanwhile, fireballs had begun to fly off Holly's fingertips, and Jer found himself suddenly busy dodging those. One struck the Golem next to him full in the face and it, too, fell, the paper in its mouth turning instantly to ash.

That left two, and looking at them, Jer wasn't sure they would be so easy to kill. The one had Holly by the throat. Her eyes were bugging out of her head, and the fireballs were still shooting off uncontrollably from her fingertips. Suddenly her face changed, took on a demonic appearance. *"Gande ipse rodal!"* she roared, in a language he had never heard. He watched in amazement as an invisible hand slowly rubbed out the *e* on the creature's forehead. The Golem and Holly tumbled together to the ground, both still.

"Holly!" he cried, rushing forward. He knelt beside her and felt for a pulse. There was none. He laid his hands on her chest and willed electricity to flow from them into her. Her body convulsed as the charge hit. He checked for a pulse and could feel one, though it was faint. He turned just in time to see Eve rip the paper from the final Golem's mouth. It picked her up and began to crush her, but she tore the paper in half and he dropped her before falling.

She stood panting and tore the paper into a dozen tiny pieces, which she then tossed to the wind. She put her hands on her hips.

"So, what's with her?"

"Unconscious."

"Sounds like a good thing."

"It probably is," he said grimly.

She walked over and crouched down to look at Holly. She didn't look impressed. "So, she's what everyone's making a fuss about?"

Jer nodded.

"I don't see it," she said, and stood back up.

"Well, I'm wasting my time here. I've got to find

your father. Got any idea where he's headed?"

Jer looked down at Holly. His father had left her to kill him and be killed herself. Wherever he was going, he must have considered her a liability. Given all of her power, that was hard to believe. *Where would he be going that he wouldn't have to worry about watching her?* he thought.

It came to him in a rush. He was right, he knew it, he could feel it. "He's headed to London."

Tri-Coven: San Francisco International Airport

Amanda sat next to Tommy on the Mother Coven's jet, holding his hand and wishing she were somewhere else. It was relatively crowded: Sasha, Alex, Amanda, Armand, Pablo, Philippe, Barbara, Tommy, and Richard were aboard. Any minute they would be taxiing for takeoff and it was back to Europe for the lot of them. The copilot, a woman and a witch, came back to address them.

"We've received a message from the tower. It seems someone in Albuquerque is requesting that we land there and pick up three more passengers. The message was sent by someone named Jer."

Amanda's mind raced. *Three passengers! Jer must have found Holly and Kari!* Before she could say anything, Alex spoke: "We don't have time to take a detour."

There was a sudden chilled silence in the air as the new leader of the coven found himself the focus of all eyes. Tommy was the one to speak. "As I see it, if he has Holly with him, we can't afford not to stop. She's our greatest asset and, in the hands of the enemy, our greatest liability. We need her and we can't afford to not know where she is."

Alex narrowed his eyes, and Amanda knew he was judging how best to respond to this challenge to his authority. He smiled after only a moment, and the tension passed. "Well-spoken, Tommy. To Albuquerque it is."

The copilot nodded and returned to the cockpit. Several more minutes passed, and then the plane maneuvered itself into position. As soon as the wheels left the ground, Amanda breathed a sigh of relief. *What can Michael Deveraux do to us in the air?*

"Quite a lot, probably, if all I've heard is true," Alex said.

Amanda stiffened. She had let her guard down for a moment, and he had gotten in. She didn't mind Pablo reading her thoughts, but Alex was different. Maybe it was because he was older, or the leader of the coven or a relative. *Maybe it's because I don't entirely trust him.* Whatever it was, she needed to watch herself more closely.

Still, she wasn't going to allow him, or his allusions to Michael's power, to ruin her flight. She sank down in the seat, put her head on Tommy's shoulder, and promptly fell asleep.

She woke when the wheels touched down in Albuquerque. A hard knot settled in her stomach. *What if Jer didn't send the message?* she thought, sudden fear gnawing at her. *Well, we'll know soon enough.*

"Soon enough" took twenty minutes. At last the hatch opened, and she heard a collective intake of breath from the group. When she saw Jer, she sagged in relief. In his arms he was carrying a woman. Her face was turned inward into his shoulder, but she recognized her, anyway: Holly!

Philippe rose quickly and helped Jer settle Holly into a seat. She was unconscious, but Amanda could see the steady rise and fall of her chest. A new feeling suddenly washed over her, a chill dancing up her spine. She turned, expecting to see Kari walking onto the plane. Instead, it was a stranger, a woman with short hair, clad all in black, and there was something about—

"Warlock!" Pablo hissed, lunging toward her.

Jer threw up an arm and caught him. "Pablo, no! She's a friend."

"I wouldn't go that far," the woman said sarcastically.

"Explain yourself, Deveraux," Alex commanded.

Jer glanced over. "Who put him in charge?"

"Don't ask," Tommy muttered.

"Eve's tracking my father, to kill him. She and I had a common purpose. She helped me save Holly. In exchange, we're giving her a lift to London."

Amanda stared thunderstruck. At last she found her voice. "Is it such a good idea to let a member of the Supreme Coven know where we're going?"

"Technically, Jeraud's a member of the Supreme Coven," Eve pointed out.

"Not anymore. I have my own coven," he snapped.

"And where would it be?" Alex asked. His voice was light, mocking.

Amanda watched the muscles in Jer's jaw begin to jump. When he spoke, his voice was a dangerous hiss. "Someday, I will kill you."

"Not if I kill you first."

Amanda's father stepped in between them. "Down, gentlemen, let's not do this." Power and authority surrounded him, encompassing him. "I promise you that if one of you starts this, *I* will finish it."

Silence descended, neither man wanting to be the first to back down. *This is ridiculous,* Amanda thought. Into the silence, she asked, "What happened to Holly?"

★ ★ ★

Jer turned to her, the fight leaving his body. "We were fighting Golems. One of them was choking her. Something took her over, and she killed the Golem and was knocked unconscious."

"Witches and warlocks, please take your seats and prepare for takeoff," the pilot announced over the loudspeaker.

Amanda wasn't sure if she was going to laugh or cry.

Holly was asleep on her little stool in the corner of her mind. Everyone was asleep. It was peaceful, for a moment, but soon all would wake and everything would be chaos again. Chaos and fear. She didn't remember much anymore, much other than fear. Fear. How well she knew it, how she had tasted it time and again, lived with it, eaten it, slept it, dreamed it. Just like that night so long ago, in her own room in her own home. . . .

The Cathers Family: San Francisco, 2001

Holly sat, munching popcorn and watching television with her parents. It was Tuesday night, and Tuesday night was movie night. It had been tradition for as long as she could remember. Even the trip to the video store was tradition, complete with the perennially chick flick—shoot 'em up controversy.

Now, as they were watching *The Sixth Sense,* she was starting to think she should have given in to her dad's pleas for a John Wayne movie instead. When the little boy told Bruce Willis that he could see dead people, she thought she was going to cry.

"At least it's not as violent as I thought it was going to be," her mother commented.

"This is worse than violence. This is just messing with your head," her dad protested.

Holly tended to agree with her father. *I can't imagine anything more frightening than seeing a ghost.*

When the movie was over, she ran down the hallway to the bathroom, throwing on light switches along the way. She shivered as she stared in the mirror. *I can't believe I let it get to me like that,* she thought.

She thought she saw a shadow move behind her, and she jumped. She brushed her teeth and got ready for bed while avoiding looking into the mirror again.

After she had laid out her clothes for the next day, she felt a lot calmer. When her mom came by to say good night, she was in bed and her eyelids were drooping.

"I love you, honey."

"I love you, too, Mom."

"You okay?"

Holly smiled. "Yeah, are you?"

"Of course," her mom said, laughing lightly.

Holly's smile widened. It was her mom's nervous laugh. The movie had gotten to her, too. "Sleep tight, Mom, don't let the bedbugs bite."

"You either," her mom said, shaking her head and laughing.

My parents are great. I can't imagine having grown up with different ones, she thought as she slid into sleep.

"Wake up, Holly," a female voice cajoled.

Holly squirmed and flipped onto her back. She could tell through her closed eyelids that the room was light. "Don't want to," she said sleepily.

"Wake up," the voice grew more insistent.

"No."

"You must wake up, Holly."

"Mom, let me sleep."

"I am not your mother," the voice snapped.

Holly's eyes flew open, and she sat bolt upright.

It was still nighttime. The light in the room was coming from a woman. She stood in the center of Holly's room, in an old-fashioned dress. Her dark hair hung in waves down her back. Her eyes burned like coals, and she was glowing.

"I'm dreaming," Holly said out loud. "This is just a dream."

"It's no dream," the woman assured her. "I am

Isabeau. I am your ancestress, and it is time for you to discover who you are."

"I know who I am. I'm Holly Cathers."

"No, you are Holly Cahors of the House Cahors, and you are a witch."

Holly began to shake uncontrollably. "I must be dreaming."

"And I tell you that you are not."

"Are you dead?"

"Yes."

She thought she would faint. The room began to swim before her eyes. "This isn't real, this isn't happening."

"It is real," the woman said, drifting closer. She sat down on the edge of the bed next to Holly. "You are of my House, my blood. You are a witch and you need to discover what that means now rather than later. The Deveraux are your enemy, you must remember this. They will kill everyone you love if you let them."

She reached her hand toward Holly, and Holly tried to scramble out of her reach. Her body seemed frozen, though, and she wanted to scream as dead, cold fingers touched her cheek. "*Ma petite,* so much to learn and so little time. I will help you."

Isabeau pressed her hand to Holly's forehead. "I will be with you, sharing my strength, my power with you. Now," her voice deepened into a commanding tone, "light the candle on the dresser with your mind."

Holly felt compelled to obey, as though she had no will of her own. She turned and stared at the candle in question and suddenly, with a whoosh, it was on fire.

Holly began to scream. Within moments she heard footsteps pounding down the hall, and her parents burst into the room. Her mother screamed, and Isabeau turned to look at Holly's parents. For a moment they all stayed, frozen as though in a tableau, and then Isabeau was gone and the only light in the room was from the candle.

"Holly! What happened?" her mother cried as she rushed forward. Holly threw herself into her mother's arms, and they both collapsed onto the bed, crying.

"Mom," she gasped between sobs, "I'm a witch and I see dead people!"

"It was the movie, that's all, it gave you night-mares, it was nothing," her mom said, her hysterical tone belying her words.

"But, Mom, you saw her, she was here."

Her mom was silent, and Holly pulled away to look at her. There was fear in her eyes. "What am I going to do, Mommy?"

Just then her father stepped in close. He placed his hand on her forehead, much as the woman had done.

When he spoke, his voice was deep, deeper than she had ever heard it. "Sleep and forget."

She slipped into blessed oblivion.

When she woke in the morning, Holly had the nagging feeling that something was wrong. She had slept well, but she was tired, and something just felt off.

Downstairs in the kitchen she found her parents at the breakfast table. Both were silent when she walked in, and both looked as though they had been crying.

"What's wrong?" Holly asked, feeling herself begin to panic.

"Nothing, honey," her father said with a forced smile that made it nowhere near his eyes. "How'd you sleep?"

"Like a log."

"No nightmares?" her mom asked.

Holly turned, puzzled and worried. "I don't think so, why?"

"Nothing. I just thought I heard you tossing a lot last night."

"No, no nightmares, no dreams. I just slept really solid. Are you two okay?"

"Fine," her father said quickly, too quickly. "We're fine, honey. We just didn't sleep well."

"I told you not to let the bedbugs bite," she tried to tease her mother.

The joke fell flat, but her mom gave her a sickly smile. Not sure what was going on but convinced they weren't going to talk about it, Holly ate quickly.

Finished, she headed for the stairs to get her backpack. She was halfway up the stairs when she heard her mother say, "She doesn't remember anything about last night, what she saw, what she did."

"I told you she wouldn't," her father said.

She froze, listening. *What happened last night?* she wondered, her pulse beginning to race. They had stopped talking, though, and she slowly finished climbing the stairs. In her room she picked her watch up off her dresser.

She turned to go but froze in midmotion. On her dresser was a candle made in the shape of a horse that her best friend, Tina, had given her for her birthday. It was beautiful, and Holly had never used it, happy to have it more as a figurine.

The top of the horse's head had melted, the wax dripping down and covering its eyes. *Someone burned the candle,* she thought, stunned, *and the horse is blind— just like me.*

Tri-Coven: Over the Atlantic

On her stool in the corner, Holly dreamed, and she remembered. Isabeau had come to her long before, and her father had hidden it from her. Her mother had been frightened, so had he. That was why they had fought. That was what had happened.

Still sitting perfectly upright on her stool, Holly slowly opened one eye and looked around. The demons were all sleeping, crashed out on the floor, lying in heaps, some atop one another. Past them, now that they were lying down, she could see more, she could see outside, and she saw Amanda.

The hairs along the back of Amanda's neck lifted on end, and she had the sudden and unnerving sensation of being watched. She turned her head sharply and saw Holly, her eyes open, staring at her. "Tommy," she whispered, "look!"

Tommy did, and came to the same conclusion she had: "It's Holly."

Amanda quickly unbuckled her seat belt and moved over in front of Holly. "Holly, it's Amanda. Do you recognize me?"

Holly blinked her eyes once, strongly and clearly.

In a moment, Pablo was beside Amanda. "I can feel her," he said.

"Holly, can you help us get rid of the demons?" Amanda asked.

Holly just stared straight ahead, and Amanda wasn't sure she had understood her.

"She can't," Pablo said. "She's afraid."

"Holly, honey, don't be afraid. We're going to help you, we're going to get them out of there. Do you understand?"

She blinked. Then, slowly, her eyelids closed.

"No, Holly, come back, come back to us," Amanda begged.

Pablo laid a hand on her arm. "She's retreated. I can't feel her anymore."

"But at least we know that she's in there," Tommy said.

"We need to find a way to bring her back," Jer said.

"We tried exorcism. It didn't work," Sasha told him. "That's how Tante Cecile was killed."

"I believe I can do it," Armand said.

Amanda turned to him. "Armand, I'm not sure we can risk losing another person."

Philippe interjected. "Let him help. Armand studied to be a priest before he began to explore the ways of the Goddess. He knows things and has seen things that none of us have. I believe he can do it."

"I say we take the risk," Jer chimed in.

Amanda turned on him. "You weren't there last

time. You don't know what it's like. We have to find a way to help her, but I'm not sure an exorcism is it!"

"Amanda, if he's willing to try, I say we let him."

She looked from face to face. They all looked so earnest, so hopeful. At last she turned to Alex. He hadn't said a word. "What do you think?"

He raised an eyebrow. "If multiple demons are in there, they might not all be from the same faith paradigm. Someone who has experience with multiple religions might succeed where others have failed. I say you let the priest try."

It made sense. She wasn't sure if that's because it was what she wanted to hear or because it really did. She looked at Holly. *We need her back. We're returning to the mouth of hell, and we need her with us.* She turned to Armand. "What will you need?"

ELEVEN

MARY

☾

Time now to make our move
Deveraux have much to prove
We show them now all our power
We rule them all in this hour

God and Goddess hear our cry
We lift our hands unto the sky
We cast out those who cause us fear
Enemies both far and near

Tri-Coven: London

Amanda's nerves were frayed. Getting from the airport to the safe house had been harrowing. They were treading on Supreme Coven ground. Moreover, at least one member, the woman Eve, knew that they were here. *What's to keep her from alerting the others to our presence? I know Jer trusts her, but that doesn't mean I do.*

As soon as they had landed Eve had taken off,

thanking them flippantly for the ride. She was hunting Michael Deveraux, and in that, and only in that, they were on the same side.

She looked around the house where they were now. It was located just outside of London and was quite large. Armand had roamed through it like a lion, until he had found the room where he wanted to perform the exorcism. Everyone had spent the last hour stripping the room bare so there would be nothing Holly or her demons could use as weapons.

The witch who owned the house had left before they'd arrived, but had left them with all the supplies they could use and carte blanche to use the property as they needed to. *I don't blame her for taking off. I would, too, if I could.*

Her father had left half an hour before, to get . . . something . . . he hadn't said what. He had had a hard look in his eye when he'd left, though, and it had made her nervous.

Tommy came up beside her and kissed her cheek. She smiled and turned into his arms. It felt so good to have him hold her. She just wanted to be held, forever.

"I love you."

"I love you too," she whispered.

"We'd better see if Armand needs anything else."

She looked up at him. He looked like a man.

Where was the boy she had once known? How had he managed to change before her eyes without her noticing? He smiled, and she saw the boy again, but it was only part of him now. There was something good and strong about him. He was more than she had ever known, more than she had ever dreamed. He was everything she needed and wanted. *I will do anything to keep hold of him.*

Arm in arm, they walked into the room. It was empty. Even the paintings were gone. It was more than just furniture and paintings, though. Pablo and Sasha had worked hard and scrubbed the room clean of any psychic imprints as well. She had never felt a place so hollow. It chilled her. *Is this what death is like? No, it can't be. I refuse to believe that it's emptiness.*

They all stood together in the room, gathered around, staring quietly at Holly. She was slumped in the middle of the floor. She hadn't come to again on the flight, or in the car ride here. Amanda had begun to fear she wouldn't wake up again.

"When you leave, close the door and stand ready with the swords we prepared. If anything comes through that door, kill it," Armand instructed.

Pablo spoke. "The demons are beginning to stir."

"Everyone leave," Armand said quietly.

"I want to stay," Amanda protested.

"No, you must go, quickly."

"Come on, Amanda, it will be okay," Tommy said, half-dragging her from the room.

Armand turned back to Holly and breathed in deeply. In a strange way, he had been preparing his whole life for this. His grandfather had been a priest and an exorcist. Armand himself had studied to be a priest. Then, on the eve of taking his vows, he had turned aside to study the ways of the Goddess. Still, in his heart, he had never betrayed his first God. Instead, he worshiped them both, and he had found others who did the same.

Holly's eyes snapped open, though it wasn't Holly who stared at him from their depths. Gazing at Holly as she sat shivering, madness flickering in her eyes as untold demons battled one another within her, Armand thanked both deities for all the years of training. It was all that was going to save him and her.

He lit the purple candles and began.

The words flowed off his tongue, though it had been years since he had studied their meaning and memorized them. *"Exorcizo te, omnis spiritus immunde, in nomine Dei."* He made the sign of the cross over her. *"Patris omnipotentis, et in noimine Jesu."* Another cross. *"Christi Filii ejus, Domini et Judicis nostri, et in virtute Spiritus."* He inscribed a third cross in the air over her.

"I exorcise thee, every unclean spirit, in the name of God the Father Almighty, and in the name of Jesus Christ, His Son, our Lord and Judge, and in the power of the Holy Spirit."

"Filthy creature, you are of witchblood and have no right to invoke that name," a demon hissed, speaking through Holly and twisting her face into a hideous reflection of its own features.

"God loves all His children, and He aids those who have faith in Him and call upon His name."

"He won't listen to you," another spirit taunted. "He will not share you with the Goddess."

"I don't believe that's true," Armand forced himself to answer calmly. "But even if it is, he is also a merciful God, and I am sure He will forgive me. Depart from her, all you demons within, in the name of the Goddess who rules her heart, you have no place within her."

"She likes us," a third demon spoke in a high, shrill voice. "She wants us to stay."

"I command you to leave. Sancti, ut descedas ab hoc plasmate Dei, Holly Cathers, *per eumdem Christum Dominum nostrum, qui venturus est judicare vivos et mortuos, et saeculum per ignem."* Depart from this creature of God named Holly Cathers through the same Christ our Lord, who shall come to judge the living and the dead, and the world by fire.

Holly began to thrash back and forth as the demons

fought her, one another, Armand, and the Deities he invoked. There was a sudden scream, and one flew out her mouth, a tiny, red-spotted thing with a tale like a dragon and wings like a sparrow.

Armand drew his sword from his belt. He sliced through the creature's body. "I send you back to the hell from which you came."

The creature exploded in a small, sulfurous cloud of red dust. It sprinkled to the ground.

Only one. This is going to take a long time.

He picked up a large wooden bowl filled with frankincense, crushed garlic, peppermint, cloves, and sage. He touched the flame of the purple candle to the mix and then set it on fire. He blew on it gently until the flame went out, but the mixture continued to smolder. The scent filled the air, and the demons inside Holly began to squeal.

Armand walked to Holly. He spit carefully into his hands and then touched her right ear then the left. *"Ephpheta, quod est, Adaperire."* Be opened. Next he touched her right nostril, then the left. *"In odorem suavitatis. Tu autem effugare, diabole; appropinquabit enim judicium Dei."* For a savor of sweetness: And to you, O devil, begone! For the judgment of God is at hand.

"Holly," he commanded her. "Holly, listen to me. Help me cast out these demons."

There was a flicker in her eyes, a moment of what he could only call understanding, before the demons pushed her back down with a roar.

"You cannot have her, priest. We shall not leave this body. We are grown . . . comfortable . . . here," one of the voices hissed.

"How many are you?" Armand demanded.

"Hundreds."

"Then hundreds of you shall die."

Holly sat on her little stool and watched in surprise as a little red demon left. It went, crying the entire way. She almost felt sorry for it, but she remembered it had spit on her earlier, so she didn't feel so sorry anymore. Rather, she was glad it was gone. There was one less voice ringing in her ears, one less body blocking her view.

Then she heard a man, commanding her, pleading with her to help him get rid of the demons. The demons were busy, looking out, talking to the man. They weren't looking at Holly. She moved her little toe, and this time no one noticed, no one cared.

She sat very still again. In a moment, she would try moving her entire foot.

Armand took the holy water and sprinkled salt in it. Demons were supposed to fear salt water—it was supposed to hurt them. That was what he had learned. That was why, when Jesus had cast demons out of a man and let them enter a herd of pigs and the pigs had stampeded into salt water, the demons had died. At least, that's what was said. He confessed in his heart that he didn't know. *But then again, that's what this is all about: It's all about faith.*

He picked up the bowl of water and crossed over to Holly. He looked down at her. Her hands and legs were bound with rope—something you're never supposed to do to an exorcism recipient, but, then, nothing about this was normal. There was magic binding her as well, courtesy of Alex. It made sense. Holly knew what the rest of them knew, practiced the same magic, knew the same spells. Alex, at least, was a bit different, as were his ways.

He poured the water over her head in the shape of an X. He did it three times. Demons screamed, and he could smell sulfur and burning flesh. A dozen demons poured out of her, and he let them go. They were dying—he could tell it by the way they rippled, as though they were fading in and out of being. If they even made it to the door, Philippe would handle them.

He put down the bowl and picked up another filled with herbs. He pressed his thumb into the dried herbs and then anointed Holly with them, touching first her forehead, then her chin, then her right eyelid, then her left.

"Pax tibi." Peace be unto you.

"Blessed be," Holly wanted to say, but she didn't. She was afraid. The stench of death filled her nostrils. More demons had gone, but the ones who remained were growing more agitated, more dangerous. She twitched her left foot. None of them noticed, though. She exhaled slowly, and no one turned to look at her.

She licked her lips; maybe she should try speaking, maybe it would help. Her heart began to pound louder, so very loud and so very fast. She parted her lips, and nobody stopped her. She flicked her tongue across her teeth. The demons were all jumping up and down, shouting and screaming at the man outside.

They hated him, and she could feel their rage; it bubbled around her, making her heart pound faster. It frightened her and exhilarated her at the same time. It had been so long since she had felt something other than fear. *I'm going to do it!*

"Blessed—" a dozen demons jumped on top of her. One clamped a hoary hand over her mouth while the rest began to hit her and spit on her. They whispered vile things in her ears, told her that she was nothing, no one. *They must be right. After all, they would know.*

***

A wizened, dying demon slid underneath the door, and Philippe stabbed it, sending it into oblivion. "Something he's doing is working," he noted. "That demon was all but dead already."

Amanda paced in front of the door, playing with her sword as though it were a baton. He felt sorry for her as he watched her. *She has lost much, and stands to lose so much more.*

"Have I mentioned how much I hate waiting?" she asked.

"You have mentioned that," Alex commented. "We need to start gearing up. As soon as Armand is done, we need to move out. Half of us will go to Avalon to rescue Nicole. The other half will begin the assault on the Supreme Coven."

"Isn't it dangerous to split up like that?" Tommy asked.

"It's dangerous not to, at this point. We need to move, and do so quickly. We can't brook anymore delays. We must strike before we are expected." Alex glanced at Jer. "For all we know, we're already expected."

Philippe noticed that Jer bristled, but said nothing. He turned his attention back to the door. *Goddess help him,* he prayed for Armand as he kept watch for more demons.

★★★

Armand heard Holly speak, or at least try to. "That's it, Holly, work with me, fight them off, you can do it. You are stronger than they are. Cast them out. You have the power."

"She has no power over me," a voice hissed. A wind suddenly whipped through the room, and Holly seemed to be at the center of it. "Neither do you."

"Who are you? What is your name?" Armand demanded.

"Bunyip."

Bunyip? Where have I heard that? The wind continued, and that seemed familiar. *Bunyip. Whirlwind.*

"You're an evil spirit that lurks in the whirlwind. Stories are told about you amongst the aboriginal people."

"You know of me, good. Then you know to be afraid."

Armand gestured to indicate the wind. "So far, I am not impressed. So, unless you have plans to turn Holly into a bird, I think you should leave." He stood, awaiting the creature's response and racking his brain as to how to expel it.

In aboriginal legend, the rainbow serpent shaped the land and created all the spirits. It's a start, at any rate.

"I command that you part, Bunyip, in the name of

the spirit that breathed life into the people of your land. In the name of the rainbow serpent, I bid you depart!"

There was a howling as the wind picked up in the room. Armand saw the demon flow out of Holly's mouth in a rush. Then the whirlwind began. Round and round, the wind swirled, harder and faster. It tore at Armand's clothes and stung his eyes.

He opened his mouth to shout out an incantation, but the wind ripped the words from his lips and they were lost even to his own ears. *Goddess help me,* he thought as the wind continued to pick up speed, twisting in upon itself, *else it will rip both Holly and me apart.*

In the corner of the room, a tornado began to form. Fear raced through Armand as he realized the creature could destroy them all.

The door suddenly opened, and Alex stood in it, his arms lifted. He was screaming something, but Armand could not tell what it was. The wind died instantly, leaving an eerie stillness in its wake. The door slammed back closed, and Armand was once more alone with Holly and all her demons.

I'll have to thank Alex later, he thought, turning back to the job at hand.

There was only chaos in her mind. At least the wind was gone, but it had left a lot of bodies strewn around, demons dazed, demons unconscious. None of them were looking at her. She took a deep breath and stood up.

Nothing happened. No one noticed her. There was a brown, scaly demon lying on the ground next to her stool. He was small, only about half her size, and very scrawny. His mouth was open, and he was drooling thick yellow liquid all over the floor of her mind. *Gross.* She nudged him with her toe, but he didn't move. *He's not so big. I could take him,* she thought, glancing around furtively at the others.

She made small movements with her left hand, inscribing a pentagram in the air over the creature. "Goddess, cast this creature out, it does not belong here about," she whispered.

The demon's eyes flew open, and it made a gasping noise before it went flying out, out through her mouth. The rest who were awake turned to her. *Uh-oh.*

Armand stared in surprise as a tiny brown demon flew out of Holly. He grasped his sword and sliced it in half. Brown goo dripped off the edges of the sword and tumbled to the floor before slowly dissolving in midair.

"Good, Holly, keep it up."

★★★

Holly, however, wasn't listening. She was back on her stool cringing as they all stood around screaming and striking her with fists and biting her with teeth. She was crying and bleeding, and there was no one there to help.

Armand stared hopefully at Holly, but there was no sign that she understood, and no more demons forthcoming. Holly suddenly started babbling; it sounded like Aramaic. Armand lifted his hands and placed them in the air over Holly's head. *"Allaahumma jannibnash-shaytaana wa jannibish-shaytaana maa razaqta-naa."* O Allah, keep Satan away from us and keep Satan away from what You have bestowed upon us.

A dozen demons came screaming out of her, and Armand whirled this way and that, skewering one, dismembering another. The last one he had to chase around the room for a minute. He stood panting after he had slain it, trying to regain his breath.

"Help me!" he heard Holly gasp behind him.

He jerked around and saw her sitting, staring wide-eyed at him. "Help me!" she cried again.

He rushed back to her. Just as he reached her side, her eyes rolled back in her head and her body started convulsing. She fell backward, and Armand caught her and held her. "Fight them, Holly, fight them," he urged her. "You can do it, I believe in you. Come back to us. Cast them out. Goddess, I beseech you, remove the unclean things from Holly, restore her mind and soul. Let all the creatures who lurk within be banished and shine your light upon her."

More demons went flying, and Armand let them go, praying the others would catch them.

"I command thee, unclean spirits, begone from this girl. You have no business here, and I command you, in the name of Jesus Christ, whose blood was spilled on the Cross, to leave now!"

Anguished screams ripped through the air as more demons poured out. He could feel a couple of them clawing at him, trying to latch on to him, but he brushed them away with hand and mind.

"In the name of the Lady and the Lord, depart from here every evil thing. I claim Holly as a holy vessel for the Goddess. Consecrate her and make her clean."

From his pocket he drew a white linen cloth and placed it on her head. *"Accipe vestem candidam, quam perferas immaculatam." Receive this white garment, which mayest thou bear without stain.*

There was something like an explosion. There was a blinding burst of light and the rush of air and *things* passing by him. Holly's eyes flew open, and she looked up at him.

***

Holly was standing in the center of her mind. *Where are they all going?* she wondered in awe as demons flew past her. One reached out and grabbed at her, its claws raking down the length of her arm. She shook it loose, and it, too, went flying.

At last she was alone and everything was silent. Quietly, cautiously, she tiptoed forward until she pressed her face to her eyes and she could see out. She took a deep breath, and air rushed into her lungs. She looked up, and there was Armand.

He was holding a white candle. The flame flickered bright and clear. He handed her the candle, and after a moment she was able to lift her hand and take it from him.

"*Accipe lampadem ardentem. Amen. Blessed be.*"

"Blessed be," she whispered. *I'm back.*

She began to cry.

Armand held her as she sobbed, thanking the Goddess and Christ that he had been able to bring her back. After a few minutes there was a tenuous knock on the door. "Come in," he called hoarsely.

The door opened slowly, and he glanced up. Philippe walked forward slowly and knelt down beside them. "How is she?" he asked.

"Philippe," she whispered.

He smiled and touched her cheek. "It is good to see you again."

"The demons?" Armand asked.

"We killed them all," Philippe answered.

Relief flooded Armand, and he felt himself sag slightly. His body began to shake as the exhaustion overwhelmed him.

"Holly?" Amanda called from the door, her voice filled with uncertainty.

"Amanda," Holly choked out.

Then the two cousins were embracing, Holly still lying half in Armand's arms.

A sound from the doorway caused Armand to turn and look. Alex stood there, an inscrutable look on his face. "She's back?"

Armand nodded.

"All right," Alex said in a loud voice. "Everyone get ready to move."

Richard: North of London

Richard was driving on M-11 North. He was about a half hour outside London. He slowed slightly, eyes searching. Finally he saw a tree-lined country lane, nothing imposing. He turned down it. He drove for a while until at last the lane dead-ended at an abandoned

World War II U.S. Army airfield. He parked and got out, cautiously.

Every sense was hyperalert as he looked around slowly. He walked quietly, barely touching ground as he glided forward toward the buildings. He made his way inside and quickly found what had once been the officers' bar. The room looked as though it had been untouched since 1945. Dust lay thick along the tables. Broken glass lay everywhere, and several windows were missing.

Cobwebs hung from the ceiling, and a mouse scuttled across the top of the bar as he passed by. He headed for the back of the room, where there was a door. It would have been easy to overlook, tucked back in the shadows, but he moved to it with surety. As his hand touched the knob, he knew he was in the right place. The doorknob was free of dust.

He opened the door and started down a long flight of stairs. He walked carefully, waiting to be challenged. He reached the bottom and came face-to-face with the guards he had been expecting.

Wordlessly, he reached into his pocket and pulled out his identification. The guards took it and examined it. After a minute they nodded him over to a machine on the wall. He placed his eyes against it and held them open as his retinas were scanned.

Mary

Almost immediately the guards opened another door, and one escorted him through the halls of the underground structure, a training ground for a British commando unit and the SAS. Within moments he was seated in a British army colonel's office.

The other man leaned forward across his desk, peering at him intently. "Richard Anderson?"

Richard nodded.

"Your reputation precedes you, sir."

"I was just a guy trying to serve his country."

The colonel raised his eyebrows but didn't respond to that. Instead, he asked, "What can I help you with?"

Richard took a piece of paper out of his pocket and passed it across the desk to the colonel. "I need a few things."

The colonel read the list twice before nodding. "I think we can take care of this." He pushed a buzzer on his desk, and a soldier came in. The colonel handed him the list. "Please assemble these items for the gentleman."

The two rose to their feet and shook hands. "Would you mind if I ask exactly what you need them for?"

Richard shook his head. "It's better you don't know. Besides, I don't think you'd believe me if I told you."

"Fair enough," the other grunted. "Good luck to you."

"Thank you, Colonel."

Ten minutes later, Richard was back in the car and on his way to the safe house.

Tri-Coven: London

Amanda hugged Tommy and prayed she would never have to let go. She didn't like the idea he would be heading to Avalon while she would be staying in London with the group that was going to launch the attack on the Supreme Coven.

She needed to stay with Holly to help keep an eye on her, to help keep her grounded, especially since she had only just met Alex. If Tommy stayed with her, though, that would leave her father, Sasha, and Philippe to sneak onto Avalon alone. They really needed another person. Philippe had to go, since Amanda could not. Because he and Nicole were in thrall to each other, he would be the one most likely to be able to find her.

Still, the tears coursed down her cheeks at the thought of being apart from Tommy. *It isn't fair!* she thought. She'd had all the time in the world to get to know him as a friend, but they were just now truly discovering each other in the love that they shared. *In fif-*

teen minutes we'll have to part, though, and what if something happens to one of us?

"I have an idea," he said, his voice husky.

"Yeah?"

"Why don't we do a spell to, you know, keep us together."

"Throughout eternity?" she breathed. "So that if we die, we'll be together?"

"You're such a dork," he said affectionately. "To keep us safe, and together, no matter what."

"Yes, we can do that. We must hurry, though."

Amanda quickly drew a rough circle on the ground while Tommy found and lit some incense. In a minute they were in the circle together, their knees touching.

She grasped his hands in hers, and for a moment all the world seemed to slow and then stop. She breathed in and he inhaled at the same time. She could feel her heartbeat slowing to match his, could feel the pulse in his fingertips mingling with her own.

An athame lay between them beside a single white candle. She let go of Tommy's hands and picked up the athame. Tommy lit the candle. "Future and past, we remain together until the last," he intoned.

She sliced her palm with the athame, wincing at the pain. She then sliced Tommy's. They clasped their bleeding hands together over the candle. Blood dripped down into the flame, causing it to hiss.

"As pure as the flame, my love for you," Amanda whispered.

"I am yours in this life and the next," Tommy replied.

Next Amanda pulled a hair from her head, and Tommy pulled one from his. Together they dropped the hairs onto the flame.

"Goddess, keep us in safety in this life. And grant we live together in the next," Amanda implored.

"Eternity," they whispered together. They leaned forward and kissed over the candle. As their lips touched, Amanda felt a great surge of power ripple through her and then leave.

When she pulled back, Tommy was staring at her wide-eyed. "Did you feel that?"

She nodded. "I don't know what it was."

"Well, let's hope it was good luck, 'cuz we're going to need some about now," Tommy said, looking over Amanda's shoulder.

"It's time," Alex said from behind her, making her jump.

TWELVE

BRIGITTE

☾

Death and destruction we always bring
Evil is what makes our blood sing
Deveraux will finally rise to power
See us in our most wicked hour

The Goddess has made us whole again
Made us stronger women and men
The circle has come full round at last
Cahors make up now for the past

Richard, Sasha, Tommy, and Philippe: Avalon

"Would someone mind telling me again—why are we in a boat?" Tommy asked.

Philippe had to admit it was a reasonable question. Given that the loved ones of Cahors witches died by drowning, what they were doing would qualify them for the Darwin Awards.

"Because this is the only way we may reach Avalon," Sasha said, answering seriously.

"Thanks to our last rescue, they've obviously warded the island against teleportation."

"So, what, the Mother Coven didn't have helicopters?"

Philippe shook his head, images of Tommy hanging from one of the struts filling his mind. "What, and miss out on all this bonding time?"

Tommy made a sour face, and Philippe's heart went out to him. *He is worried about Amanda, and I understand that. Half of me is lost until Nicole is found.* He grimly turned back to the job at hand.

A dozen times they wanted to turn the boat, but didn't. Twice, the boat tried to turn itself, but they straightened its course back out. All the magic had been put in place years ago to keep the island from being accidentally discovered.

The magics used to hide the island weren't the only strange thing he had noticed. He kept catching himself glancing backward, trying to see something in the water behind them. Always, though, nothing was there. Still, he couldn't help but feel as though they were somehow being followed. He closed his eyes and tried to reach out with his mind, to touch something, but he only touched air and sea. Frustrated, he gave up. *It's just in my imagination.*

They didn't see the shore until they were nearly on

it. Her breath catching in her throat, Sasha whispered a spell that Philippe hoped would allow them to land safely and without detection.

The boat ran ashore. After a few seconds and nothing had happened, they all breathed a collective sigh of relief. Philippe hopped out, and together he and Tommy tied the boat up so it wouldn't slip off the rocky shore back into the water.

"Can you feel her?" Sasha asked as she joined them.

Philippe shook his head in frustration. He glanced over at Nicole's father. Richard stood a few feet apart from them, tension evident in every line of his body.

A sniper rifle was slung across his back, and he was carrying ammunition on his person—and a few other things he hadn't bothered to identify to the group.

We really are at war, Philippe thought.

They were standing on a rocky shore. A faint path led upward, wrapping around the base of a mountain. Sasha set out upon it, and the rest of them fell in behind her. Philippe strained his senses. *Nicole is somewhere on this island, and I should be able to feel her.*

They wound their way up and around the mountain, tripping on loose stones that seemed to suddenly twist beneath their feet. "This whole place is cursed," Tommy muttered, and Philippe had to agree.

At last they stopped for a rest on a small plateau.

The trail blanched here, part of it continuing upward and part of it beginning to head back down. A large rock stood on otherwise level ground, and all but Richard sank to a seat on it. The wind whipped past them, taking Philippe's breath away.

He touched Sasha's arm, and she turned to him. "How do you know where we're going?" he asked.

"I've spent much time on this island," she admitted.

"A prisoner?" he asked.

She smiled faintly. "Yes, and no."

"I don't understand."

"I used to come here at night, when I was sleeping. I would astral-travel—my body lay in my room in Paris, and my spirit roamed here."

"What were you doing?"

She shook her head. "I never really knew. It wasn't an active choice on my part. At first I thought there was something here I could use to help my sons, but all I ever found here was evil. When they brought Jer here, I was overwhelmed with sorrow and joy. I tried to speak with him, to comfort him, but I don't think he ever heard me.

"Holly heard me, though. She came one night to see Jer."

"You were the one who showed her where the island was," Philippe said.

She nodded. "I thought then that maybe that was why I had roamed the island every night for so long. If it freed my son, it was worth it."

Her eyes took on a faraway look. "There's something here, something I can't explain. . . ."

As she drifted off, Philippe felt a cold chill sweep through his body. She was right: There was something here. It felt ancient, evil. It tainted everything. Sitting beside Sasha, he could barely even sense her; the evil was acting as some kind of filter, muting the feel of her presence. He closed his eyes, trying to ignore the evil, trying to push past it, to reach beyond it . . . and then, he felt—Nicole!" he exclaimed, leaping to his feet.

"She's not far away," he said excitedly.

"Which path?" Richard asked, his voice strained.

"Down," Philippe said. He could feel it in his soul.

Eli was angry with himself. *The witch is playing me, she has to be.* Still, part of him didn't care, and that's what got to him. Fantasme sat huddled in a corner looking miserable and angry at the same time. *He's probably as confused as I am by the fact that I'm sitting next to a Cahors witch and I'm not trying to kill her.*

"Fantasme, find us a way out of here," he ordered.

The hideous, birdlike creature screeched once and then disappeared.

"Alone at last," he joked.

"Uh, not exactly," Nicole answered, staring toward the back of the cave.

"What do you—"

And then he saw the three Golems lumbering out of the darkness.

Philippe, Sasha, Richard, and Tommy: Avalon

They had been on the island for almost two hours. They had worked their way down the path and were now standing on the crown of a hill facing east.

"Where is she?" Sasha said in a voice that was barely above a whisper.

"She is here. I can feel her presence, and she is very frightened," said Philippe. He had been able to keep her presence with them since he had first felt her on the plateau. The hard part was, they had probably been only within a few hundred feet of her then, but the winding of the trail had taken them on a circuitous route.

At that instant there was a loud rumbling down the hill by the shore. A large dust cloud was rolling along the sand, and when it cleared, Eli and Nicole were lying in the water and three very large creatures were emerging from the ground.

"Golems!" yelled Philippe. With that, Tommy was

off running, stumbling, and rolling down the hill toward Nicole. He was still over a hundred yards away when one of the Golems reached Nicole. Nicole tried to kick it but to no effect. It reached down and picked her up by the front of her dress like a rag doll. A second Golem was reaching for Nicole's legs as if to tear her apart.

"Do something, hurry!" Sasha yelled in a near panic.

At that moment the hairs on the back of Philippe's head lifted, and four more Golems raced past him, heading directly for Tommy. Philippe shouted, panic flooding him.

Richard, who had been slightly higher up the hill than the others and was looking the other way, whirled around. In a movement so sudden and yet incredibly smooth, he had unslung the sniper rifle, raised it, and fired twice. There was almost no sound, just a soft *phfft, phfft,* and two Golems dropped to the ground, the first *e* on each of their foreheads neatly replaced by perfectly round little holes. Philippe was stunned by the look of controlled rage on Richard's face. Before he and Sasha could even react, Richard was racing past them and was about fifty feet behind Tommy.

Tommy reached Nicole just as the two Golems were beginning to pull her in opposite directions. He jumped on the back of the one closest to him, bringing his right arm up and around the Golem's forehead. The Golem tried to shake Tommy off, but that only served to wipe away the *e*. Three down. As Tommy was riding the back of the Golem to the ground, three more shots rang out and the Golems who had just reached Tommy fell. Philippe felt his jaw grow slack.

The last remaining Golem had Nicole by the head. *He's going to kill her.*

Another *phfft* sound, and the final beast dropped to the ground still clutching Nicole. Richard had fired again while at a dead run.

As though in slow motion, Philippe watched as Eli rolled up to a sitting position and raised his hands into the air. He could see his lips moving but could not hear what spell Eli was chanting. Richard reached behind his head and unsheathed a long, wicked knife that had been resting between his shoulder blades. It went sailing end over end before driving itself into the ground between Eli's legs. Even from that distance, Philippe could see the warlock turn ash white.

"You just sit still," Richard boomed. "Breathe wrong and I kill you."

As Philippe scrambled down the hill, his heart was pounding. Eli was sitting absolutely still, not even blinking.

Tommy rolled off his dead Golem, turned, and

shouted at Richard, "You could have hit her."

"No, there was six inches above her head," Richard said as tears of joy rolled down his face. He was cradling his daughter in his arms, and she was clutching him and sobbing.

As Philippe ran up, Richard extended an arm to him and he joined them in the circle. He reached out and touched Nicole's arm, and an electric shock went through him.

He gasped and looked down at her distended abdomen. *She's pregnant!* His head reeled with the possibilities. He reached down with a shaking hand and touched her stomach. *What magic is this?* Then, with a sudden, devastating certainty, he knew—*it's not mine!*

"Where, where did those other Golems come from?" Tommy panted.

"I think they were following us," Philippe said.

Sasha stood, taking in the whole scene. Dead Golems lay everywhere. She reached down and touched one lightly, shuddering at the contact. "These last went after you, not Nicole," she noted to Tommy. "I think they're the same ones that were trying to find Amanda."

"But that makes no sense. Amanda's not here," Tommy protested.

"It makes perfect sense," Philippe answered quietly. "We've blocked Amanda's essence from them, so they turned to the only person who carries a piece of her inside himself."

"Yes, you and Amanda are in thrall, a part of each belongs to the other. When we left the group, the Golems must have been able to sense Amanda in you and came after you."

Tommy shuddered. "Do you think there are any more?"

Sasha shook her head. "Jer said four came after Holly. We know these four"—she gestured—"were after Amanda. We may be able to assume they are searching in groups of four. If that's the case, though, only three were attacking Nicole."

"One of them was dead already," Eli said quietly. "I killed it back in the castle."

Sasha turned to stare at him. "Thank you for getting her out."

"Don't thank me," he snarled. "I didn't do it for you, or for her. Trust me, I'll kill all of you the first chance I get."

"I say we don't give him that chance," Tommy muttered.

Sasha could tell that Philippe agreed wholeheartedly but compassion for her kept him from voicing his feelings.

She looked down at Eli. There was hate raging in his eyes. He stood slowly, head half-turned toward Richard, who kept his eyes riveted on him. "The Horned God will destroy you, all of you," he hissed.

"Eli! I did not raise you to be a servant of evil."

"No, that's right. You didn't. You didn't raise me at all," he snapped. "No, you bailed out and left that to Dad. Now you want to come back into my life and judge *me*? How dare you! Instead, you are the one who needs to be judged. You are the one who abandoned your children and never once looked back! And now, what, you get to act all surprised and hurt that we take after Dad. Gee, big surprise, he was the one who was there. He gave me my first lessons in magic, he taught me how to drive a car, he told me how to treat women. You left me with him knowing what he is and you're surprised at how I turned out?" He was screaming at the last, his face crimson, and spittle flying from his mouth.

He raised his hands as though he was going to attack her. From the corner of her eye she saw Richard draw another knife, and then suddenly a shiny black demon knocked Eli off his feet.

The thing resembled a giant cockroach, complete with exoskeleton. It scrabbled on six legs and twisted around, its fangs headed for Eli's neck. He punched the thing in the head, though, and it whimpered and skittered away while he leaped to his feet.

"Say good-bye," a voice hissed from somewhere behind her. Sasha twisted around to see a nymph aiming a crossbow at Eli.

"No!" she shouted, lunging at Eli and trying to knock him out of the way.

She hit Eli, and both of them began to fall. She felt the arrow as it pierced her back, burrowing through her body and toward her heart. Then, there was a great *whoosh* and a blinding light.

They hit the ground, which was made of stone and covered with straw.

"Welcome," a silky female voice purred.

Sasha looked up, amazed that she could still do so, and began to laugh hysterically.

"Who is she?" Eli asked, his voice dripping with fear.

A stately woman in black and silver robes, crowned with black veils and a diadem of silver, stood over him. Her mouth twisted. "I am Isabeau of the House Cahors, and you are most welcome."

"Where did they go?" Nicole shouted.

A moment before, Eli and Sasha had been falling.

They had hit the ground and vanished. Their disappearance had been accompanied by a sound like a sonic boom.

The demon who had shot Sasha staggered backward, a dagger in its chest. It collapsed to the ground, wheezing and gurgling. Tommy had grabbed the cockroach creature and twisted its head off.

Tommy stood slowly, looking sick. Purple blood covered the lower half of his face.

"I'm not sure, but I think it might have something to do with a spell Amanda and I cast."

"Explain," Philippe demanded.

"We did a spell so we would stay alive and together. When we were done, there was a surge of power. Just now, I felt it again, just before they disappeared."

Nicole felt a wave of nausea rush over her. "Maybe Pablo can figure out where they went," she gasped when it had passed. "Where is everyone, anyway?"

She saw Philippe and Tommy exchange a quick glance. *They're wondering how much to tell me,* she realized.

"Let's just say they're on the Continent," her father said cautiously.

She glanced up at him, seeing him with new eyes. "You never wanted to fight again, to use your training again, did you? You never wanted us to know who or what you are, and Mom never wanted to know either."

The look on his face was validation, and she could feel all the pain that he had kept to himself for so long. "Mom recoiled from your scars and never let you talk, so your soul could heal. So you just turned into a simple, quiet, fade-into-the-background kind of person. Well, it's out now, Dad. You are—"

"Ssh, honey. It's okay," he said, interrupting her. "All that matters is that you're safe." His face was full of tenderness, but slowly his look changed to one of grim resolve. "Now, let's go find your sister."

With her father on one side and Philippe on the other, Nicole rose shakily to her feet. "My men," she joked weakly, and they both laughed, humoring her.

She could feel the baby move inside of her and she winced. *What I wouldn't give for a nap.* She glanced around quickly, wondering if Fantasme had come back, but the hulking creature was nowhere to be seen. *Go, find your master and Sasha,* she bid him silently, knowing he would never listen to her.

France, 13th Century

"We're dead," Sasha said as she rolled over onto her back and stared up at Isabeau.

"No, Madame, you are not," the Cahors witch assured her, and though she was speaking in medieval French, Sasha understood every word she said.

"If we're not dead, then where are we?" Eli asked, looking around suspiciously. "How do we know if—"

"You are in my home, my time." The beautiful princess inclined her head. "Inside the castle of my husband, Jean de Deveraux, and his father, Duc Laurent."

Sasha sat up slowly, confused and unsteady. She saw the gray stone walls, adorned with battleaxes, picks, and maces. A long wooden table was covered with the remains of a recent feast, and rushes were strewn on the floor.

"We're in France, six hundred years ago?" Sasha asked her. "How did this happen?"

A cloud passed over Isabeau's face as she regarded her surprise visitor. "A portal was opened between our two times. It was an accident. I stepped through and pulled you from your time."

"Why?"

"To save your life," Isabeau answered.

Sasha slowly stood to her feet. She wanted desperately to reach out and touch the other woman, to assure herself that she was flesh and blood. *Is it she, or her spirit? Does the woman still live, or has the Massacre already occurred?*

Isabeau reached out her hand and touched Sasha's. Her skin was soft and warm. "I am flesh," she said simply. "I was told to look for you."

And then in her mind, Sasha heard her speak. *He is Deveraux.*

He is my son, she replied.

"You worship the Goddess," Isabeau asked her out loud.

"I do, yes."

Then you understand my pain.

"Your husband. Jean."

My love.

Sasha felt a sudden rush of giddiness. *I can stop it,* she thought. *I can keep it all from happening.*

"You can stop nothing," Isabeau told her, her voice filled with sadness. "Nor can I. All we can do is watch and pray."

"What are you two talking about?" Eli asked, standing.

"Her future," Sasha whispered.

Isabeau smiled, and it broke Sasha's heart. *She knows! On some level, she knows all that is to come.*

"A choice has been placed before you both. You may remain here, to live out your days, or you can return to your own place and time."

She nodded to Sasha. "If you should choose to return, you will die from your wound."

The arrow! So, I was not far wrong in thinking I was dead already.

"Indeed," Isabeau said to her. "But how many days you will live, I cannot say. Wild days and nights will unfold soon. Of your own fate, I have no knowledge. Of my own . . ." She turned her face away and sighed. "I have it in me to stop it from happening."

Sasha's lips parted in surprise. "Would I be able to do anything to help you? Could we manage it together?"

Isabeau stared at her. "I have no idea," she answered frankly.

"Perhaps the Goddess sent me here," Sasha told her. "So many die, do they not, once our families clash in the flames? If you and I could change the future, would the Supreme Coven still rise? Will the Mother Coven become so weak, if you and I together worked magic now, in your time?"

"I . . . I don't know," Isabeau murmured.

"What of your mother?" Sasha asked, her blood warming. "Would she join us?"

Isabeau smiled bitterly. "For her, the fate of all in this castle is sealed. They shall all die."

"I shall stay," Sasha replied. "Even if we fail to change what is to come, I'm a survivor. Better to live, no matter what century. And no matter if for a few days or a hundred. And whether we can stop the Massacre or not."

Eli stood, emotions that she couldn't read colliding inside him. She could see the struggle, but there was nothing she could do to help him. Death could conceivably await him no matter which he chose. He could die in the Castle Massacre along with dozens of Deveraux, or he could die in his time by the hand of the Supreme Coven, or his own father's.

She could see his fear, his confusion, and for the first time since she had left, she felt close to him. *He's just a child, still searching for his way in the dark,* she thought.

He turned to her, his eyes full of questions she could not answer, and her heart began to break. She reached out and touched his cheek, and for a moment he let her before he jerked away.

Our whole lives have been leading to this, she realized.

He took a step back and turned to Isabeau. "I choose to return."

The young woman inclined her head.

He lifted a hand. "Can you return me to London instead of Avalon?"

Isabeau nodded. "The portal was initially formed in London by two who wanted to shield themselves and their love for eternity. I can return you there."

"Good."

"What do you intend to do?" Sasha asked.

He looked her in the eyes. "I don't know yet."

She grasped his hand and swallowed around a sudden lump in his throat. She hadn't been a part of his life for years, but there had always been the possibility that that could change. Now, that would be lost to them both. "I will try to come to you," she whispered.

He nodded that he understood, but he didn't say anything. He let go of her hand, Isabeau made a motion in the air, and with a rush of wind, he was gone.

Michael Deveraux: London

It was nearly time. In a few hours it would be Wind Moon and blood would be shed. Michael Deveraux smiled. In a few hours House Deveraux would take its rightful place as head of the Supreme Coven. His ceremonial robes flowed about him as he walked toward the altar. He had prepared several sacrifices to appease the Horned God, that he might look with favor upon Michael.

Duc Laurent was there, smiling wickedly and dressed from head to toe in black leather. "Tonight, the Black Fire will consume our enemies, and will visit destruction upon all who stand in our way."

Considering that the Black Fire had, at least, indirectly, been the death of the Duc, Michael admired his fearlessness. "You're sure my son will be there?"

Laurent nodded. "He and what's left of the Cahors Coven are planning to attack the Supreme Coven tonight."

Michael shook his head at the audacity, and at the foolishness of it. "What can they hope to achieve by such an assault? They are weak, divided, and Holly is still possessed." *At least, last my imp saw her, she was.*

Laurent laughed. "Who cares—so long as they are there, we can use them."

Jer is the key, Michael thought with bitter amusement. *That was why we were able to conjure the Black Fire in the high school gym. Eli and I were chanting, but his presence was key. The son who disobeys me and tries to break with our magic will lead to the destruction of all. How poetic. I guess he can't help it. Deveraux are just born bad.*

"What do you think, pet?" Michael called out.

Kari walked in from the other room, listless and dazed. "That's nice," she said, though she clearly had no idea what was nice.

"How long do you plan on keeping her like this?" Laurent asked, pursing his lips.

"Oh, a little while longer, at least."

"You should kill her now, before the battle. The mesmerism takes some concentration, concentration you could easily lose during the fight."

Michael shrugged his shoulders and sneered. "Look at her. Do you really think she's a threat? Besides, I'm saving her for the after-Massacre celebration."

Tri-Coven: London

Jer was nervous. The coven wasn't prepared to take on both the Supreme Coven and his father, yet in a few scant hours they were going to war with them both. He touched his face, feeling the scars that lingered there. The last battle his father had been involved with hadn't ended well.

Now I'm hideous, disfigured, a monster outside to match the monster within. He searched his heart and still found himself lacking. He knew not which deity he owed his allegiance to, and he was filled with rage and bitterness.

What would I have been like had I grown up in a different family, one who worshiped the Goddess? Would I be more like Alex? Can he really be as good and pure as he seems, or is it all a masquerade?

He wasn't going to find the answers to his questions, at least not in time to help with the battle to come.

"Jer?"

He looked up. It was Holly. She seemed different to him—older, quieter. *I would be, too, if I'd gone through what she has.*

She came and sat beside him, the springs of the bed creaking ever so slightly. In the darkness she couldn't see his scars, and he was grateful for that. She touched his hand, and he flinched.

"Jer, I want to be close to you. Don't shut me out."

"You deserve someone who is whole," he whispered.

"There's nothing wrong with you," she answered, her voice cracking slightly.

"We both know that's not true, Holly."

She laced her fingers through his, and he thrilled at her touch. "I need you."

"You need someone who can take care of you, someone you don't have to hide in the dark with."

"Your face is not our problem," she answered, her voice gaining strength. "Your fear is. I've seen horrors I can't even express. You think a few scars bother me, especially when they're yours?"

"You don't know what you want," he said bitterly. "You and I, if we begin something, it's going to be forever. 'Till death us do part,' even if we're the cause of that death. You're not ready for that. You're a child."

"I'm not a child," she said, her voice rising. "I'm a woman, but you've been too wrapped up in your own self-pity to notice."

He turned toward her. He could see her eyes gleaming in the dark, large and round like a cat's. He ached for her. He wanted to take her in his arms and never let go. He had dreamed of it for so long. . . .

She lifted her hand to touch his cheek, and he jerked back.

"Don't pull away from me. I'm not afraid of you, of us."

"I am," he whispered.

"Don't be."

And then her lips were on his, hungry, demanding, and he could not deny her. He kissed her with all the passion that was in his heart, his soul. He felt her hands plucking at his shirt, unbuttoning it, and then her warm hands moved against his chest.

With a groan, he closed his eyes. *It would be so easy to make love to her, we have both wanted it for so very long.*

Yes, oui, take her, he heard Jean whisper in his mind. *She is ours, and we will have her.*

"*Mon amour,*" whispered Holly—or was it Isabeau?

"You are the fire that burns me," he answered, his lips against hers.

"And you, me."

Holly stared into Jer's eyes and could see the passion within. His face swam in her sight as Isabeau began to take her over, even as Jean was claiming Jer. She felt everything that Isabeau had felt as she had lain in the marriage bed with Jean: the passion of a lover, the duty of a bride, the fear of a virgin. Holly knew all these because the same emotions coursed through her, the same feelings held sway in her heart and mind.

Our lord, our husband, we must be with him, Isabeau demanded, her words ringing clear in Holly's mind.

"I love you, Jer," Holly whispered, gazing at him through lowered lids.

He paused for a moment, staring into her eyes, and all the world around them seemed to stand still. "I love you, Holly," he answered in a voice so savage, it made her quake.

His hands were on her shoulders; she could feel the weight of them, and their heat burned through her shirt. He slowly slid his hands downward to the front of her shirt. Her back arched uncontrollably, pushing her harder against his hands. She could hear his breathing heavier now, and his breath warmed her neck.

"My husband, *mon homme, mon amour,*" she whispered.

With a groan, he tore her shirt open and pulled it off her. She gasped as he trailed kisses down her neck and to the tops of her breasts. A fire kindled in her belly, and all she wanted was to be his. Bodies moving, flesh entwining, as it has been it always shall and must be. He circled his arms around her and crushed her to him.

And then he pushed her away again with hands that shook. "No," he said, voice hoarse.

She felt as though ice water had been poured into her veins. She tried to lift her hands to touch his face, but he grabbed them and held them still.

"This is Jean and Isabeau, not us, Holly."

"It *is* us," she breathed. "It always has been. They can only play upon the emotions we already feel. We belong together."

"I can't pull you into my world of darkness. You deserve to live your life in the light."

"I want to live my life with you."

"No, we have to stop, even if that means I have to be strong for both of us. We need to stop before there's no turning back."

She stood abruptly, pain rolling off her. "You say that you are being strong, but you are weak. A strong man embraces his emotions, he doesn't run away from them."

Jer sat helplessly watching as she clutched up her shirt and threw it back on, awkwardly holding together the ripped edges in front. His heart ached for her. He could feel her pain and humiliation as though they were his own.

She started to leave, and he wanted to call her back but knew that he couldn't. At the door she stopped and turned back toward him. Her voice was quivering as she told him, "Jeraud Deveraux, you are nothing but a coward."

And as she left, he knew that she was right.

THIRTEEN

DIANA

And now at last our journey's done
We give praise to almighty Sun
We kill and maim and claim our right
To triumph using power and might

Bleeding we lay in the dust
Goddess protect us, you must
With our last breath we pray to thee
If you wish us dead, so mote it be

Tri-Coven: London

Wind Moon. It had come at last. Holly didn't know whether to feel fear or relief. One way or the other, it would be over tonight. Everything would be done. She looked down at her hands, clasped tight in her lap. It still seemed so strange to see them, to know that she could control them. She breathed in deeply, centering herself. One thing she had learned from the possession, and that was the value of patience, *and how to be still.*

She was still now, waiting and listening for the voice of the Goddess. Isabeau sat beside her, impatient but quiet. At last, Holly turned to her. "If he doesn't want me, then there's nothing I can do."

"But he does want you, you can feel it, you know it as well as I."

"Maybe I do," Holly answered. "But he is going to have to come to me."

Isabeau made a hissing sound but said nothing.

Holly sat for a few more minutes, gathering strength, focusing her thoughts and calming her heart. At last she rose to her feet. She was wearing a black turtleneck and loose-fitting black trousers. She had removed all her jewelry and braided her hair back, entwining it with silver and black thread.

All the others were similarly dressed. She took her place in the circle they had formed in the living room of the safe house. She looked at their faces and was stirred by sorrow. *Not everyone is going to survive tonight. Maybe none of us will.*

Armand met her eyes and nodded encouragingly. He had been very kind to her the last couple of days. He alone of the group truly understood what she had gone through.

Nicole smiled bravely, but Holly's eyes were fixed on her cousin's belly. *She shouldn't be fighting.* The cat

Astarte sat on her lap. The cat had found Nicole before she and the rescue party had left the island. The cat gazed at Holly as though she knew exactly what was happening and the nature of that which they were about to undertake. Philippe sat next to Nicole, one hand protectively on her stomach and the other stroking the cat. *He'll die before he lets anything happen to Nicole.*

Amanda and Tommy huddled together, arms entwined and legs touching. *The magic they did opened the portal that Sasha disappeared through. Their magic alone, though, couldn't have done it. They must have combined it with someone else's inadvertently. It wasn't mine, so that could only leave . . .*

Alex. He sat there staring levelly at her. *We know so little about him, but he's a Cahors, and he's helped us so much already. The extent of his abilities is unknown to us, though, perhaps also unknown even to him.*

Next to Alex sat Jer. She could feel the hostility flowing through them both. *Something has passed between them that the others haven't told me about. Goddess, let them put it aside for the battle.*

Pablo stared at her, clearly reading every thought she was having. Since she had come back she had noticed that he had given up every pretense of not reading people. *We may need your insights yet,* she told him. He nodded.

Barbara sat looking nervously at the rest. *Of us all, she doesn't belong here, and I don't know what help she can be. It's likely we sacrificed so much to rescue her, and she will be killed tonight, anyway. The others have worked hard with her, repairing her mind, teaching her some protection skills. Goddess, let it be enough.*

That left Richard. He sat, dressed all in black, but with black markings on his face. They made him look like some sort of devil. He had cut his hair to within a half inch of his head as well, military style. Of all of them, he had surprised her the most. Everyone had written him off so long ago, and that had been a mistake. His particular skills were going to prove especially useful now. Her uncle had spent the last forty-eight hours discussing the layout and security of the Supreme Coven with Jer.

The two had formed a plan that was brilliant and daring and, Goddess willing, that just might work. Richard sat quietly, and it was clear that he, too, was preparing himself mentally. Around him lay a small arsenal. She hadn't asked where he had gotten the weapons; she didn't want to know.

Just as Jer and Richard had worked on a plan of attack, Alex, Tommy, and Philippe had worked on enhancing the weapons magickally. *That should surprise Sir William,* she thought. *I wonder if anyone has thought before to combine technology and magic in the way that we have?*

Her army waited. It was a good army, one that had stayed loyal despite all the hell she had put it through. Many had been lost, but those who remained were undaunted by that. They were ready to fight, and to die, for what they knew was right.

"Tell me again about the weapons," Holly said quietly.

Philippe let go of Nicole and Astarte and picked up a bullet. "These are depleted uranium bullets. As I understand it, they are incredibly deadly on their own. One bullet can rip through a tank, turn into shrapnel, and shred anything inside so that it is unrecognizable."

"That's correct," Richard said.

"What we've done is, tried to put a charm on each bullet so that it can also punch its way through a magic ward. Most wards are designed to block much larger things—a creature, a melee weapon, or other magic. We figured that something this small, if enhanced slightly, might be able to make it through the barrier."

"Excellent," Holly said, impressed.

Philippe put down the bullet and picked up something that vaguely resembled a grenade. "This is a concussion grenade. Instead of spraying shrapnel, it compresses sound waves and air."

"It's like when you have the bass on the TV set

really high and you can feel it more than hear it."

"Like when the sound vibrates your breastbone?" Holly asked.

Philippe nodded. "These should cause a ripple effect that can theoretically tear through wards as well."

Philippe put down the grenade and held up a knife and a baton like police used. "We only have a couple of these. Barbara's going to show us all some of the most effective places to strike to cause damage or death."

Barbara? Holly's eyebrows shot up as she turned to look at the woman.

Barbara stood up, her hands shaking slightly. "Well, who better than a doctor to teach all of you how to hit someone to cause the most damage? Tommy, will you help me out?"

Tommy rose with alacrity, and the two positioned themselves in the center of the circle. "First off, some basic physiology," Barbara said, her voice growing stronger. "As I understand it, most of the warlocks you'll be fighting are men, so we'll focus on gender-neutral techniques, and then some that will work specifically on men.

"If you hit your opponent hard on the nose, it will cause him to lose his vision for a couple of seconds. If you hit his nose really hard, it can drive blood and bits of bone into his eyes, further impairing his vision. If you can hit the nose at the bottom with the palm of your hand and push upward hard enough, the breaking bones will drive up into his brain and kill him."

Barbara slowly and gently mimicked the motion she was describing. Tommy looked distinctly uncomfortable. Holly glanced over at Amanda. Her cousin looked green, and for a moment Holly thought she was going to throw up.

Apparently ignoring the reactions around her, Barbara continued. "If you take your hand like so," she said, demonstrating, "and drive it upward just under the breastbone, you will crush his heart. Avoid actually punching your fingers into the chest cavity, because you could get your hand caught in there."

Amanda got up and fled from the room, her hand pressed over her mouth. In a moment the sound of retching could be heard coming from the bathroom. Even Holly was beginning to feel queasy, and the sound didn't help.

"Kick your opponent in the side of the knee to fell him instantly," Barbara continued.

"Now for some gender-specific points. Men have Adam's apples. Strike the Adam's apple, and he won't be able to breathe for about thirty seconds. Strike it harder and you can dislodge or crush it, causing him to choke to death. Notice even the slightest pressure there is uncomfortable," Barbara commented as she gently touched Tommy's Adam's apple with one finger and he instantly backed up.

"Now, men and women stand differently. Women stand straighter, whereas men hunch their shoulders forward slightly. This makes a man's collarbone more vulnerable. If you can strike it, you can break it, and it is one of the most excruciatingly painful bones to break. That is because of its proximity to the head and neck. The nerve centers in the collarbone link up with the head as well as the chest, so the pain will pretty much incapacitate most people."

Holly felt herself start to sweat slightly and she squirmed as she imagined the pain.

"Now, this is especially important," Barbara said, pausing to look at them all. "You all know that you can kick a man in the groin to cause him extreme pain. It's more effective, though, if you actually grab the testicles and crush them."

An anguished shout rose from every man in the room, and Tommy leaped back, shouting, "Stay away from me!"

Amanda, who had just made her way back into the room, went running again.

Barbara sat down, her lecture done. It took a minute

for everyone to calm down, and Holly noted that when they did, every man was sitting with his legs crossed.

"There is one other thing," Philippe said, still visibly shaken. He picked up a pair of ice picks. "Richard wants each of us to carry a pair of these with us. He's going to show us what to do with them later."

Pablo's face suddenly went deathly white, and he, too, went running from the room, his hands clamped over his ears.

"Okay," Holly said. "And now for the plan."

Headquarters of the Supreme Coven

The plan was simple, and it involved marching into the Supreme Coven's headquarters. Of course it helped that Michael wasn't going alone. He was being smuggled in by James Moore. Between the two of them, they knew where all the trip alarms and wards were. With Duc Laurent and Kari in tow, they made their way into the heart of the underground kingdom as the last ray of the setting sun touched the earth above them. *Sunset for Moore, how poetic.*

The alarm wasn't raised until they were nearly to the throne room. Guards caught sight of Michael and shouted, there was the sound of footsteps as warlocks came running, and Michael smiled, knowing many of them were loyal to him.

Then, from the darkness behind him, he heard a female voice purr, "Hello, Michael, I've been waiting for you."

He threw himself to the side just as a lightning bolt ripped through the air where he had been standing. He glanced up to see a young female warlock standing, smiling wickedly.

Eve.

Tri-Coven: London

Jer hated Alex. There was something about him that drove him crazy. *Maybe it's the fact that he threatened to kill me on Wind Moon,* he thought dryly. *Maybe it's because he's everything I'm not. He's what I could have been had my father served the Goddess and not the Horned God. Whatever it is, I'm not going to let him out of my sight. Of course, that's going to be difficult since I'm point and he's bringing up the rear.*

Next to him, Richard lifted his hand in the air and Jer stopped, bringing his mind back to bear on the task at hand. They had already passed through the outer defenses that the Supreme Coven had placed on the streets of London surrounding the entrances to the Coven. They were thin wards that acted more like "magic detectors" than actual barriers. Richard had been able to pass through easily, having no witchblood in his veins. Jer had passed through easily, though not without notice. He was a warlock, though, so no alarms were raised.

Through the fog, two men converged on them, warlocks both. They were sentries, guarding the entrance to the underground headquarters. Jer didn't recognize them—a good thing, else they might have raised an alarm upon seeing him.

"Hail the Green Man, guardian of the day," Jer murmured as they stopped before them.

"You have entered ground consecrated to the Horned God. Woe be to any who trespass here."

"I come as a fellow servant."

Satisfied, the two men turned, indicating that Jer and Richard should follow. Jer pulled his two ice picks from his belt and waited for Richard to nod. When the other man did, they both moved in tandem. Jer jabbed one ice pick into each ear of the man in front of him. The warlock died without a sound, without even a breath being expelled from his body. Holding on to the ice picks, Jer lowered him slowly to the ground so there was not even the thud of his falling to alert anyone. Beside him, Richard did the same. Then they stepped over the bodies and moved forward.

Jer was shaking from head to toe. It was the first human he had killed, and he felt like he was going to be sick. He glanced over at Richard and saw the steely look in his eyes. *It's not his first, and if this night goes as planned, it won't be his last,* Jer realized.

He shuddered. Adrenaline was rushing through his body so that all his senses felt alert, heightened. *He would have killed me if I'd let him,* he told himself, thinking of the fallen guard.

They entered a dead-end alley. At the back was a door, set low into a brick wall and blending so well with it that it would go unnoticed by most. The glamours on it were strong.

Jer nodded to indicate that this was the entrance. He took one of the concussion grenades from a pouch on his belt. He pulled the pin and sent it sailing through the air. It exploded against one of the wards with a low boom. Windows rattled in the buildings around them, and Jer could feel it in his bones. *Hope that did the trick,* he thought.

Moments later, the rest of the Coven raced up to him. When no portals opened spilling forth demons, Jer realized that it must have worked.

"All right, everyone inside quickly before they realize what's happened," Jer instructed, opening the door.

They all spilled inside. Holly touched his hand as she passed. Once they were all in, he stepped in and closed the door behind him.

"'Into darkness deep as hell,'" Alex muttered.

"What?" Jer whispered.

"It's a *Phantom of the Opera* reference," Holly explained quietly.

She and Alex exchanged a glance that made Jer instantly uncomfortable.

"Quit the chitchat," Nicole hissed.

Jer moved back forward to re-establish himself at the front, leading the way through the twisting corridors. They hadn't gone more than a hundred feet when all hell broke loose.

Suddenly there were warlocks everywhere, bursting from side passages and hidden doors. It seemed as though they were coming out of the walls. And, then, bewilderingly, they rushed past the group and kept going.

Jer blinked. *What is this, the Twilight Zone?* And then he heard it, a deep keening sound—it was supposed to indicate a breach of the premises. *If we're not it, though, what is going on?*

Another warlock came thundering down a side passage.

"What's going on?" Jer shouted.

"Michael Deveraux," the man panted. He turned to glance at Jer and then stopped dead. "Hey, you're—"

Before he could finish his sentence, he died in his

tracks, a knife buried in his chest. Philippe strode forward and yanked the weapon back out, wiping the blood on his clothes.

"All right then, let's go," Jer said.

"Can you tell where they're headed?" Holly asked.

"Looks like the throne room," he said grimly. "Makes sense. The Deveraux have been wanting to take that throne back from the Moores for generations."

Eli Deveraux stood next to James Moore as they both surveyed the carnage. *I had no idea my father had recruited so many of the Supreme Coven,* Eli thought.

He ducked as a stray fireball exploded in the air above his head. He straightened slowly and turned to look at James. "You know they don't care about us," he said.

James turned to eye him coldly. "What?"

"Your father and mine—they don't care about us. Neither of them has ever been able to see beyond himself. We'll always be pawns in their games."

A warlock raced by, engulfed in flames, and Eli watched him for a moment before turning back toward James.

"He threatened to kill me," James said so quietly, Eli had to strain to hear him. "He told me it was time to choose sides and that if I sided with your father, he would flay me alive. For starters."

"I think the only reason I'm still alive is my father's been too lazy to kill me."

James snorted. "They think we'll be content to live our lives in their shadows, never wanting more than what they give us."

"I'm tired, tired of watching my back. We need to stop fighting each other and start fighting those who oppose us."

James nodded. "We should do something about it."

"Agreed," Eli said. "And, James, just one more thing."

"What?" the other grunted.

"When this is done, I want you to divorce Nicole."

A lightning bolt shot into the wall between them. When the smoke cleared, James turned full toward him. "Divorce her? I planned on killing her. Why?"

"Because I want to marry her," Eli said, hardly believing the words that were coming out of his mouth. "I think the kid could be mine."

"It could as easily be mine," James said, a subtle threat in his voice.

"I'm willing to take that chance," Eli told him, looking him square in the eye.

A week before—hell, an hour before—they would

have tried to kill each other. Now, though, James nodded slowly. He extended his hand. "Agreed. Now, let's go kick some ass."

Holly couldn't help but gasp as she stood surveying the scene. Everywhere she looked, warlocks were engaged in combat. *They're so busy fighting one another, they don't even notice us,* she marveled.

The same could not be said of the other denizens of the dark. The demons she had been expecting at every turn suddenly exploded upon them, as though they had all been waiting to attack at once.

"Heads up!" Holly yelled, hurling fireballs off her fingertips. Several demons dropped to the ground. One, though, continued to stride forward, laughing. It looked human but for its twisted face and the fact that the fireballs splatted against him with no effect.

Before Holly could react, Amanda exploded into action. She rushed forward, shouting and twirling a baton. For one moment she looked like a crazed member of a marching band. The illusion faded, though, when Amanda smashed the end of the baton into the creature's nose.

With a roar of pain, the thing fell to its knees, clawing at its face. Amanda pulled back and then drove the end of the baton upward into the nose again. The creature fell backward, dead.

"Works," Amanda said shortly. Another demon rushed them, roaring. Amanda twisted around and drove her fist up into the creature's abdomen. It, too, fell with a thud. Amanda turned and gave Holly a brief nod.

Holly said the first thing that came to mind: "You go, girl."

Then there was no more time to stand and wonder how her cousin had soaked up so much information while in the bathroom puking her guts out. It was Holly's turn to put down some demons.

She spun in a circle, fireballs rolling like waves from her fingers. A high-pitched scream caused her to twist and throw her hands up. *Too late!* A shiny black demon breathing smoke was upon her. Then suddenly it exploded before her.

As bits of demon fluttered to the ground, Holly stared through the smoke to see Eve. The warlock gave her a brief salute before limping on toward the fray. Holly stared after her. She had seen only a glimpse of Eve, once, but Amanda had told her enough about the warlock that there was no mistaking her.

Something hit Holly hard, and she tumbled to the

ground. She lay still for a moment, the wind knocked out of her. She glanced up expecting to see a demon and instead came face-to-face with a grinning warlock. He slammed her head into the floor, and her vision dimmed for a moment.

Jer knocked the warlock off of her with a sideways blow. Amanda stepped up from behind and hurled a fireball directly into the man's face. He fell to the ground, writhing in agony for a moment before dying.

Suddenly a wave seemed to ripple through the air, and Amanda gasped aloud. *Wind Moon, anyone who kills a witch or warlock on this night gains their power,* Holly thought.

Then Amanda and Jer were off again, whirling dervishes dealing out death at every turn. Holly lay still a moment, trying to regain her breath as she assessed the battlefield. Everyone seemed to be holding their own. She struggled to a sitting position.

"Holly!" Barbara Davis-Chin shouted. "Are you okay?"

Holly turned to look at her just in time to see a demon walk up behind Barbara and cut her in half.

"No!" Holly screamed. Shock ripped through her. All the effort to save Barbara had been in vain.

A hand grabbed the back of her collar and hauled her to her feet. She swung around, a fireball in hand.

"Keep moving!" Richard shouted at her, his face inches from hers.

She nodded through the haze of pain. Richard clapped her on the shoulder and then he was off.

Holly turned in time to see a wave of warlocks descending upon them. Suddenly they were all flung backward as though by a gale. Out of the corner of her eye she saw Alex, his hands raised in the air. The warlocks hit the far wall and were pulverized against it, bits of blood and bone flying everywhere. A ripple shimmered back across the room and slammed into Alex. The powers of the dead warlock were bestowed upon him in that moment.

Shaking her head in amazement, Holly turned to punch a horned demon that had its hand around Pablo's throat. She waded into the creature, and it dropped Pablo. She poured all her rage into every blow and kept pounding until the creature slumped to the ground. She didn't know if it was dead or only unconscious, so she took a step back and fried it with a fireball for good measure.

There were more demons to fight, and Holly loosed her rage on them. From time to time the others entered her line of sight, and so she knew they were still alive.

She downed one and turned just in time to see

Tommy ripping the head off another. She heard the sound of the rifle as Richard shot monster after monster. They exploded in a fabulously grotesque manner, showering each of them with gore. She noted that in every case Richard fired at creatures only when they were in front of walls, careful not to send bullets toward any demon standing in front of a member of the Coven.

She stood panting, looking around at the bodies of the dead demons. She glanced at the others, and they all shook their heads, not knowing if that was all.

Jer motioned them to follow, and in moments they were in another room. In the middle of it she saw Michael Deveraux.

"Jer!" someone screamed.

Then she saw Kari, running toward them. Michael Deveraux must have heard her as well, for he looked up and threw Holly a mocking salute. To his son, he called, "Welcome, Jer, the devil take you."

He threw a metal sphere toward Jer. Holly screamed a counter-spell but was unable to deflect it. Kari twisted, saw it coming, and dove in front of it. It hit her full in the chest, exploding as it struck her, and she fell backward against Jer.

Jer grabbed Kari as she fell against him, falling to his knees and lowering her to the ground. Her head lay on his leg, and she stared up at him, eyes wide. Around them the battle began anew, Holly's coven against his father's followers, but he didn't care. All he cared about was the shadow that was passing across Kari's eyes.

Kari lay in his arms, her blood covering his hands and face. "Jer," she gasped, looking up at him.

His father had tried to kill him, and Kari had sacrificed herself to save him.

"Ssh, it's all right now. Everything is going to be okay," he lied, looking down at what was left of her chest.

"No, it's not," she gasped. "I'm so sorry. I was wrong, and afraid. I thought you were dead. All I ever wanted was to love you, be with you."

"And you can, Kari, I swear. You'll be okay," he told her in a shaking voice. He tried to take her pain, tried to pass healing warmth through his hands, but he couldn't. Deveraux hands could only give death.

She whispered to him, *"Je suis la belle Karienne. Mon coeur, il s'apelle Karienne. Ah, Jean . . . mon Jean . . . "*

"Oui, ma belle," he found himself answering in French, finding love deep inside himself for her. *"Vives-toi, petite."*

The light began to fade from her eyes, and he felt himself begin to die. He had been so cruel to her, had treated her so badly. He had loved her once, or, at least, he thought he had. She had been shallow and vain, but no more so than he was. And when it had counted, she'd been there. *She'd always been there, even when I had refused to see,* he realized. He felt as though he couldn't breathe, as though his heart were being squeezed in his chest. "Live," he begged her, knowing that she could not.

"Kill me, Jer," she whispered. "Don't let your father get my magic."

"I can't," he sobbed.

"Yes, please, for me," she whispered.

His tears fell on her cheeks.

She reached up and touched his scarred face. Her fingers were cold. "You are beautiful," she said. "Like Jean."

He turned and kissed her hand. Then he pulled his dagger from his belt and cut her throat.

The ghost of a smile touched her lips. Then her hand fell, her eyes rolled back, and she was gone. And nothing he could do would bring her back. He felt the power passing from her into him, strengthening him and bringing him some bleak comfort. *A part of her will always be with me.*

Karienne.

★★★

Eli saw Jer and Holly enter the throne room, but they were the least of his worries. Eli maneuvered close to his father, who had nearly reached the throne of skulls. Only four guards stood between Michael and the leader of the Supreme Coven. Eli hazarded a glance toward Sir William and saw James at his side. With a wave of his left hand, Michael Deveraux sent three guards flying and, with his right, hurled a fireball into the chest of the fourth.

And then Eli was standing beside his father in front of the throne. Sir William had changed to his demonic appearance, his visage a terrible thing to behold.

"Deveraux," he bellowed. "You will pay for this."

"I think not," Michael said with an arrogant laugh.

Eli pulled his athame from his belt. "Actually, Father, you will."

Michael turned to look at him, surprise on his face. At that moment, Eli plunged the athame up under Michael's breastbone and into his heart. From the corner of his eye he saw James do the same to Sir William.

Michael tumbled to the ground, a look of astonishment on his face. Blood began to spill from his lips. They moved as though he was trying to speak.

Eli knelt beside him. "Why so surprised, Dad? You were the one who taught me to kill. You also taught me one other thing: 'Do unto others before they do unto you.'" He bent and kissed his father's brow before twisting the dagger and pulling it out.

In a moment, the light faded from Michael Deveraux's eyes and he was gone. A wave of power washed over Eli. It had belonged to his father, and now it belonged to him—not as his heir, but as his killer.

Eli stood shakily as a roaring sound began to fill the room. He looked up and saw James kneeling over the body of Sir William. The corpse shook and convulsed; Sir William's eyes bulging and then popping from their sockets. His chest expanded, contracted, then blasted outward. His skin slithered and steamed; and then, a hideous-looking demon clawed its way out of Sir William's chest, howling. Its form was black and leathery, and as it got free, its many-jointed, skeletal limbs began to unfold like collapsed metal rods. With a series of cracks and scraping noises, it unfolded itself until its furled, lizardlike head brushed the ceiling of the great chamber.

Its eyes were snakelike, yellowing and glowing, with a pinprick of darkness in the center. Its tongue was black and forked, and it flicked it once, twice, at James, who repelled the attack with fireballs, one of which lodged itself just beneath one of the monster's eyes, where it continued to burn, apparently unnoticed by the creature.

It roared, and then it flung back its head. Sir William's human laughter cannonaded out of it, making the walls shake. Then it hopped forward on massive, taloned feet, raced across the room in three steps, and disappeared into the far wall.

The skull throne cracked from top to bottom with the sounds of thousands of dying animals pouring from it and everyone stopped to stare.

Eli fingered his athame for a moment before hurling it at James. At the same moment, James threw his weapon. Eli fell, the dagger lodged in his shoulder. He turned his head slowly and saw James lying on the ground as well, his body draped over that of his father's ruined corpse.

Eli turned away. *Bastard*. Then, slowly, everything went dark.

Pandemonium broke out. Warlocks raced toward the fallen bodies of their leaders as Holly stood, mouth agape. She turned and glanced at Nicole. The other girl was white as a ghost, and her hand was pressed to her stomach. Then she began to totter, and Holly watched in horror as her cousin's knees buckled and she began to fall as though in slow motion.

Philippe threw himself forward, hitting the

ground beneath Nicole and reaching up to wrap his arms around her, cushioning her fall with his body. "She's going into labor," he shouted.

Holly turned and stared toward the remnants of the skull throne. Those they had come to fight were dead, the Supreme Coven was in a shambles. *Time to go, to get out while we can,* she thought, *before they turn their attention to us.*

Too late, she realized almost instantly as several nearby warlocks launched a sudden volley of fireballs their way. She lifted her hands to spin a barrier, but before she could, a rushing wind filled the room, extinguishing the fireballs.

"Everyone out!" Alex boomed in a voice that rolled and echoed like thunder. He stood, the center of the windstorm, his eyes flashing like lightning.

Holly didn't have to hear the scream that issued from Nicole to agree that it was a good idea. Philippe and Armand picked up Nicole and, carrying her, set out at a run led by Richard.

Pablo, Tommy, and Amanda followed close on their heels. Jer stood, stock-still, a look of shock on his face as he stared toward the throne. Holly touched his shoulder. *What must he be feeling about his father's death? Joy, sorrow, both? Only he knows,* she thought. "Let's go," she urged.

He let her lead him out of the room and into the passage. She could hear Alex as he brought up the rear behind them.

Getting out would prove harder than getting in, she soon realized. Demons crawled out of the walls. A strange sucking sound exploded around her, though, and the demons suddenly were trapped, pinned to the walls as though by some invisible force. She could feel a slight movement of air.

Wind, she realized, *Alex is keeping them at bay, somehow.*

As they raced through the seemingly endless tunnels, her thoughts flew ahead to where Nicole was. She could feel her pain; it rippled in waves off her, and her screams bounced off walls and ceiling and floors. *Nicole is strong, but none of us knows what to expect.*

Then, suddenly, they were at the exit and they all burst up onto the street outside and into the fresh air. Alex slammed the door behind him, muttering a spell to bar the way.

Holly stood, gasping in the clean, crisp air and listening to the labored breathing of the others. The stench of death and decay still hung about her clothes and being, and she worried that all the showers in the world would not change that.

A cloud moved in the sky, and directly above them

the full moon burst into sight, shining down upon them. *Wind Moon and most of us are still here, praise the Goddess.*

Back in the safe house, Holly felt as if an age had passed since they had left. Nicole lay in a bedroom upstairs, in the final stages of labor. Armand was tending her and had chased all the rest but Richard out with a worried look on her face.

I can't believe that it is over, Holly thought. *Michael Deveraux is finally dead. I am free of him—we all are. It is done. I feel strangely robbed that he did not die by my hand, but relieved as well.*

"It is not over," Alex announced, standing and facing the group. "Michael Deveraux and the Supreme Coven were just the barest tip of the iceberg. There are thousands of covens, on this world and others, and not all of them worship as we do. For every Michael Deveraux who falls, there are a dozen who stand ready to take his place."

And Sir William escaped, Holly thought.

"Indeed he did," Alex said, gazing at her. Then he said to the others, "I belong to the Temple of the Air. My coven and I have spent years fighting those who use the dark magic."

"You mean, tonight, this was not new to you?" Amanda asked.

"Hardly," he said, his face inscrutable. "I and others of the House of Cahors have fought many battles in the name of good and light."

"Other Cahors?" Holly asked, astonished. "But we—"

He nodded. "We four here are not the only descendants of House Cahors. There are many, many more, and we are all fighting to bring the covens together, to lead Coventry into a new era of peace."

"You didn't tell Luna any of this," Amanda accused him. "You let her think you were ignorant of your heritage."

"Yes, I did," he said. "The Mother Coven is weak. I have no use for them."

"I have a lot of experience with people who want 'to lead Coventry,' none of it good," Jer flung at him.

"Your experience all comes from the dark side of magic," Alex retorted, and it was clear that no love had been gained between the two of them. "Join us and help bring light. You can atone for your family's evil."

"I don't think so," Jer said. "Not that way."

"The Supreme Coven and the Mother Coven are both just two covens in a much larger world. The time for age-old battles is past. Covens need not fight each other. Houses need not fight each other," Alex said pointedly. "Not even yours and mine," he added, looking straight at Jer.

"I'm tired of fighting," Holly said quietly. "But I can't allow others like Michael Deveraux to roam free, killing all those in their path."

"You would be welcome in our coven, Holly," Alex said, pinning her with his gaze. "You have lost so much in this battle, and you have become so hard. You don't need to stay that way, though. We can help you. We can restore your faith."

Suddenly there were tears streaming down Holly's face. She *was* hard inside; her heart was a piece of flint. And yet . . . tears. They were magical, a miracle. "Is such a thing even possible?" she found herself asking.

Alex came and sat beside her. He picked up her hand and stared into her eyes, and she felt his heat, and his strength. His power.

"It *is* possible, Holly. We can help you, and you in turn can help us. You could be my High Priestess, and I will be your Long Arm of the Law. Together, we could lead with strength and mercy. Imagine what we could accomplish *together*."

And as he said that, she knew what he meant by the last word. *Together*. She broke his gaze and turned to Jer.

He locked gazes with her and for a moment, one

single instant, she saw . . . something. And then it was gone—extinguished or hidden, she couldn't say which.

Jer shook his head bitterly.

And Holly's heart hardened again.

Alex was still holding her hand. Warmth suffused her skin, and where the heat traveled, feeling returned to her. Alex was offering her something that Jer couldn't—or, more accurately, wouldn't.

Alex released his hand and stood. Holly could feel the weight of Amanda's stare on her, but she wasn't quite yet ready to meet her cousin's eyes.

When Amanda spoke, though, it was directed at the group at large. "We've done our bit for Coventry; we've fought our battle. Tommy and I need time to rest, to just be together. And I'll be honest, I don't know if we'll ever be ready to go back to fighting again."

Holly risked a glance at her. Amanda sat, arm entwined with Tommy, who was nodding agreement. *They are so close, so in love. What would it be like to have the kind of bond that they do?* She glanced again at Jer. *If I wait for him, I may never know.*

"I understand," Alex said. "Nicole should also stay behind. She has a baby to raise—a very special baby, unless I miss my guess."

Holly cocked her head to the side, wondering what

he meant by that. He didn't elaborate, and she knew that now was not the time to press him.

Philippe cleared his throat. "The survivors of the Spanish Coven wish to join yours."

"But your heart is torn," Alex answered.

Philippe nodded. "I wish to fight with you as well, but I must be with Nicole."

"Then you have a choice to make, for you cannot do both," Alex said.

"I'm going out," Jer announced abruptly, grabbing a coat and heading for the door.

Holly watched him go with an aching in her heart.

Everyone was silent for a moment. Holly heard her heart beating; it was a sound so foreign that she wondered if it had actually stopped for a while . . . ever since she had sacrificed Nicole's first familiar, Bast . . .

"So, Holly of the Cahors, what will you do?" Alex asked her.

She looked at him and felt a blush mounting her cheeks. She loved Jer, but he was damaged. He had worshiped the darkness for so long that his soul was more deeply scarred than his body.

Then again, so is mine.

She looked at Alex. His straightforwardness was refreshing, and he was offering her a chance for healing, a relationship with one who worshiped as she did and a place in the battle against evil.

His face shone with an unnatural beauty, and she knew that it would be easy to say "yes" and go with him. She was tired of fighting losing battles, and it felt good to know she could be on the winning side. She glanced at Pablo and Armand. She trusted them both, and they were going with Alex. *I won't have to be alone.* She looked in Alex's eyes and realized she would never be alone again.

He extended his hand to her.

EPILOGUE

(

Anne-Louise Montrachet had been gone a long time, her body still, but her spirit seeking the answers to so many questions. Whisper, the cat, walked slowly around her, careful not to tread a paw on her. The woman should be coming back soon, with answers to old questions and more new questions than she would be able to count.

At last Whisper walked gingerly up onto Anne-Louise's chest. Slowly, the cat sat down, an Egyptian Goddess waiting for her tribute.

Then, with a gasp, Anne-Louise awoke, eyes flying open, body twitching. Blood began to appear oozing from wounds that seemed to spring up in the witch's flesh as if by magic.

Anne-Louise looked wildly around for a moment before bringing her eyes to bear on Whisper. "You?" she asked.

The cat dipped its head in acknowledgment.

"We must get to the others, warn them," Anne-Louise gasped. "We need to tell them *that's not Alex Carruthers.*"

Aaron Corbet isn't a bad kid—he's just a little different.

On the eve of his eighteenth birthday, Aaron is dreaming of a darkly violent landscape. He can hear the sounds of weapons clanging, the screams of the stricken, and another sound that he cannot quite decipher. But as he gazes upward to the sky, he suddenly understands. It is the sound of great wings beating the air unmercifully as hundreds of armored warriors descend on the battlefield.

The flapping of angels' wings.

Orphaned since birth, Aaron is suddenly discovering newfound—and sometimes supernatural—talents. But not until he is approached by two men does he learn the truth about his destiny—and his own role as a liason between angels, mortals, and Powers both good and evil—some of whom are bent on his own destruction....

the
fallen

a new series by Thomas E. Sniegoski
Book One available March 2003
From Simon Pulse
Published by Simon & Schuster